"**Well, at least ya've brought something of** value." Culloden MacPherson muttered as he headed the horses along a trail that led out of the village and upriver through the trees. He gestured, with his hands holding the reins, toward the little dog in her arms. "I dunnae know a lot about pigs, but I vow, I've never seen such a one as this."

"Perceval most definitely isn't a pig!" Her drenched cloak clinging to her, Isabella clutched her pet closer, shielding him from the elements as best she could. From beneath the water dripping from the hood of her cloak, she glared over at her companion on the driver's bench. "He's a Pug dog and one of the finest of the breed."

"Whit?" He stared at her through drifting rain and sleet. "Niver! With a face like that? I saw its tail stickin' out from under yer cloak. Curled as tight as on one of the best porkers I've ever come across."

"He's my devoted friend and companion, and I'll thank you to treat him as such, Mr. MacPherson."

A chuckle from Fletcher Atkin, sitting with Lucinda and Horace in the cargo space behind them, made her turn to glare at him. The wagon lurched in a rut. She and her dog might have been thrown from the seat if Fletcher hadn't caught her arm to steady her.

Praise for Gail MacMillan

Heather, of *HEATHER FOR A HIGHLANDER*, was chosen as Best Heroine by the Trans Canada Romance Writers Maple Leaf Awards. Dr. William MacTavish (same book) placed as second favorite hero. The book's ending also received Honorable Mention.

"I love, love, loved this book [*HEATHER FOR A HIGHLANDER*]! It…begins in England with a murder, and ends with a fiery romance in British North America. And it's all because of a horse bet between brothers. I mean, isn't that how all good stories begin?"

~*Romance Novels for the Beach*

"Read in one sitting, which hardly ever happens for me. Truly engaging. I would definitely pick up another book by this author."

~*a judge at TransCRW competition*

"Be prepared to be hooked on the first word of the first page [of *COWBOY COUNTRY CONFESSIONS*] and go on to the next with anticipation."

~*Rebecca Melvin, Publisher, Double Edge Press*

"Gail MacMillan's stories delight the senses and brighten the dark days of winter like a candle glowing on a windowsill."

~*Sue Owens Wright, author, newspaper columnist*

"I love this little adventure [*HOLDING OFF FOR A HERO*]!…surprises…one light, wonderful read."

~*The Romance Reviews (4 Stars)*

"Not sure who I like better, [the] German Shepherd, the Pug, or the sexy next door neighbor."

~*Matilda, Coffee Time Romance & More (5 Cups)*

"Not your typical romance story [*SHADOWS OF LOVE*], but I couldn't put it down."

~*Michelle, Cocktails and Books (4 Cups)*

A Baron's Bartered Bride

by

Gail MacMillan

Riverhaven Rogues, Book 5

A Baron's Bartered Bride

Cover Art by *RJ Morris*

The Wild Rose Press, Inc.
PO Box 708
Adams Basin, NY 14410-0708
Visit us at www.thewildrosepress.com

Publishing History
First Tea Rose Edition, 2018
Print ISBN 978-1-5092-1962-9
Digital ISBN 978-1-5092-1963-6

Riverhaven Rogues, Book 5
Published in the United States of America

Dedication

To Linda and her beloved beagle Molly.
Thank you for being a friend.

Chapter One

Lumber baron, thirty years of age, in good health, well regarded in his community, seeks a lady wife to be mistress of a large manor house situated on an excellent and spacious estate. Reply to Culloden MacPherson, village of Riverhaven in the British North American Colony of New Brunswick.

Her left hand concealing it from the room's other occupants, Isabella Marston reread the dog-eared advertisement she'd cut from a newspaper the previous autumn. She remembered how her heart had pounded when she'd written a reply and sent it off on the last ship destined for America that day in late November of 1814. Now she felt only a depressing sense of disappointment.

Spring had come, ships had begun arriving from across the Atlantic over a month earlier, but none, up to this last week of March, had brought an answer to her interest. Perhaps the man had found a more acceptable lady. Knowing her father could provide little or nothing in the way of dowry, she'd avoided the subject in her response. Perhaps, by this omission, he'd surmised she was wanting in that area and decided against taking a pauper bride. Certainly a woman with several thousand pounds as accompaniment would be a much more attractive acquisition.

She stared out the window of Hollybranch Hall

into the spring rain that had been falling for what seemed like weeks. Blurring the sodden landscape, long, languid streams slithered down the panes. It precluded one of her favorite pastimes…working in the kitchen garden. Although her mother disapproved, Isabella enjoyed weeding the vegetables and watching the tiny sprouts mature under her care. These seemingly constant downpours were keeping her from even this simple pleasure.

Will it never stop!

"Lizzie, I can't imagine how you could have been so stupid as to let such a golden opportunity pass you by!" Across the morning room, her mother was berating Isabella's eldest sister. "When Mr. Henderson purchased the estate across the park, I saw him as a heaven-sent gift, yet last evening at the ball, you let him slip right through your grasp after only two dances! He ended the evening with that Tenderly girl, the conniving little wench. I've no doubt we'll be hearing of their engagement any day now. If you'd shown him some affectionate attention, you could have secured him."

"Mama, he's not at all handsome." Elizabeth stuck her nose defiantly in the air. "I've no wish to attract such a scrawny, bandy-legged creature. Furthermore, aside from his purchasing Eastside, we have no proof that he's rich. He may have spent his last penny to buy it."

"Foolish, impudent child!" Shaking her head in disgust, Maud Marston dropped her needlepoint into her lap and turned her scowling countenance on her twin daughters, who'd been born barely a year after Elizabeth. Mary and Ann were bickering in front of the hearth. "And you two! Do stop that ridiculous quarreling! Your father will spend no more on finery for either of you until we get Lizzie married off. I'll hear nothing more of who needs a new gown or gloves or bonnet. Izzy, what's that you're hiding?" She swung on her youngest child. "Not another of your daft stories, I hope."

"No, Mama." She hastened to shove the scrap of newsprint into the pocket of her gown.

"I should hope not! I live in dread of seeing one of your tales come into print. If it did happen, my hope is it would be published as being by an unknown authoress, such as that recent bit of rubbish called *Sense and Sensibility*. I shudder to think what that poor girl's family must be suffering as a result of their daughter's foolhardiness. I'll not have it, Izzy, do you understand? I'll not have it!"

"Have you read *Sense and Sensibility*, Mama? It's a beautiful story of love and…"

"Of course I haven't read it! Managing this household takes every minute of my day and every ounce of my energy. Just mind you don't get carried away by the so-called success of this unknown writer. Oh, Mary and Ann, do stop that incessant quarreling! You're setting my nerves on edge."

They paused only a moment before renewing their dispute with fresh vigor.

Isabella sighed as her little dog, a Pug, jumped up against her knee. Eyes round and bright, he gazed at his mistress.

"What do you think, Perceval?" The advertisement in her pocket rustled as she gathered him into her arms and whispered in his small, black ear. "Has our offer been refused?"

He muttered a Pug sound, wiggled his curl of a tail, and grinned.

"Always the optimist." She cuddled him close. "Thank goodness."

"Izzy, what are you doing? Are you talking to that infernal dog again? I declare, you're becoming as batty as Great-Aunt Agatha. Where are you going?" Maud Marston's rancor continued as Isabella stood and headed for the door, the Pug in her arms. "I hope you're not planning to ride in this weather. Duchess is our only decent saddle animal. I won't have you getting her sick. Or"—she added as an afterthought—"letting Horace catch a chill by accompanying you. I don't want our coachman becoming too ill to drive us to the ball at Eastside next week."

"Do not concern yourself, Mama." She paused and spoke over her shoulder. "I'm simply going to inquire when Horace will be fetching the next post."

"There's no need. Lucinda brought in all of today's letters at breakfast." Mrs. Marston paused a moment before narrowing her eyes to frown at her youngest daughter. "Expecting something, are you?"

"Who would be writing to me, Mama? I'm simply hoping for a copy of this week's newspaper. This rain keeps one indoors, and I would be delighted to have something fresh to read."

"Very well. Go along then." Her mother heaved an exasperated sigh. "While you're about it, remind him not to take out any of the horses. Now, Mary and Ann, I'll not hear another word…"

"Yes, Mama." She closed the door on her mother's continuing rant and headed for the kitchen where, at this hour, Horace their groom would be having a cup of tea with Mrs. Potsworth, the cook.

****

Once free of the morning room and its petty squabbling, Isabella heaved a sigh. Desperation had emboldened her to answer that unusual newspaper advertisement, desperation to escape the strictures and mores of societal demands, but most of all to get away from her discontented mother and sisters and the seemingly constant rain that forced her into their company.

She'd heard stories of fine weather in this new country of British North America, of sunny summer days and blue skies, even in winter, when snow of the purest white blanketed the fields and forests. Her father's brother, a sea captain who frequently traded along its shores, had talked of autumns when shortening days and cooling nights turned the leaves of deciduous trees magnificent tones of red, gold, and orange. Captain Edgar Marston told of lush forests and meadows and a society where the rigid manners of England had largely fallen into an abyss, where a person was free to do one's own bidding...and of the peace and quiet to be found in these bucolic reaches.

It had all sounded wonderful. Perhaps in this new country women were permitted to ride astride, to let their hair blow free in the wind, even to swim naked in waters warmed by summer suns.

Most of all, it would offer an escape from the ignominy of being the youngest of four daughters. She was weary of waiting until Elizabeth, Mary, and Ann were married before she had even a hope of a husband who would free her from Hollybranch Hall.

The possibility of this happening any time soon appeared slight to nonexistent. Elizabeth acted as if the Prince Regent wouldn't be good enough for her. The twins, ill-natured, hollow-headed, and not sufficiently attractive to make a man overlook the petulant aspect of their characters, appeared unlikely to attract any sensible man.

Added to these negative aspects was her father's inability to provide decent dowries for his daughters. That fact barred the possibility of even a financially desperate man taking on one of Phillip Marston's girls.

"Miss." The house parlor maid stopped her with a bobbed curtsy as Isabella headed down the corridor. Lucinda Welsh was a pretty girl with a thatch of dark curls caught up under her cap, dark eyes that sparkled with the suggestion of a lively disposition, and a face blessed with a creamy complexion and pink cheeks. Her figure, a tad on the plump side, was dressed in a black woolen dress topped with a snowy apron.

"Yes?" Isabella paused and smiled at her. Over the years, due to financial restraints, Lucinda had frequently served as lady's maid to Isabella and her sisters and mother. As a result, Isabella had become close to the servant, enjoying the maid's bright, effervescent company to that of the forever wrangling female members of her family.

"Mr. Marston has requested you join him in the library. Captain Marston is with him."

"Uncle Edgar has come? How wonderful! Thank you, Lucinda." She handed the Pug to the maid. "Please take Perceval into the side garden. It's sheltered there, and he does need an outing."

"Of course, miss." Lucinda gathered the little dog

into her arms. "Come along, Master Perceval. We'll see if we can shed rain like a duck."

"Thank you, Lucinda." With a dash that began with a skip, Isabella headed toward the room that ran along the side of the manor. The arrival of her sea captain uncle each spring was an event to which she eagerly looked forward.

"Uncle Edgar!" she cried, bursting into the library. "How wonderful to find you returned!" She had to restrain herself from rushing to encompass him with an inappropriate embrace. Instead she dropped a quick curtsy before continuing, "How fit you look! Your voyages of late must have agreed with you."

"My dear." A tall, gray-haired man in his late fifties, Captain Edgar Marston exuded a dignity that inspired respect. He took her hand and bowed over it before straightening to peruse her, a twinkle in his bright blue eyes. "You're even prettier than I remembered."

"Your uncle has brought something for you." Her father, standing with his back to the fire, raised the tails of his coat to enjoy its warmth. "Something that has rather surprised me, I must say."

"Uncle?" Isabella looked inquiringly up at him.

"A letter, I believe." He drew a paper from his waistcoat. "From a place named Riverhaven, in the North American colony of New Brunswick."

Inside Isabella Marston, something jerked and jumped. Astonished, she didn't at first reach for the missive, simply staring at the sealed document in her uncle's big hand.

"Are you not curious, daughter?" Her father's words brought her out of shock. "I had no idea you knew anyone across the ocean."

"Yes, yes," she stammered out the words as she extended her hand. "May I please have it, Uncle?"

"Of course."

Once the travel-stained document was in her hand, she stood staring down at it. It was sealed with wax. Fear of its contents held her immobile.

"Well, my dear, don't keep us in suspense." Her father's admonition startled her back to action. "Will you not open it? Surely, since you are unaware of the sender, it cannot be anything sufficiently secret for you to need to scuttle off to your room to peruse?"

"No, no, of course not, Papa." With a trapped feeling, she eased it open and spread out the communication, which consisted of two pages. Her gaze fell on the topmost. With a hammering heart, she scanned the lines.

My dear Miss Marston, it was with great pleasure that I received your positive response to my published advertisement in which I expressed the desire to acquire a wife. The charming likeness you chose to include was most appreciated. Your explanation that your lady's maid drew it leads me to believe that this servant has a talent for capturing beauty in its purest form. Paramount, however, was the description of your character and expectations for the future, both of which give me to believe we can make a successful life together.

I am therefore delighted to reply in the affirmative. If you have not altered your position in this matter, I will anticipate your arrival at the soonest instance. I have sent a communication to my London banker advising him to advance any funds you may require for the journey. Enclosed you will find the letter of introduction which you will need when approaching him.

> *Most respectfully, your servant,*
> *Culloden MacPherson*

"Well?" Her father had moved away from the fire and was heading for the brandy decanter and snifters on a nearby table. "Are you not going to share the contents of this mysterious missive? Since I'm not aware of your being acquainted with any young men who have gone out to the colonies, I cannot credit it being of an amorous nature." He poured two measures and handed one to her uncle.

Isabella heard her father's words vaguely through a hum of astonished disbelief. Culloden MacPherson wanted her to join him, to journey to the wilds of North America and marry him. And as soon as possible.

She could no longer hide what she'd done. Wordlessly, she handed the pages to her father.

Casting her a quizzical look, he set his drink aside and took his spectacles from his waistcoat pocket. As he set about reading the letter, her uncle gazed at her fondly.

"Not going to be too great a surprise for the old fellow, is it?" He chuckled. "Nothing that will give an ancient heart reason to pause?" He sampled the brandy.

"Uncle Edgar, you know Papa is only a year older than yourself." Isabella tried to take up her uncle's lighthearted tone, but her mouth had gone dry. A pulse pounded in her chest.

"Nevertheless, let us give him a few minutes to digest the contents of those pages in his hands."

Captain Edgar Marston indicated a chair for her to

sit, but she shook her head. Instead she went to stare out the window into the rain. She couldn't bear to see her father's reaction when he'd finished reading.

"Bella, my dear, this comes as quite a surprise." After what seemed the longest hiatus of her life, she heard his words. "A suitor, no less. And apparently a serious and generous one, since he's offering you the resources of his London bank."

She whirled to see an amused smile tipping his lips.

"Papa…"

"You appear astonished by my reaction." He crossed the room to lay the letter and its included document on a desk. "And rightly so. If this had been my first inkling of the contents of this communication, I most likely would have been taken aback. As it is, I've been forewarned."

"Forewarned?" She sat down abruptly. Her knees had weakened. Too much was happening too swiftly.

"Your uncle informed me of this bit of post before we summoned you." Phillip Marston returned to stand, back to the fire. "He told me he'd received it from a fine-looking young gentleman on the docks in this village of Riverhaven in the colony of New Brunswick. Well groomed and neatly dressed, the fellow had ridden onto the wharf on a fine bay horse just as your uncle was about to cast off. He called out to inquire if the captain knew a Miss Isabella Marston. He said he'd learned the captain had a similar surname. Once Edgar had informed him he was your uncle, the young man held up a letter and asked if he'd be so kind as to deliver it. Your uncle, busily engaged in last-minute preparations to cast off, called out his compliance and sent one of his sailors down the gangplank to fetch it moments before the board was raised and the *Lady M* set sail."

"Are you very angry, Papa?" Isabella found her ability to speak returning as she gazed at her father.

"Angry, child?" He came to stand beside her and placed a hand on her shoulder. "How could I be, when I can understand all too well your desire to escape from this house of howling harridans? Believe me, if I didn't have responsibilities to this estate, I would be sorely tempted to join you."

"Papa"—she could barely believe her ears—"what are you saying?"

"Edgar has described your intended as appearing to be a man of some quality." Phillip Marston took his pipe from the mantel. "His clothing, although ruggedly typical of the area, was neat and in good repair, his manners in accordance with those of a gentleman. God knows, you'll have few enough prospects here, what with your mother's determination that first Elizabeth and then the twins must be married off before you. Therefore"—he began to stuff tobacco into the bowl— "I'm willing to leave the decision to go or stay to your good judgment...and desire."

"Furthermore, my dear, you shall have an escape from marital commitment should you choose to make one." Edgar Marston looked down at her, weathered face crinkling into a kindly smile. "I will take you and that pretty little maid servant of yours back with me on my next voyage to Riverhaven. There, suitably chaperoned by Lucinda, you may stay at the village inn and get to know this young gentleman before you make the decision to marry, have a courtship, as it were. If, by the autumn, you have decided you do not wish to wed, on my voyage back from the Caribbean I will collect you both and see you safely back to England." He turned to his brother. "These days the seas are much safer, with the war ended. Of course, there's always the danger of storms and piracy, but not the villainous threats by privateers such as previously was the case during the days of the conflict."

"So you see, all that is possible is available for your convenience and safety." Her father took a slender bit of wood from the fire, touched it to the bowl of his pipe, and puffed heartily. Once the pipe smoked, he removed it from his mouth to continue. "Your uncle informs me this young man, this Culloden MacPherson, is a person of considerable wealth, regarded as what is known in the colonies as a lumber baron."

"Not an official title, mind you," Edgar Marston was quick to explain. "He's never felt the touch of the royal sword on his shoulder, but in the New World, riches can make one become regarded as the equivalent of an aristocrat in this country."

"And you've seen him, Uncle?" Isabella looked up at the captain hopefully. "You say he's not... unseemly?"

"Not in the least. I was most impressed from our brief acquaintance when he brought that letter for me to deliver." Edgar paused to draw a deep breath before continuing. "As to his foreman who came to oversee the loading of my ship, well, now, he's a horse of a very different color, a raw backwoodsman if ever there was one. Well over six feet tall, broad shouldered, dressed in buckskins, and able to bellow orders to his men and mine as well or better than my first mate, he proved a creature not to be trifled with. Roughshod to the core, he never showed so much as the common courtesy to introduce himself. After he'd identified his wares as being from the MacPherson Mill, he boldly spouted the price expected for the cargo, not a trace of gentlemanly courtesy involved."

Captain Marston crossed the room to lean a shoulder against a corner of the fireplace before continuing. When he did, he spoke more slowly. "That being said, I believe your Mr. MacPherson has chosen well in picking this man as his lieutenant under the conditions to be faced in the lumbering trade in New Brunswick. A timid man would be eaten alive under the necessities of the timber business in that province."

"Well, what say you, daughter?" Phillip Marston allowed her only a brief, speechless hiatus before pressing on. "Your uncle will be staying overnight. Tomorrow he will be going back to his ship, which will sail on Monday's tide. You must decide if you wish to accompany him."

"I will." Every bit of body and mind tingling with a mix of anticipation and apprehension that set her innards trembling, Isabella Marston squared her shoulders and gave the answer she'd decided upon the previous autumn. She drew herself to her full five feet and six inches of height and looked straight at her father. "Yes, Papa, I most definitely will."

****

"What?" Maud Marston's response was a shriek. "Going to some Godforsaken country full of wild animals and savages...to marry a man...a creature you've never met? Child, you have gone quite mad! You always were a willful one, but this...this is pure insanity!"

"Mama…" Isabella tried to interject, but her mother had taken to pacing up and down the morning room, wrenching her handkerchief through her hands as she continued her rant.

"Mrs. Marston, I beg you to be quiet." Her father, ever the voice of reason over the irrational group composed of his wife and three eldest daughters, imposed himself in front of her to still her movements and blather. "Bella has good reasons for her decision."

Phillip Marston had requested a conference in the morning room with only his youngest daughter and his wife. Now, as more rain battered its windows, he drew a deep breath and prepared to do verbal battle with his wife.

"Oh, and I suppose you knew of this lunacy for some time and gave your approval?" She glared up at her husband. "Mr. Marston, what can you be thinking? Where is your common sense?"

"I fear that over the years it's become badly bruised and battered by the present company…Bella excepted. Now, my dear, if you'll compose yourself for a moment and allow me to speak, I think I may lessen some of your objections. Please"—he indicated a chair by the fire—"sit and listen."

Shaking her head and continuing to abuse her handkerchief, Maud Marston obeyed.

"The man Bella is proposing to marry is a baron." As Isabella opened her mouth to qualify the statement, her father, behind her mother's back, frowned her to silence with a shaking of his head. "Now, I realize such an aristocrat is at the bottom of titled society, but still it will give Bella the right to be addressed as 'her ladyship,' if not 'my lady,' and will allow her children to place 'the Honorable' in front of their names. Certainly, not a position to be scoffed at, I think you must agree."

As he spoke, his wife's demeanor had begun to change. When he'd finished, she fidgeted on her chair for a moment, then sniffed and drew herself up to question.

"A baron, you say, Mr. Marston?"

"Yes, my dear, and better still, an extremely wealthy one, according to my brother. Edgar knows of the man and confirms he's a person of more than considerable means. As well, my brother has met him and describes him as young, about thirty years of age, and not ugly of face or form."

"Well, well, perhaps we might come to live with such a situation." Mrs. Marston calmed to look over at her youngest daughter. "At any rate, it will be one off our hands and comfortably, I suppose, situated...even if it is most unconventional that she should marry before her sisters."

"Good, good. Now I hope you will also acquiesce to what I intend to send along with Bella in the way of a dowry."

"Not too much, I hope. You've already said this man she's to marry is wealthy. We've never a penny too many ourselves these days."

"Do not worry your pretty head, my dear." Henry Marston's expression was smug. "No money will change hands. I intend to send Duchess with her."

"Duchess?" The mare's name was a shriek. "She's the only decent riding animal our girls have. Surely you cannot be serious!"

"I'm deadly serious. Bella will need a means of transport, and Edgar has given me to understand the roads in the country to which she's going are little more than trails." He drew a deep breath before continuing, "Horace will be going along to tend the mare, as well as assure our daughter's safety. Lucinda will accompany them as Bella's lady's maid."

"Our coachman and our house parlor maid! Our best servants! Surely, husband, you've taken leave of your senses!" Maud Marston's words were a scream as she jolted to her feet to glare up at him.

"Papa, perhaps you need not send Duchess and Horace." In an attempt to quiet her mother's rant, Isabella turned to her father. "I feel confident Lucinda and I can manage on our own."

"No, no, my dear." He looked down at her, his face crinkling into kindly lines of affection. "This is the best I can offer by way of a dowry. I'll not have my future son-in-law thinking he's married into a family of paupers. Now run along and begin your preparations for the voyage. Your uncle leaves on Monday's tide."

"But there will be no time to send him a reply, to announce my coming."

"You accepted his offer already, I believe. If you write a quick reply, I'll see it gets off on the Tabusintac tomorrow. It's the fastest ship on the North Atlantic run just now. He'll get it in time to prepare for your arrival."

Isabella paused only long enough to give her father a quick kiss on the cheek before darting off to find Lucinda. She located the parlor maid coming in from the garden through the kitchen entrance, the Pug under her arm. Before removing her wet cloak, Lucinda

16

placed Perceval on the floor, where he proceeded to shake vigorously.

"It's a day fit for neither man nor beast," Lucinda commented as she hung the garment on a peg near the door. "This weather is enough to turn a decent girl like myself to drink."

"What would you say to an opportunity to leave it all behind...including my mama's harping and my sisters' whining?" Isabella's excited anticipation couldn't be contained.

"I would say you're describing a bit of heaven, miss." Lucinda brushed damp hair back from her face. She narrowed her eyes to peer at Isabella. "Just what do you have in mind? I know that look. You've something up your sleeve."

"Do you remember my telling you of an advertisement I saw in a newspaper last autumn, placed by a gentleman in British North America, in which he expressed the desire to find a lady wife?"

"Yes." Lucinda's response was tinged with suspicion. "You're not telling me you replied?"

"I did. And, oh, Lucinda, Uncle Edgar has brought *his* reply. The gentleman has accepted my offer!" She grasped her maid's hands and swung her about in a gesture she'd never before felt free to do. "And Papa has agreed you're to come with me. Don't you see what this means? We'll get away from this annoying household! We'll be able to do as we please!"

"Miss, miss." Lucinda stopped their whirling and stepped back to look Isabella squarely in the face. "Have you given this...plan...serious thought? I know you, like myself, are weary of your mother and sisters, but to leave your home, all you've ever known, and journey across the ocean to marry God only knows what kind of creature…probably never to see your family again…"

"Lucinda, do not make it sound like a sentence of transportation." Isabella picked up the Pug, who shivered as his small, wet body cuddled against her warm one. "The first months in this new land will be spent in courtship. If, by autumn, when Uncle Edgar returns, we have not found this new situation tenable, he'll bring us back home."

"But you know nothing of this man you'll be expected to marry. He might be a great, hairy oaf, not fit for any woman, never mind a lady like yourself."

"If he turns out to be so horrible, then we'll return to England, simply having had an adventure. At any rate, I know such will not be the case. Uncle Edgar has met the man, albeit briefly, and he assures me he's a fine-looking gentleman…even if he does wear the clothing of a working man."

"And what is to become of us if this handsome bloke has not the restraints of a gentleman? Although I've sent many a stable lad off cringing and clutching his nether parts when he made unwelcome advances, I'm not so sure I can battle off a frontiersman."

"Horace is going with us." Isabella gave her head a toss. Surely this fact would temper the maid's reluctance.

"Well"—Lucinda gave a resigned sigh—"since I can see there's no changing your mind, I will have to throw my lot in with yours. You'll be needing me. Furthermore, I'd never get a peaceful night's sleep knowing you'd gone off to wed some barbarian all on your own."

"He's not a barbarian. Uncle Edgar has met him and assures me he's a decent gentleman, if a trifle rough in his manner of dress." Isabella paused to catch her breath before she continued more calmly, "I wish there were a book or even a pamphlet describing the province of New Brunswick. It would be helpful to know more about the country. An illustrated publication would be best." Optimistic joy gushed over her. "Perhaps we will produce such a document, Lucinda. I'll write the words, and you can draw the pictures."

"I doubt I'll be drawing many more pictures." Lucinda's response was a grumble. "I suspect it was that drawing I made of you which you saw fit to send off to this savage that influenced his decision to send for you. Now I wish I'd shown you as being fat and ugly, with a great wart on the end of your nose."

"You couldn't be so dishonest. And you're brave and strong and kind, the perfect companion for the adventure we're about to undertake."

"Yes, well, I'll just be making my way down to the stable to select a good sturdy cudgel to take along. I can land a fair blow with such a stick."

"Although I doubt you'll need such a weapon, I thank you, Lucinda, for being willing to fight for our welfare. I knew I could depend on you. I'm so glad"— she danced backwards away from her companion— "Papa has decreed that you will accompany me. Now I must write a note to tell Mr. Culloden MacPherson of my coming."

With a delighted giggle, Isabella Marston turned and half-walked, half-skipped away.

Chapter Two

"She answered aye last autumn, but we've heard nothing this spring. She would have gotten my reply by now. Ya gave it ta that Captain Marston in early March and now it's nigh on the end of May. She had fittin' time ta respond. I'm thinkin' she's changed her mind."

Culloden MacPherson leaned back in his chair in the Riverhaven Tavern and narrowed dark eyes as he looked across the table at his friend. Wearing buckskins, his black curling hair gathered into an untidy queue at the back of his neck, and sporting a heavy beard, the man appeared the epitome of a frontiersman. His companion, although in woolen homespun, was neat and clean shaven, remarkably civilized by comparison.

"Could you blame her?" The tall, broad-shouldered, sandy-haired man heaved a sigh, a twinkle in his eyes. "Poor innocent creature. Little does she know what a great lout she's agreed to wed."

"She'll be gettin' a fine, large house and the wherewithal ta furnish and embellish it." Culloden drew himself upright to meet his friend's taunt. "And I'll not be stintin' with her allowance. I gather, from what she's replied, she's ta come with little more than the clothes on her back."

"I hardly read that condition in her answer," he replied. "She simply said her father could provide no dowry. I'm supposing it's this lack of financial means to attract a suitor in England that led to her taking a chance on a pig in a poke across the sea. As for yourself, as I've told you time and time again, a local girl would be more suited to our way of life. I cannot envision this lady, this Miss Isabella Marston, milking a cow, churning butter, cleaning your house, and washing your drawers."

"None of the local women air ladies ta a manor born." Culloden MacPherson reached forward to encase the tankard of ale in front of him in both large, strong hands. "I'm plannin' on bein' a man o' consequence in this province, Fletch, even governor someday, and that will include bein' able ta present a lady wife ta government officials in Fredericton. I need someone who can speak, act, and dress like a lass of refinement, not a creature who wears homespun, keeps her hair in braids, and grinds out her words like a doxy."

"Someone who can teach you to read and write?" Fletcher Atkin lowered his voice and shot him a smirk.

"Aye, that, too, since ya've declined ta do it." Cully took a long drink before continuing. "And I'll thank ya ta lower yer voice, laddie. Yer the only livin' creature that knows my secret, and ya'll keep it that way or forfeit yer position as my foreman and general manager."

"Your temper is too short to make you a good student. Maybe some pretty young woman will be able to tame it sufficiently to make you sit down and learn."

"I've managed well this far without any of yer book learnin'."

"Of course, but you have to admit it was my words in that advertisement and in the letter of reply that won

21

the lady over."

"Or maybe it was mention of a mansion and a fine estate." Culloden narrowed his eyes as he looked over at his companion.

"What I can't fathom is how a man as clever at ciphering as you, who can estimate a pile of lumber down to the exact number of board feet in a wagon load, never learned letters and words." Fletcher leaned toward his friend and spoke softly.

"I had ta learn numbers and measures if I wasn't ta be cheated blind, but as ya well know, I've worked dusk ta dawn week in and week out fer years since I was a lad. There was no time for the fancy frills of writin' and readin'."

"So when this young lady, this Miss Isabella Marston, arrives, she'll find teaching a part of her wifely duties?"

"Aye, after we're married and she's had time ta adapt ta the country and get my household up and runnin' smooth."

"Cully, I've no desire to discourage you, but you did advertise for a lady wife. This lady who has agreed to come in answer has described herself as Miss Isabella Marston of Hollybranch Hall."

"Aye, and yer point would be?"

"She sounds very much to me as if she's definitely been to a manor born. I hardly picture her gutting fish for your dinner, cleaning manure out of a barn, or scrubbing mud from your floors."

"Ya'll recall she is 'miss,' not 'lady.' Furthermore, lackin' a considerable dowry…it hardly speaks of a woman who's comin' from rich and pampered circumstances."

"Have it your way." Fletcher heaved a sigh. "Molly," he summoned the barmaid. "Please fetch us more ale. My friend's convoluted reasoning has left me parched."

"It's yer convoluted English ways that's left *me* fair parched," Culloden snapped. "I cannae countenance hirin' that Irish woman ta tend her in yer house and act as chaperone until such time as this highfalutin lady sees fit ta name a weddin' day. I see no reason not ta take her ta the church the minute she arrives and have Reverend Edward Morgan marry us at once. 'Twould save a deal of bother, never mind the coin ta pay Irene O'Malley."

"I'll provide Mrs. O'Malley's wage, meager as it is, if that's what's troubling you." Fletcher smiled up at the barmaid as she placed two tankards in front of them. "Thank you, Molly."

She gave him a coy glance before sauntering off.

"Mark my words, laddie, that one has a likin' for ya, and no mistake." Culloden gave his companion a sly nod. "I'm sure a young buck such as yerself is in need of her kind of attention."

"Well, any serious liking will remain on her side." Fletcher took a sip of his ale.

"Because she's a barmaid? Laddie, laddie, I thought part of the reason ya left England was because ya were fair sick of what ya called class distinctions with its rules and regulations."

"It wouldn't be her position that would keep me from her if I felt a sincere attraction." He lowered his tankard and looked across at his friend.

"Well, then, whit?"

"She takes a fancy to any man who might share a

23

bit of his wealth with her. I've no taste for such a money-grubbing creature."

"Then perhaps ya'll not have a likin' fer my future bride? I'm guessin' she was attracted by my wealth, as ya so elegantly outlined it in that advertisement, a lot more than the prospect o' marryin' a pig-in-a-poke Scotsman." He scowled over at his companion. "Or air ya suggestin' ya'd be better suited ta marry such a lass? Ya might have better manners than me, me fine laddie, but chust remember ya've more than a few dark spots in yer past."

"I've never denied that I have. I'm simply saying Miss Isabella Marston won't be my problem, at least not after she vacates my house to marry you. Furthermore, I doubt she'll present much difficulty to a purse-clutching Scot like you. In my acquaintance, you've always kept a tight rein on your finances." He let a wry grin curl his mouth. "At any rate, I wouldn't give up hope of her arrival. It's early spring yet. No telling when that sea captain uncle of hers will see fit to offer her the transport she mentioned in her letter. You'll just have to wait for his ship, the *Lady M*, to arrive before you go despairing of her coming."

"Murderin' bastards!" A tall, broad-shouldered, sandy-haired man burst into the tavern and strode across the room to confront the pair at the table. A swagger in his step and bellicose lines contorting his face, he exhibited all the power of a chieftain of one of the legendary Highland clans Fletcher knew could be dangerously fierce. The newcomer's hand was on the hilt of the sword in the scabbard at his side. "Dirty, underhanded English swine!"

"Aye? Whit's that yer sayin', laddie?" Culloden

was on his feet, facing the newcomer, his expression matching that of his accuser. "I'm no more murderin' than I am English, Brodie MacMillan."

"Dunnae play dumb with me, MacPherson! You know damned well what I'm talkin' about! You and your dandy of an English foreman have been spikin' trees on our patch! This mornin' one such molested pine went through our mill. The big junk of metal implanted in it fair ruined our best saw, but that was small cheese. Pieces flew. My bosom friend Harry Wallace was hit and all but killed. Now he lies near death with only my wife's tendin' to keep him alive!"

"Whit!" Culloden MacPherson stared at his accuser. "Good God, man, whit do ya take me for? Spikin' is a despicable trick. I've had no part in it or ever will!"

"Aye, well, you can protest all you like, but if Harry dies, rest assured you'll be followin' him to the grave in short order!"

"Damn ya ta hell, MacMillan!" Culloden glared at his accuser, hands clenched into fists at his side. "Yer nothin' more than a footpad, a bandit married ta a witch!"

His big hands clutched the edge of the table in a grip that Fletcher, familiar with his friend's movements, knew would shortly upend the bit of furniture toward his accuser and start a major tavern brawl.

"Hold there!"

A wave of relief flooded over Fletcher as he recognized the voice of Captain Caleb Cameron, magistrate for the community. He watched the tall, powerful figure striding into the room, flanked by his deputy, the former first mate on his ship during the recent war, the big Scotsman Duncan MacDougal.

"I'll not have you two coming to blows in a public place—or anywhere in this community, for that matter." The captain stopped by the table and drew himself up to his over-six-foot height. "The rivalry between your two lumber operations is well known, but if you're hell-bent on beating each other to a pulp, you'll have to do it outside of Riverhaven."

"Brodie, this isn't the place, laddie." Duncan MacDougal placed a hand on the shoulder of the man gripping the hilt of the sword and spoke with the soft Highland lilt that characterized their kind. "You don't want to go about breakin' up Mr. Miller's place. He works as hard as you do to make a livin'. Come, now. I've a mind to ride out to your homestead and take a look at that fine foal your stallion fathered last year. I hear she's right bonnie, and wild as a Highland breeze."

"I'm not a wee bairn!" Brodie MacMillan jerked from beneath the man's placating touch. "I'll see this bastard pays for his infamy before I give an inch of ground."

"Just exactly what are your charges, Mr. MacMillan?" The captain stepped to the side of the table to stand between the two pugnacious men.

"This poor excuse for a human bein' spiked trees on our patch! This mornin', while we were cuttin' logs in our mill, the saw hit one such dastardly device. Bits of steel and wood splinters as big as my hand flew like shrapnel. Harry was grievously wounded and now lies near death, bleedin' like a stuck pig, with my wife fightin' to keep him alive."

"Is this true, Mr. MacPherson?" Caleb Cameron turned penetrating blue eyes on the buckskin-clad man.

"Did you spike trees in Wallace-Fowler territory?"

"I did no such thing!" The denial snapped out. "I'm lookin' for an apology from this man for puttin' forward such a foul accusation."

"There'll be snowball fights in hell before that happens!" Brodie MacMillan adjusted his hand on the hilt of his sword.

"Perhaps." The captain remained calm. "But there will be the same activity in this village in July before I allow anyone other than myself or Duncan to enforce the law. I must say"—he continued in a more conversational tone—"I find it difficult to believe Cully would resort to such a despicable practice, Brodie. I've known him for some time, and I cannot attribute such a cowardly act to him." He drew a breath before continuing. "I'd be much more inclined to see him doing exactly what he is now, spoiling for an out-and-out fight. Now"—he cleared his throat—"as magistrate, I order you both out of the village and to stay at least a mile apart until you've cooled down sufficiently to settle your differences in a civilized manner."

Silence fell as accuser and accused stood glaring at each other. Tavern customers, enthralled by the drama, watched.

"Come on, Cully." Fletcher, feeling impelled to make a move before more fuel was added to the fire of the dispute, jerked his head toward the door. "It's time we were heading back to the mill."

Culloden MacPherson paused a moment longer, then with a final scowl and guffaw in Brodie MacMillan's direction, headed for the entrance. There he paused and swung back, dark eyes snapping outrage.

"Ya've no' heard the last of this, MacMillan, not

by a long shot."

"I'm countin' on it, MacPherson. I'm countin' on it."

****

"Never thought I'd see the day the great Culloden MacPherson got backed down by a bit of trash like Brodie MacMillan." Two burly, bearded men followed Culloden and Fletcher out of the tavern. As Culloden began to untie his waiting team from the hitching post, the speaker leaned a shoulder against the building and grinned tauntingly. "Afraid his wife will put a curse on you, MacPherson?"

As Culloden whirled, fists knotted, Fletcher put a hand on his friend's shoulder.

"No, Cully. Don't let the likes of Tom Bracken and Clem Reid goad you into a fight."

"We heard you're buying yourself a woman," the second man yelled. "Sad when the only way you can get a wife is to purchase one who's never seen you!"

"Ignore him." Fletcher tightened his grip on his friend as he felt muscles knot beneath his fingers.

"Go ta hell, ya muck-rakin' bastards!" Snarling out the curse, Culloden returned to untying his horses. He jumped aboard his wagon and swung the conveyance about with such vehemence that Fletcher barely had time to scramble to the seat beside him before Culloden had, with a yell and violent flapping of reins, urged the animals into a gallop.

"Swine!" Culloden didn't speak until they had left the village street and were heading down the trail toward their holdings. He slowed the team to a trot. "Tavern trash, both of them!"

"Tom Bracken and Clem Reid are troublemakers

who aren't worth your getting sent off to jail over." Fletcher relaxed the hold on his seat necessitated by his friend's earlier mad pace. "You know that as well as I do. If you hadn't been riled over what had just happened in the tavern, you wouldn't have let them tempt you toward a fight."

"Yer right, laddie." Culloden MacPherson squared his shoulders. "Gettin' inta fisticuffs at the moment wouldn't be wise. I must preserve me good looks, what with my lady comin'. I don't want ta be greetin' her with black eyes and broken teeth."

Fletcher shook his head ruefully. He suspected that, under all that hair, Culloden MacPherson might not be an unattractive man. Could he possibly persuade him to shed some of it before the arrival of Miss Isabella Marston?

"Damn that MacMillan to hell!" Animosity over the recent incident apparently returning, Culloden muttered the words as he adjusted the reins between his fingers. "Accusin' me of spikin'! What manner of cur does he take me fer?"

"A determined rival. I'm astonished he didn't confront you about damaging the bridge that prevented him and his crew from delivering their timber to the docks before you did. And I've been amazed he hasn't come after you before now."

"Aye, well, there's a sight of difference from removin' a few sticks over a brook ta doing the kind of mischief that could get a man maimed or killed. Yer forgettin', laddie"—the big man's ire receding, he cast a sideways glance at Fletcher, a twinkle in his eyes— "we put a log across the road just afore it. If Wallace's team has half the sense my fine beasts have, they'd stop dead the minute they spied it. There was no danger ta man or creature. Any road, MacMillan has no proof it was me as did it. Those two great nuisances Tom Bracken and Clem Reid were more likely candidates ta be guilty fer such a prank. God knows they've a sharp ax to grind with MacMillan, seein' how he was responsible for the death of their mistress."

"True, Brodie's horse trampled Cassandra Carmody when the woman was threatening to burn his wife alive."

"Aye, well, that's the tale MacMillan tells, him and his sorceress mate bein' the only witnesses."

"I've heard Mrs. MacMillan lost the child she was carrying this past winter." Fletcher shot his companion a glance. "A child, I understand, for whom Brodie held high hopes. No doubt this loss has affected him."

"Aye, well, I'm right sorry." Culloden's tone softened. "No man deserves ta lose a bairn. Still, grief does not give him the right ta go accusin' me of such a dastardly thing as spikin'. Whoa." He stopped the team and handed the reins to Fletcher. "Now I've got ta take a great piss. See if you can manage ta hold this pair quiet until I get back."

"Relieve yourself…if you must explain at all."

"Whit?"

"That's the proper way to refer to a call of nature."

"Argh!" With a disgruntled wave of his hand, Culloden jumped to the ground. Fletcher ran his free hand over his mouth.

God help that young lady who is bound for this place. She's no more idea than a goose does about God of what she's coming into. Cully will be a big enough shock without her discovering she's arrived in the middle of what can easily erupt into a timber war. And I'm responsible. I wrote those damned letters that convinced her to come.

Chapter Three

"So we're about to embark." Staring up at her uncle's ship moored by the wharf and holding Perceval cuddled inside her cloak, Isabella stood at the gangplank, wet her dry lips, and willed the butterflies in her stomach to settle down. A heavy gray mist all but blotted out the spars that rose into it. The damp cold of the day penetrated her woolen cloak, and she shivered. Surely this new country would be more hospitable.

"I had no idea masts were so tall." She glanced at Lucinda standing beside her, carpetbag in hand, and forced a smile. *This whole mad adventure is of my doing. I must put a brave face on it.*

"Looks as if they're fair capable of tipping over the whole kit and caboodle." Lucinda adjusted her baggage in her hands.

Slanting a glance at her maid, Isabella saw her face was unusually pale and rigid. Isabella experienced a rush of guilt.

What have I gotten Lucinda into? I'm dragging her off into the unknown. What if her loyalty causes her to be injured...or worse? If I hadn't encouraged her to come, hadn't longed for her company, she'd be safe at Hollybranch Hall. Maybe in a year or two there'd be a gentleman farmer or a groom who'd be looking for a wife, and who better than Lucinda? As it is...

"Come aboard." Her uncle broke into her thoughts.

He stood beaming down at her from the deck. "We can't afford to miss the tide."

"Good-bye, Mama." She turned to her mother, who'd accompanied the emigrants to the dock along with her husband and daughters. "I wish you good fortune," she called over to Mary, Ann, and Elizabeth, who were standing well back, handkerchiefs over their noses against the wharf smells. "Perhaps you'll soon be sending me news of your nuptials."

"Rest assured *we'll* be choosing civilized men!" Elizabeth shot back.

"Lizzie, that's enough!" Mrs. Marston silenced her eldest daughter. Turning to Isabella, she caught the hands of her youngest daughter in hers, a simpering smile on her face. "My dear, I cannot wait to receive your letters signed by Lady Isabella. You must visit in a year or two and bring the dear baron with you. I should be delighted to introduce him to the neighbors."

"Isabella." Her uncle summoned her again.

"Papa." She turned to her father, tears suddenly welling in her eyes. "I shall miss you, Papa."

"And I you, my special girl." He leaned to plant a kiss on her cheek and murmur in her ear, "If all goes well with you, daughter, you may perhaps expect a visit from me next year."

"I shall look forward to it, dearest Papa."

"Isabella." This time her uncle's voice brooked no dallying. With a wave to her family, she headed up the gangplank, Lucinda close behind. Horace had already boarded and settled the mare Duchess in the hold. Now he stood on the deck beside the captain, raising a hand in farewell salute to Mr. Marston.

A few minutes later, as the *Lady M* slipped away

33

from the wharf amid the bellowed orders of her uncle's mate to the crew, Isabella Marston raised a gloved hand to her family waving on the pier. Inside her cloak, Perceval sneezed and shivered.

"I must say, I'm not sorry to see the back of that lot." Lucinda rubbed a hand across her nose. "Your father excepted, miss."

"You've no regrets about agreeing to come with me to New Brunswick?" Isabella blinked away the tears.

"Not yet, at least." Lucinda again hefted her carpetbag. "Now let's find our cabin. It won't be long until we're on the ocean, and I've been told it can rock a ship something fierce."

"I'm sure we'll manage. Actually a bit of gentle rolling might prove soothing."

                    ****

Beneath her, the ship rocked over the waves. Isabella Marston leaned over the edge of her bed and retched over a bucket in her uncle's cabin, which he'd vacated and left to her and Lucinda that they might have the best accommodations possible for the voyage.

What ever made me think this infernal rolling to and fro might be soothing?

"Lucinda, tell me again that we're doing the right thing, that the man I'm going out to consider marrying will be worth this suffering." She fell back on the pillows and looked up at her companion, who discreetly replaced the cover on the pail.

"He will be, miss." Lucinda took a cloth from a basin of water, squeezed out the excess, and placed its cool dampness on her mistress's forehead. "He's a baron, you must remember...and a rich one, at that.

Best of all, we'll be away from those blessed sisters of yours. Their whining and fighting near drove me to do them violence."

"Not to mention Mama." Isabella mustered a weak grin.

"Your mother can be a trial." Lucinda dipped the cloth back into the water and repeated her ministrations. "Now, you lie back, close your eyes, and rest. In three weeks we'll be docking in our new home."

"Three weeks." Isabella closed her eyes and sighed out the words. It seemed an eternity. Beside her in the bed, the Pug Perceval moaned. His stomach made rumbling sounds. He was as seasick as she.

"Poor little mite," she murmured, placing her hand gently on his small, round head. "You don't deserve to suffer. It's all my doing. Hopefully, the new life we're to begin in New Brunswick will be worth all this misery."

****

"The *Lady M* is comin' upriver with the tide." The man burst into Angus Harper's mercantile store. "She'll be here midday, no later."

Fletcher Atkin jerked about from where he'd been looking over the purchases the shopkeeper had laid on the counter before him. "The *Lady M*? Are you sure, Billy?"

"Certain sure, Mr. Atkin. Mr. MacPherson has ordered everyone to keep a sharp eye out for her. I seed her myself when I went downriver to fetch some salted fish for my missus. I was ridin' hard…the wife's in a family way again, and havin' all manner of cravin's. Says she can't stand another minute without the blessed things. So I bought a sack full and jumped aboard me horse to get back as fast as possible. It was then I saw the *Lady M* makin' her way across the bay into the mouth of the river. What with the wind blowin' rain and sleet into me face, I had to squint somethin' fierce to make her out, but I'm sure, certain sure. She's one pretty…"

"I'll send a man to pick these up, Angus." Swinging out a hand to indicate his purchases, Fletcher spoke to the shopkeeper. He started for the door, then paused and turned back to pull a coin from his waistcoat pocket. "Billy, thank you for the intelligence." He tossed it to the hard-breathing, shabbily dressed workman. "Mr. MacPherson will be grateful."

"Thank you, sir." Billy caught it and touched his forelock. "It's a gentleman you are, sir."

A gentleman? Hardly, but let the fellow think the best of me.

Long strides took Fletcher outside, and a smooth swing put him into the saddle of his bay gelding. A touch of booted heels urged the animal to a flat-out run as they left the village.

****

"You might at least have shaved that bush from your face." Fletcher glanced over at his friend. Watching the *Lady M* being lulled into mooring position, he and his employer stood on the Riverhaven wharf. "You did get that message she sent aboard the Tabusintac, on Monday last, informing you of her imminent arrival. It gave you ample time to prepare."

"She'll take me as I am, and no fussin' about it." Culloden squared broad shoulders and kept his focus on the approaching vessel. "Any road, I don't see as how ye've done a deal of tidyin' about yer own self. Yer still in yer workin' clothes."

"That's because I've no one to impress. Furthermore, you gave me scant time to change after I told you your intended's ship was moving up the river. What with your ordering me to help harness the team…"

"Look!" Culloden raised a hand to indicate a woman standing at the rail. "There she is! And a right bonnie lass if ever I saw one!"

Fletcher followed his friend's gaze. Through the drifting rain and sleet he saw a young woman standing at the bulwarks, cheeks pink in the biting east wind, dark curls lashing out from beneath her bonnet.

Good God, what a miserable day to try to make anyone feel welcome to this country. It's enough to cause her to take the next ship back to England.

As he got a better view of the object of Culloden's attention, his thoughts skidded to a halt. Surely this wasn't the young woman depicted in the sketch that had been included with her letter of acceptance. This person at the rail was buxom, with a round face. Miss Isabella Marston had been drawn as a slender creature with a heart-shaped countenance.

He had no time to speculate further. Culloden was striding forward across the planks of the pier, eagerness reflected in his every step as the gangplank was lowered.

"Miss Marston." He stopped at its foot to look up at her. "Culloden MacPherson." Then, apparently remembering some of the manners Fletcher had struggled to teach him in the previous days, he pulled off his hat and inclined his head. "Yer servant, ma'am."

For a moment, the woman stared mutely. Fletcher didn't have to guess the reason. Confronted by this tall, bearded, long-haired creature in buckskins, any woman might be struck dumb.

"I thank you, sir." Finally she found words, but stayed where she was. "I fear you're mistaken. I'm not Miss Marston. I'm Lucinda Welsh, her lady's maid. This is my mistress." She turned to indicate a pale, thin creature getting slowly to her feet from a capstan by a mast. A small creature with a black mask and ears peered out from beneath her cloak.

Fletcher Atkin bit his lip. *Bloody hell!*

****

"You're Isabella Marston?" Culloden MacPherson recovered his power of speech as the women joined him and Fletcher on the wharf.

"*Miss* Isabella Marston." The dark-haired woman drew herself proudly by her mistress's side and glared at the big, unshaven man.

"Welcome, Miss Marston." As Culloden stared at the pale woman beside the haughty one with flashing dark eyes, Fletcher stepped forward. "Fletcher Atkin, at your service, ma'am." He bowed. "I hope you had a decent voyage?" Although her appearance spoke to the contrary, he could think of no more appropriate words.

"You're…you're not Culloden MacPherson?" The question stumbled out. Her countenance appeared to grow even paler as she looked from one man to the other.

"No, I'm his foreman." He tried to regain the composure he'd lost at his first sight of the woman. "This, as he's introduced himself"—he turned to indicate his companion—"is Culloden MacPherson."

"Ah, I see you've met." Captain Edgar Marston, who until that moment had been involved in seeing his vessel safely docked, came down the plank to join the four people on the wharf. Rain spouting from his hat, he strode to Fletcher, hand extended. "Mr. MacPherson, a pleasure to meet you again, sir."

"I fear there's been a misunderstanding." Fletcher coughed as he turned to the captain. "You see…"

Fletcher Atkin spent the next few moments explaining. When he'd finished, Captain Marston stood staring at the quartet. Finally he found his voice.

"This is a major mix-up." He looked down at his niece, shivering in the miserable day, the little dog in her arms trembling inside her cloak. "My dear, I made a serious mistake in identifying the man I believed to be your intended. You will not be forced into this unexpected situation because of my error. I'll have no objection if you wish to continue on with me to the Caribbean and then back to England."

"I don't like what yer implyin', sir." Culloden confronted the captain. "Air ye sayin' I'm no fit ta marry this young woman? I'm no' a poor man. I have a prosperin' lumber business and a house as good as any you'll come across in this country. I'd have a care, sir, or I might not find this lass"—he pointed to Isabella—"guid enough for me. She's fair skinny as a rake and white as a sheet."

"Mr. MacPherson, I'll thank you not to make disparaging remarks about my niece." Edgar Marston's rugged, wind-darkened face scowled at the man. "She's taken a great risk coming to this country. She deserves to be treated civilly." He turned to his niece. "I repeat, Isabella, if you do not wish to stay, I will gladly take you along with me to the Caribbean and eventually back to England."

"I thank you, Uncle, but no." Isabella glanced back at the *Lady M* and shuddered. "Not all the tea in China will induce me to get back on your ship. Perhaps by the time you return this autumn I will have sufficiently forgotten the horrors of this past voyage or found this village so repulsive I will be happy to face a journey back to England. For the present, Lucinda, Horace, Perceval, Duchess, and I will remain here. I'm sure we can find accommodation at the local inn."

"Horace? Perceval? Duchess?" Culloden stared down at her.

"This is Perceval." She indicated the little dog in her arms. "The man endeavoring to bring my mare Duchess from the ship is Horace, her groom."

I can't believe my eyes. Through the driving rain, Fletcher squinted at the horse prancing and throwing up her head, long weeks below deck having made her fractious as a big, burly man attempted to lead her down the gangplank. *This is absolutely incredible. What are the chances…?*

"Hell and damnation!" Culloden's bellow snapped Fletcher's attention back to the people around him. "I didnae bargain for half of England!"

"Hardly that." Fletcher fell into the role of peacemaker. "You wanted a lady wife. It's only to be expected that she would bring along her amenities."

"Miss Isabella has had an unpleasant voyage." The one who'd identified herself as Lucinda Welsh spoke up. "She needs a comfortable bed and decent food."

"Of course." Fletcher took command, since he could see his flummoxed employer was presently incapable of doing so. "As soon as your belongings are unloaded, we'll take you to my house. I've moved to live with Mr. MacPherson until the wedding. You'll have my accommodations to yourselves. My housekeeper, Mrs. O'Malley, will be on duty there to serve you and act as chaperone."

"I'll see to my mistress, thank you very much, sir." Lucinda Welsh drew herself up to what he fancied was about five feet four or five inches in height and gave him a saucy glance. "We've no need of an Irish wench."

"I'm sure you've made your mistress comfortable back in England." Recognizing the maid's pride in her duties, Fletcher was quick to compensate. "But in this country where the woman of the house is expected to carry in wood to feed the hearth, milk cows, tend chickens, clean stables, and any number of other domestic duties, Mrs. O'Malley's assistance may be appreciated."

"Well, then, perhaps, given such a list of unseemly chores, a scullery maid might come in handy." She cast him a belittling glare. "Very well, we'll accept the services of this creature." She gave her shoulders a haughty shake.

A corner of Fletcher's mouth quirked. He could imagine the sparks that would fly when this high and mighty lady's maid tried to put Irene O'Malley in the position of scullery maid.

"Come along, then." With a rueful shake of his head, Culloden MacPherson brought himself back to the moment and turned toward the cargo wagon, a team of large black horses attached, waiting at the backside of the wharf. "There's no sense wastin' further time.

Captain." He spoke over his shoulder to Edgar Marston, who still bore traces of the shock the unexpected situation had given him. "I'm assumin' these people have baggage. Order a couple of yer lads ta fetch it ta my wagon. This nor'easter is a bit of a…witch"—he caught himself over what Fletcher knew would have been his normal word—"and I've no desire to have any of this English gaggle catchin' their deaths of cold…not after I've paid dear for them."

"Paid dear?" Isabella Marston turned on the big man, pale face suddenly engulfed in an outrage that astonished and delighted Fletcher. *The lady has spirit.* "What have you paid, sir, may I ask? Nothing beyond our passage, and there my uncle was most reasonable in his fares. You'll not find undue expenses charged against your London bank. Therefore, do not think that you've overpaid for me or any of my company! Furthermore, if you're so petty as not to wish to pay our passage, I'm sure my uncle will acquiesce to your reneging. *He* is a generous gentleman."

"Argh!" Culloden MacPherson turned and headed for his wagon.

"Isabella, my dear, are you genuinely certain you wish to stay?" Her uncle frowned down at her. "Surely even the unpleasantness of another voyage would be better than enduring this unfortunate mix-up for which I most humbly apologize."

"Mr. Atkin has offered the hospitality of his house, including a suitable housekeeper." She stuck out her chin and squared her shoulders. "We'll remain until you return in the autumn. I must give this country…and its people…an opportunity. Farewell, Uncle Edgar." She turned to her maid and groom. "Come along, Lucinda and Horace. Let us see what kind of hostelry Mr. Atkin has to offer."

She adjusted the little dog in her arms and strode regally toward the man who waited beside the cumbersome-looking wagon, a scowl distorting the face above the beard.

****

"Well, at least ya've brought something of value." Culloden MacPherson muttered as he headed the horses along a trail that led out of the village and upriver through the trees. He gestured, with his hands holding the reins, toward the little dog in her arms. "I dunnae know a lot about pigs, but I vow, I've never seen such a one as this."

"Perceval most definitely isn't a pig!" Her drenched cloak clinging to her, Isabella clutched her pet closer, shielding him from the elements as best she could. From beneath the water dripping from the hood of her cloak, she glared over at her companion on the driver's bench. "He's a Pug dog and one of the finest of the breed."

"Whit?" He stared at her through drifting rain and sleet. "Niver! With a face like that? I saw its tail stickin' out from under yer cloak. Curled as tight as on one of the best porkers I've ever come across."

"He's my devoted friend and companion, and I'll thank you to treat him as such, Mr. MacPherson."

A chuckle from Fletcher Atkin, sitting with Lucinda and Horace in the cargo space behind them, made her turn to glare at him. The wagon lurched in a rut. She and her dog might have been thrown from the seat if Fletcher hadn't caught her arm to steady her.

"You must forgive Mr. MacPherson his ignorance

43

of your dog's fine pedigree," he said, and she saw not only humor but a kindly concern reflected in the man's features. Even through her distress and the misery, she realized he was a handsome man. "He's not acquainted with the fads and fancies of English society."

"And you are, I suppose?" Recovering her balance, she snapped at him and gave him what she hoped was a haughty scowl, although she found herself weakening in confrontation with the expression in his blue eyes.

"Once upon a time, Miss Marston, once upon a time." He turned away.

The wagon jolted again. Puzzled, she was forced to center her attention on maintaining her balance on the seat. Drenched, shivering, and utterly miserable, Isabella Marston wished she could recant her decision to stay in this miserable country, which seemed even worse than the one she'd left behind, but it was already too late. Her uncle, having delivered her and her entourage, the full extent of his cargo destined for Riverhaven, had already set sail.

"Hold up there!"

Isabella's heart seemed to bound to her throat as, ahead of them in the downpour, a horse and rider appeared, blocking the trail. "Culloden MacPherson, a word!"

The team, apparently as startled as Isabella, jolted sideways, shaking their heads and rattling harness.

"Get out of my way, MacMillan!" her companion yelled as he brought his horses under control. "It's a right miserable day, and I've a desire ta get home."

"Aye, well, seein' you're already as drenched as a drowned cat, a few more minutes won't matter." The man brought his horse abreast of the wagon seat and squinted up at Culloden MacPherson. Even with water dripping from his cap, the man cut an imposing figure. Broad of shoulder, a sword belt slung across a powerful-looking chest with an impressive weapon in a sheath at his hip, he wasn't about to give way to Culloden's order. And even though his face was encompassed by the darkest of scowls, she recognized this stranger had a handsome countenance beneath his anger.

"I see ya weren't long availin' yerself of yer master's goods." Culloden jerked his head to indicate the charcoal mare the man rode. Although wet and mud-spattered, the creature with its silver mane and tail stood out as a magnificent animal. Isabella, an equine fancier, in spite of her present discomfort and misery couldn't help admiring it.

"You know my stallion was murdered. The filly he sired is still too young to ride. Scotia, here, was the only mount available. Now, enough of that. You've gone back to spikin' trees, I've discovered. And with my boon companion Harry still at death's door because of your last infamy! What kind of infernal bastard are you, MacPherson?"

"Whit?"

Looking over at her companion, Isabella saw what she interpreted as genuine shock cross his face.

"I took advantage of this inhospitable day when we weren't workin' the mill to do some checkin'. So far I've found six more of those killers implanted in trees on our patch."

"Bollocks!" Culloden MacPherson drew back his lips in what resembled a snarl. "I've told ya time and time again, MacMillan, I'd have no part in such a dastardly practice."

"Aye, well, we'll see. If such murderous antics keep up, if there's one more incident against me and mine, there will be a war between us, I give you my word."

"Gentlemen, this isn't the way to settle anything. Tomorrow, when we're dry and in better frames of mind…" Fletcher Atkin stood in the back of the wagon in the role of peacemaker.

"You'd be wise to keep your counsel, Atkin!" Brodie MacMillan was quick to squelch his effort. "This is between MacPherson and me. We've no need for a London dandy to smooth us down!"

He swung the mare away and galloped off into the storm.

"Bastard!" Culloden shook the reins over the team's backs and started them forward. Behind him, Fletcher staggered at the sudden movement before dropping back down onto the board seat.

Isabella struggled to bring her heartbeats back to normal. Watching these two men on the verge of all-out battle was like witnessing a pair of Titans preparing to make war. What had she gotten herself involved in? Suddenly gentlemanly practices didn't seem so frivolous, so unimportant.

"What was that about?" As the wagon jolted forward, she had to ask the driver.

"Men's business. None of yers." He focused ahead on the team. The two sentences snapped with an annoyance she realized it wouldn't be wise to challenge. "Ya chust be stayin' clear of that lad. He's a highwayman married ta a witch."

Chapter Four

Culloden MacPherson drew rein in a clearing in front of a log house. Through sheets of rain, Isabella saw a similarly constructed barn some distance back in the trees, a paddock at its rear. In the miserable day, with a gale forcing the surrounding forest to bow to its fury, the drenched dooryard appeared a mudhole full of hoof prints and roiled earth, far worse than the stable yard at Hollybranch Hall in the most terrible of English weather.

At least the house looks sound. Any shelter out of this terrible day will be welcome. There's hope of a hearth fire. Smoke is issuing from the chimney.

"Welcome to my home, Miss Marston." Fletcher Atkin jumped to the ground and held up his hands to assist her from her perch. "I hope you will be comfortable here."

"Thank you, Mr. Fletcher. Mr. MacPherson, please hold Perceval." Much as she disliked the idea of relinquishing her pet to the man who'd branded him a pig, she had no choice. If she left the Pug free on the seat, she knew he'd make an attempt to follow her. Jumping from the height this ungainly wagon presented could see him seriously injured.

"Oh, aye." He took the little dog into his arms with a tenderness that astonished Isabella, his expression softening as he stared down at Perceval.

"Chust be quick about it." Looking up at her, he hastily reverted to his former bitter self. "I've no desire to have him foulin' me."

"I assure you, Perceval is a perfect gentleman." She cast a haughty, disdainful look at the buckskin-clad man. "He's been in any number of fine houses and carriages and never once had an accident. He's…"

"Miss Marston?" Rain running down his face, Fletcher Atkin broke into her deluge of defense as he continued to hold up his hands. "We'd best be taking cover."

"Yes, of course." Gathering her drenched cloak about her, she moved to accept his offer. "Thank you, sir." She bobbed a short curtsy after he'd placed her on the ground.

"Your servant, ma'am."

Behind her she heard Culloden MacPherson scoff at their exchange of courtesies.

"That's most kind of you." Isabella found herself answering in much more congenial words and tone than she would have used when addressing a servant in the Old Country. "Mr. MacPherson, please pass Perceval down to me."

"With pleasure, yer royal highness." Instead of doing as she requested, he deftly wound the reins around the whip stand and jumped to the ground.

Held ignominiously under the man's arm, Perceval grunted from the jolt.

"I asked you to hand him down to me." Weary from the journey, cold and hungry and utterly miserable, not even years of training of how a lady never revealed her emotions could not prevent her snapping at him. Perceval was special to her. The Pug, like his father before him, was her faithful friend and companion. He'd endured that horrendous voyage, ill as she herself. He deserved better treatment.

She snatched the little dog into her arms. She would allow no one to misuse her beloved Perceval, not even this bearded barbarian. "You might have injured him," she continued, snuggling the Pug into her arms.

"I'll be doubtin' that would happen." Dark eyes flashed angrily back at her. "He's one tough little laddie, or I'm no judge of beasts."

A stout woman appeared in the doorway of the log house. A smile brightened her plump face as Fletcher Atkin hurried Isabella to join her.

"Lord bless us and save us, child, I thought you'd never arrive." After wiping her hands on the snowy apron that covered a simple cotton dress, she reached out to draw Isabella inside. Wisps of curling gray hair protruded from beneath a white cap.

"Come in, come in." She put an arm about Isabella with a familiarity no servant at Hollybranch Hall would dare. "This is a witch of day if ever there was one. There's a fine fire on the hearth and a hearty stew to warm your innards, but being English, I fancy you'll be seeking a nice hot cup of tea first. That's ready and waiting as well."

"Miss Marston, this is my housekeeper, Mrs. Irene O'Malley, and the maker of the finest caribou stew you're ever likely to encounter." Following them inside, Fletcher Atkin was quick to intervene with an introduction. "Mrs. O'Malley, Miss Isabella Marston. Now, you must excuse me while I help the others with the horses and baggage." He turned and strode back out into the stormy day, closing the plank door behind him.

"A pleasure it is to meet you, me dear." The woman stuck out a dimpled hand. "Mr. Atkin showed me the likeness you sent. I must say, it didn't do you justice. Even if you're a tad pale and scrawny at the moment, that's nothing a bit of good fresh air and decent food won't fix. I'll soon have you back to being as pretty as your picture."

"Thank you." Isabella, although astonished by the Irish woman's hearty greeting and blunt description, nevertheless managed a reply politely. "That's most kind of you." The door burst open to admit two more drenched travelers, struggling with trunks and valises. "Do you think you might have enough tea and food for my maid and groom?"

"For sure and certain, dear child." She cast an assessing look over Lucinda and Horace as they straightened from their task. "My, he's a hearty one," she continued giving Isabella a nudge and wink as she studied Horace.

Startled by this unexpected familiarity, for a moment Isabella didn't reply. When words came, they were addressed to the groom.

"Horace, what of Duchess? Has she been seen to?" Her mare had been tied to the back of the wagon for the journey to the homestead.

"Cully...Mr. MacPherson is seeing to her and his team." Fletcher Atkin stepped inside carrying a pair of valises. "He told us to come ahead and find shelter."

"Duchess?" Alarmed, Mrs. O'Malley turned on Isabella. "Lord have mercy, is there a noblewoman outside in the storm? I didn't see another soul..."

"Duchess is my mare," Isabella reassured the startled housekeeper.

50

"Oh, well, then, that *is* a relief." Irene O'Malley took Isabella's arm and drew her toward the hearth, where a log fire issued light and warmth. "What's that you're clutching under your cloak? Surely this is another newcomer," she continued as the little dog's head peeked out.

"He's my Pug. His name is Perceval."

"Poor, wee creature." She patted the dog's shuddering head. "By the looks of you, I'm assuming you didn't enjoy the voyage across the heaving sea any more than your mistress." She hastened to add another log to the fire. "I'll get the lot of you warmed up and fed in two shakes of a lamb's tail, never fear."

"Though I don't doubt Mr. MacPherson is a dab hand with horses, I will take a look at the Duchess myself." Horace picked up the shabbiest of the valises. "I'll change into dry gear...if such can be found in this bag...in the barn."

"You'll come back shortly." Mrs. O'Malley's words stopped him at the door. "I have a fine pot of stew bubbling on the hearth. I reckon, from the size of you, you can do a fair job of swallowing your share."

Horace grunted, then proceeded outside.

"He is quite a man." The Irish woman surprised Isabella with her admiration of the groom as she stood rubbing her hands up and down her apron, staring at the door after he'd gone. "Now..." She broke out of her musings and swung on Isabella and Lucinda. "Let us move this baggage into the bedrooms and get the pair of you into dry clothing." She indicated two doorways covered by curtains.

****

Isabella glanced around the room. It had one

51

window, high in the wall opposite the bed built into the log wall. The plank floor beneath her feet felt comfortingly firm after weeks of tossing about on her uncle's ship. Warmth from the fire crackling on the hearth in the outer room had spread into the small chamber, giving it a pleasant ambience.

Opening her trunk, she was relieved to discover its contents had remained dry. She rifled through neatly folded clothing until she came to a woolen gown she'd brought in anticipation of cold winters. Digging deeper, she found undergarments, stockings, and slippers. Gratefully she threw them across the bed.

"It will be so good to get out of these wet things and into something dry," she said to the Pug curled up on the bed.

Going to the curtain that served as a door, she gave it a quick twitch to make certain it fully covered the entrance. In the outer room she could hear Mrs. O'Malley humming as she bustled about preparing the meal. Sounds coming from the adjacent bedroom told her Lucinda was unpacking in the cubicle she would share with Mrs. O'Malley. Perhaps this was a peaceful household; perhaps here she'd find the tranquility unobtainable at Hollybranch Hall.

She returned to the side of the bed and stripped off her clothing. They fell into a sodden heap on the plank floor. Naked, she was reaching for the first of her fresh undergarments when she heard Culloden MacPherson bang back into the cabin.

"More stuff the lass brought with her," he muttered. His booted footsteps strode across the outer room.

"Mr. MacPherson…" She heard Mrs. O'Malley

begin, but before the woman could waylay him, he was at the bedroom entrance, flinging aside the curtain, her second trunk on his shoulder.

Oh, God! She snatched up the chemise she'd been about to don and clutched it to her breasts.

He stopped. His burden slid from his grasp. It hit the floor with a resounding thud. He stared.

"Mr. MacPherson!" The Irish woman appeared at his side, grabbing his arm. "You come away from there! You can't go charging about this house...not with ladies in residence."

The curtain fell back into place as she yanked him away.

By the time Isabella heard him slamming out the door, she was no longer cold. Instead she was suffused from head to toe with a glowing blush.

From the bed, Perceval stared up at his mistress, looking as startled by the preceding incident as she felt.

"You must forgive Mr. MacPherson." Mrs. O'Malley's words came through the curtain. "He lived here for some time with Mr. Atkin. He's accustomed to making himself familiar about the house. I'm sure he never meant to embarrass you, dearie. You must remember he's not had much truck with ladies such as yourself afore."

"Of course." Isabella let her chemise drop over her head, its hem falling to her ankles, and stood for a moment, waiting for her racing heart and burning cheeks to subside. "I'm sure he meant no disrespect."

Once fully dressed in fresh clothing, she managed to subdue her embarrassment sufficiently to return to the kitchen. With Perceval in her arms, warmed by the fire dancing on the hearth and comforted by the aromas of stew and brewing tea, Isabella pushed aside her encounter with Culloden MacPherson and began to take inventory of her surroundings.

The log house, with its wide hearth and side oven, consisted of three rooms—the kitchen area in which they sat and the two bedrooms at the rear. The kitchen contained dressers filled with dishes and pots, a sink with the amazing commodity of a hand pump, and a plank table with benches along each side and chairs at either end. A pair of rocking chairs sat on either side of the hearth. Clean and neat, board floor well swept, windows gleaming, although a long way from the size and civilized outlook of Hollybranch Hall, the structure presented a reassuring solidarity.

"Here, child, take a seat by the hearth." Mrs. O'Malley took her by the arm and led her to one of the two rocking chairs. "And you as well, young lady." Once Isabella was seated, the woman turned to Lucinda, who'd also come back into the main room dressed in dry clothing. "You must be as frozen as your mistress."

"Of course I will not." Lucinda confronted the housekeeper, head held high. "I'm not about to sit about and let others do for Miss Isabella. I'm strong and able, and I'll have you know I'm ready to do my share around here."

"As you wish." Mrs. O'Malley drew herself up to face the maid servant, her countenance every bit as defiant. "You can begin by setting the table. For six, mind. The men will be joining us shortly."

"I can count, thank you very much." Lips tightly pursed, Lucinda sashayed across the room to the dresser that held plates, bowls, mugs, and utensils. "I take it you haven't any cups and saucers about the place?"

"You are in a wilderness home." Mrs. O'Malley had gone to the hearth to stir a pot simmering there. "A long time such fancies would last here! You'll have to make do."

"Huh!" Lucinda began to take down the settings. She carried a stack of plates and bowls to the table, placed them on a corner, then ran a finger over the surface.

"You'll find no dust or dirt there, my girl." Mrs. O'Malley snapped, catching her gesture. "So if you're hell-bent on being of assistance, just set out the dishes and don't go making a great issue of it."

Isabella bit her lower lip. Were these two destined to be enemies? Quite possibly she'd have her work cut out for her in the role of keeping domestic peace.

"Now, Mr. Pug," the housekeeper put her hands on her hips and looked at the little dog in Isabella's arms. "I've a nice bowl of caribou stew cooled for you. Put him down, miss. Poor little mite, you must be starving."

"Mrs. O'Malley, Perceval has never eaten caribou. I'm not sure…"

"I'm sure he's had venison back in England. Not a great stretch to caribou. Just put him down, miss, and let him have a go."

Reluctantly Isabella placed the Pug on the floor. The housekeeper took a container from the cupboard and placed it on the floor. "There. You get your chops around that, and I reckon you'll begin to feel less peaky," she addressed the little dog.

Perceval sniffed the mixture of meat, vegetables, and thick gravy. With a mumbled combination of contented Pug sounds, he stuck his muzzle into it and gobbled.

"Seems like he's making do." The Irishwoman turned away with a vindicated swish of broad hips.

****

As Lucinda and Mrs. O'Malley busied themselves with dinner preparations, Isabella sat gazing into the flames dancing on the hearth. At her feet, snoring, lay Perceval, dry and with his hunger satiated, stretched out on a quilt furnished by the housekeeper.

Her thoughts travelled to the man Fletcher Atkin. He was a puzzle. Having identified himself as Culloden MacPherson's foreman, most likely his factotum—she hazarded the guess by the way he'd taken charge—he nevertheless demonstrated the manners of an English gentleman. A gentleman who perhaps had fallen from grace at home? He didn't have the look of a man who'd become dissipated by drink, but there were other reasons why a young man could be sent away. But then again, maybe he was simply an adventurer weary of the strictures of life in England. An adventurer...like herself.

Her thoughts were interrupted as the men filed into the cabin. Culloden MacPherson, who brought up the rear of the group, met her gaze for a moment before ducking his head in what she guessed might be embarrassment.

At least the man has the good grace to be ashamed of his brash action.

She looked away, determined to further avoid the man's glances.

"Come to the table, my dears." Mrs. O'Malley interrupted her speculation as the housekeeper indicated the table set with six places. In the center, bread that looked freshly baked, with a saucer of butter beside it, immediately caught Isabella's attention. After the coarse fare aboard her uncle's ship, these two items alone made her mouth water. Mrs. O'Malley bustled about, placing bowls of steaming stew at each of the place settings while Lucinda filled mugs with steaming, aromatic tea.

"Take a place on the benches," Mrs. O'Malley directed the women and Horace. "The chairs at either end are for Mr. Fletcher and Mr. MacPherson."

As the men made to take seats, the Irish woman stopped Culloden and Horace. "You'll not be getting a mouthful, Culloden MacPherson, nor you either"—she swung on the groom—"before you both stop at the washstand outside the door and see to your filthy hands." The Irish woman blocked their further progress, hands on her hips. "We eat clean and civilized in this house. You might take an example from Mr. Fletcher. Look how he's washed up before coming to the table."

Glancing at the mill manager, Isabella saw that his face and hands were clean, his hair freshly pulled back from his face.

"Now, Mrs. O'Malley, there's no need to make comparisons." Fletcher Atkin hung his wet coat on a peg by the door.

Scowling, Culloden gave a muffled retort as he turned and strode back outside. Horace followed.

When Culloden MacPherson and Horace returned a few minutes later and took their places, the man in buckskins dropped onto the chair at the head of the table and dug into his food as if he hadn't seen nourishment for weeks. Snatching a slice of bread with a big, calloused hand and dipping it into the gravy, he ignored the others at the table.

Barbarian. Culloden MacPherson is an absolute barbarian. Why did Uncle Edgar have to make such a terrible mistake!

Glancing around at the others, she caught Lucinda's disgusted expression. She had the distinct feeling her former maid wasn't about to tolerate such table manners for very long.

In contrast, she noticed Fletcher Atkin had taken his time beginning his meal. He'd paused to look down at Lucinda's carefully laid place setting before him, a shadow of a smile on his lips.

What was he thinking? That such care was out of place in a wilderness log house? Or was it something else...something she couldn't yet fathom?

****

When they had finished the meal, Mrs. O'Malley set to clearing the table. Lucinda was quick to join her in the task.

"No need, child." The Irish woman turned to her, a kindly smile crinkling her plump face. "You've had a long journey."

"I told you, I've never been one to sit on my backside and let others do for me," Lucinda said, her tone altered to one of mild resistance. "I'm not about to start now."

A truce. Thank God, a truce. Isabella felt like heaving a sigh of relief. Then she repressed a chuckle. Good food, dry clothing, and a warming fire had revived her. She could see the humor in Lucinda's lapsing back into the country vernacular the former parlor maid had spouted when first she came to work at Hollybranch Hall. Her mother's constant nagging had gradually refined the young woman's language, but free of Maud Marston's rebukes, Lucinda Welsh was reverting, becoming her natural self. Isabella was glad. She'd come to Riverhaven to be liberated from Old Country restraints. She wanted the same for her maid.

"Very well." Mrs. O'Malley accepted the young woman's insistence. "I'm not one to deny the occasional helping hand." She turned to the men. "It's high time you were seeing to the barn work and leaving us ladies some privacy."

"Of course, Mrs. O'Malley." Fletcher Atkin stood and gave the robust housekeeper a nod of acquiescence. "Another excellent repast. I thank you."

"Yes, Mrs. O'Malley, a fine meal indeed," Isabella agreed.

"Ah, get on with the pair of you." The housekeeper waved aside their praise, but her plump face dimpled with pleasure. "It should at least keep your bellies from sticking to your backbone until first light."

With a disgruntled mutter, the buckskin-clad man stood and headed for the door. Horace followed.

"You ladies will have this house to yourselves for as long as you wish." Fletcher faced the women after the groom and the lumberman left. "I'll stay with Mr. MacPherson at his manor, farther upriver. Your groom can join us and come down each day to tend the stock. It's but a short walk. Mrs. O'Malley will remain here as chaperone and housekeeper. I hope that will be agreeable."

"That's most generous of you, Mr. Atkin." Isabella inclined her head in his direction.

"It's the very least I can do to make your introduction to this country more agreeable. Certainly the weather hasn't done much to recommend New Brunswick as a place to put down roots. Now I bid you good evening, ladies."

He took his coat from the peg by the door, gave a short nod to the women, and left the log house.

A true gentleman in spite of his attire. What can have brought him here when he has the manners that would have made him acceptable in the finest homes in England?

****

"We'll be leaving now." Fletcher Atkin stepped into the kitchen where Lucinda and Mrs. O'Malley were tidying the room. "The stock is fed and settled for the night. Have you everything you need, Mrs. O'Malley?"

A sudden desire not to look superfluous, not to appear a lady of leisure, gushed over Isabella. She got up from the chair by the fire and added a log. As flames leaped, she turned back toward the man, head held high, shoulders back.

"We're fine and dandy, Mr. Atkin." The Irishwoman paused, hands on her hips. "You run along."

"Very well. Ladies, I bid you good evening." He went out.

"As fine a gentleman as you'll find in this country." Mrs. O'Malley returned to replacing clean plates and cups on the shelves. "We could use a few more of them. Now, dearies, we've best to bed. I reckon you're both bone weary." She indicated a lighted candle on the table. "You take that one, miss." She picked up its mate from the sideboard. "Come along, young lady," she turned to Lucinda. "We'll use this one to show us

60

the way."

"Mrs. O'Malley." Isabella hesitated as the woman, followed by Lucinda, made her way toward the second bedroom. "Are we quite safe here…three women alone?" She didn't want to ask the question, didn't want to sound a frightened female, but she knew she wouldn't sleep well without an answer.

"Bless your heart, miss, quite safe." Isabella watched as the Irishwoman pulled aside the curtain on the door of the room she'd indicated would accommodate her and Lucinda. Narrow beds along each side came into view. "No one would dare bother women under the protection of Culloden MacPherson. Furthermore"—she moved into the room, placed the candle in its holder on a small table that stood between the beds and indicated a pair of pistols on its top—"I'm a crack shot. Anyone who dares dally with us may not live to regret it. These are primed and ready. Now off to bed with you."

****

Fletcher Atkin watched, amused, as the big groom perused his log barn. In side-by-side box stalls, Duchess and his gelding, Galahad, placidly munched hay from their mangers. They'd run wild in the paddock behind the structure while supper was served in the house. Now they were content to settle for the night. Across from them, a soft-eyed brown cow chewed her cud as she watched the two men. In a pen beside her, chickens, clucking contentedly, settled for the night.

"A fine, strong place you've got here." The man finally spoke, letting his gaze roam up to the hayloft, then to the thick walls and plank doors. "I reckon as how nothing will get at your stock."

"I like to feel confident my animals and fowl are safe." Fletcher was glad to hear approval in the coachman's words. "You have a way with horses, Mr. Horace. I admired the manner in which you brought Miss Marston's mare off the ship. Not an easy task with an animal that's been contained for weeks, especially a high-bred creature like her." He indicated Duchess. "Hunter?"

"Bred as such, sir." Horace fell into conversation. Fletcher guessed horses were one of his favorite subjects. "But didn't prove out. Got sold off as a lady's mount. Oh, I reckon she could still take a few fences, but she'd never make it in the field, nor Miss Isabella neither."

He stopped short. Fletcher understood. The big man had made an unintentional faux pas in discussing his mistress's abilities with a stranger.

"I didn't mean Miss Isabella isn't a good rider"—Horace was immediately stumbling to correct his statement—"I just meant she never took to the hunt."

"No need to explain, Mr. Horace." Fletcher stilled his apprehensions. "Not all ladies enjoy the chase and kill."

"If you please, sir, it's Horace, just Horace."

"Very well, Horace it shall be. Horace, did something not strike you when you first saw my gelding?"

"Aye, sir, that it did. Downright uncanny, I'd call it. A sign, perhaps?"

"Let's hope it proves a good omen."

"Whit's keepin' you pair?" The shout from Culloden MacPherson brought them both back to the moment. "I've a pair of harnessed horses eager to be off to their own stable and out o' this bloody awful evening. Best and Timber are fair champin' at their bits."

"The man calls his team Best and Timber? Sure the mare's name would be Bess." Horace looked the question at Fletcher.

"Her name was indeed Bess when he purchased the pair," Fletcher explained. "He decided it would be a good idea to change it to something that wouldn't be too difficult for the animal to recognize but that would promote his product. Now we'd *best* be going." Fletcher grinned at the coachman. "Mr. MacPherson isn't a man noted for his patience."

"Are you sure the ladies will be safe alone?" Horace hesitated as the other man headed for the door.

"Quite sure." Fletcher turned back, his face twitching with humor. "No one in this valley would dare touch anything or anyone who comes under the protection of Culloden MacPherson. Furthermore, Mrs. O'Malley isn't a woman to be trifled with. She keeps a pair of pistols primed and ready, is a crack shot, and all and sundry know it."

"Very well." Horace nodded acceptance and followed Fletcher out to where rain and sleet filled the inhospitable evening. Trees surrounding the homestead clearing continued to bend before the unrelenting gale.

"It's high time you showed up." The lumber baron, his face above the beard wrinkled into a scowl, held the reins of his team, who stood shaking their heads in the miserable evening. "I've scant patience after a day such as this. Climb aboard."

Fletcher took his place beside Culloden on the wagon's high seat, while Horace climbed into the back and sat down. With an annoyed flap of the reins over the team's backs, the man in buckskins sent the team forward in a shambling trot along a rough broken trail into the darkening forest.

"Cully, I see no valid reason for your discontent with Miss Marston," Fletcher commented. "Back home in England, she'd be regarded as a perfect lady. That's what you wanted, isn't it, not some two-hundred-pound Amazon."

"A few more pounds wouldn't hurt her." He cast Fletcher an annoyed glance. "How can anyone that scrawny be expected ta help with the hayin' or milkin' or churnin'? As for that horse she brought with her…never been in harness in its life, I'll wager. A lady's mare, good fer nothing but a Sunday afternoon's ride. And that wee beast she calls a dog…"

"Very well, very well. Maybe a good night's sleep will sweeten your temper."

"And more than a wee dram before I find my bed. Bloody hell, what a day." He shook his head, sending moisture flying. It hit Fletcher in the face.

"Damn it, Cully, you're not a dog! Don't shake all over me." Fletcher caught himself up after the outburst. Apparently the stress of the day was getting to him as well. One of them had to retain a cool head and it would have to be him.

The remainder of the quarter-mile trek over a narrow woods road to the MacPherson house was quick, silent, and rough. Nevertheless, with Culloden's competent hands guiding the horses, Fletcher had time to reflect on events of the day and wonder how a marriage between his employer and the slip of a young woman who'd come to be his bride would ever work.

He held himself largely culpable for the debacle. He'd written the correspondence that had induced her to come to this country. Poor Isabella Marston! He'd have to do all in his power to ease her days in Riverhaven.

****

Isabella snuggled down under the quilts in the bed inside Fletcher Atkin's house. The rain she'd come to this country to escape continued to bucket down. Wind howled around the corners of the log structure and ripped through the surrounding trees until it sounded like a storm at sea.

As Perceval snuggled up under her chin, she wondered why she'd let her uncle sail away without her. Now that she'd overcome the discomfort of her seasickness, its horrors were receding in her memory, making her believe it a lesser evil than being left in this miserably wet, cold wilderness with the prospect of a barbarian as a husband.

She cuddled Perceval close and curled deeper into the warmth of the bed, surprisingly comfortable in spite of its straw tick mattress. The Pug gave her nose an affectionate lick, snuffled, and settled to sleep.

"Good night, Perceval dear." She kissed the top of his head. *Poor little creature, what have I brought you into?*

Drawing a deep breath, she came to a decision. She'd have to face the reality of her situation with all the grace and courage of a true lady. Surely she, with Lucinda's help, could keep that horrible man at bay for the months it would take for her uncle to return. Surely the pair of them, with perhaps Mrs. O'Malley's help, could manage to make him behave. Although she'd known the Irishwoman but briefly, Isabella believed she was a kindly soul who'd allow no improprieties or unwelcomed behaviors in her sphere of influence. Furthermore, she appeared to have at least some dominion over Culloden MacPherson.

Resolved to make the best of a bad situation, exhausted from weeks of sleeping poorly on a tossing ship, Isabella Marston drifted off to sleep to the familiar sounds of wind and rain.

Chapter Five

Isabella woke to a shaft of sunlight sliding in through the window. It brightened the room with a golden glow. Trying to orient herself to her surroundings, she stared up at the plank ceiling. As Perceval shifted against her, memory returned, and she shuddered. That awful sea voyage, that savage she'd agreed to wed…

As she lay steeling herself to face the day, Irene O'Malley's voice softly singing an Irish melody, accompanied by the enticing odor of food cooking, wafted into the room. Her stomach rumbled. She moved Perceval aside, stretched, sat up, and looked toward the sun-brightened window. At least the storm had subsided.

Her spirits began to revive as she listened to the housekeeper's lilting tune and the sounds of breakfast preparation. She stood and reached for her robe. This was better than awakening to her sisters' bickering and her mother's high-pitched voice ordering them to be quiet. And the room was warm, beautifully warm. Perceval got languidly to his paws and stretched.

"Lazy," she teased him. She lifted him from the bed to the floor, and he scampered under the curtain into the kitchen. Barefoot, she shoved it aside to follow him.

"Good mornin', dearie." Mrs. O'Malley turned a

bright, smiling face from where she'd been stirring a pot on the hearth. "You must have been fair worn out, you slept so long. Lucy and I have been keeping your breakfast warm. Good morning, young sir," she continued, greeting Perceval. "I reckon as how you're hungry? I have a nice bit of meat for you."

"You're looking a lot more fit this morning, miss." Lucinda smiled up at Isabella from her seat by the fire, where she sat mending a man's shirt. She looked at home in her situation.

"I'm feeling much better." She saw Mrs. O'Malley putting a bowl filled with meat chunks on the floor in front of the Pug. "Mrs. O'Malley, Perceval has his food chopped into small pieces. I don't think…"

"He's a woods dog now, dearie. He has to toughen up."

Isabella watched as Perceval sniffed the food and pulled a piece into his mouth. Stretching out beside the hearth, he uttered a contented sigh and began to chew.

"Will you look at that!" Lucinda grinned. "He likes it. And to think of all the time our poor scullery maid back home spent chopping his meal into tiny bits."

"Sit yourself down, child." Mrs. O'Malley indicated a place at the table. "I'm hoping you're partial to oatmeal porridge. It's what we have for breakfast most days. There's more of that bread I made yesterday, and butter and jam, and a nice pot of tea."

"But I should dress first." Accustomed to not appearing at breakfast unless fully attired for the day, Isabella hesitated.

"We don't stand on such formality here. Furthermore, since there're only us women about, no need to dress the minute our feet touch the floor."

Isabella took the place at the table indicated as the woman bustled about putting the meal before her. Savoring a cup of tea, she found herself relaxing in the warm, sunny kitchen with its atmosphere of easy companionship. And being permitted to eat in her nightgown and robe! So different from breakfast in the cold, austere dining parlor at home, with her sisters arguing, her mother berating Lucinda for her lack of economy in putting an extra log on the fire, and her father, his glasses perched down his nose, reading either a newspaper or the post and ignoring the melee.

"Here, my girl." Mrs. O'Malley placed a steaming bowl of oatmeal before her, her plump face beaming down on her. "Get this into your belly and I reckon you'll live to fight another day." She thrust a small jug toward her. "And lace it good with this maple syrup."

"Thank you." Isabella smiled up at the woman and did as she suggested.

"Well?" Mrs. O'Malley awaited her reaction.

"Delicious."

"Made from the sap of our trees this very spring." Mrs. O'Malley beamed at her appreciation. "I think you might find this country has a number of pleasant surprises…if you give it a chance."

She returned to the hearth, humming.

"I'm hoping so, Mrs. O'Malley. I'm definitely hoping so."

****

After Isabella had eaten, washed, and dressed, she decided a short foray out into the fine spring day would do her a world of good. Mrs. O'Malley and Lucinda had refused her offer of assistance about the house, and she wanted to see Duchess.

Leaving Perceval avidly watching Mrs. O'Malley preparing a large roast for the spit over the fire, she stepped out of the log house to survey her surroundings in sunlight. The deciduous trees were in the process of leafing out into a greenness that the previous day's rain had enhanced with a freshness that made them glisten. Lingering droplets of moisture on their foliage reminded her of diamonds. From among their branches, birds twittered and flitted, seemingly delighted in the fineness of the morning. And the sky—the sky was a wonderful, glorious vastness of purest blue.

She looked across the yard to the log barn with its crudely fenced pasture land at the rear. Like the house, it gave the appearance of strength and security. In the sunshine, the yard which the previous day had seemed a sea of muck was drying. Surrounded by grass and trees of the most verdant varieties, the entire homestead gave off an air of being an oasis in the forest. The thought reassured her. Her spirits lifted, and she drew in a lungful of the clear, fresh air.

Maybe she hadn't been entirely foolish to have made the decision to come to this country. Behind her, in the house, Lucinda had joined Mrs. O'Malley in a folk song. Yes, this was definitely a better atmosphere than the one she'd left behind in England. Then, as she remembered Culloden MacPherson, a shadow fell over the sun-bright day.

Still, she'd worry about that later. With a shrug, she lifted her dress above her ankles and stepped off the veranda that ran across the front of the house. Dodging the remaining puddles as she scampered toward the stable, she was glad she'd had the foresight to wear half boots instead of her usual slippers.

When she approached the barn, she was surprised to see the door gaping open. Surely it couldn't have been left in that condition overnight. Robbers? No, of course not! Horace must have come over to see to the chores.

That was the answer. She moved inside and paused to allow her eyes to become accustomed to the gloom. When she could distinguish her surroundings, she glanced about for the groom.

"Horace?" she inquired, moving slowly forward with the unsettling thought that it might not have been he who had opened the door, that she might have been hasty in her assumption. Perhaps in this country there were footpads who robbed stables. Certainly a fine horse like Duchess would be worth the exhibition of a fair degree of boldness.

"Miss Marston." Fletcher Atkin stepped out of a box stall which contained a shadowy outline indicating the presence of a horse. "Good morning."

"Mr. Atkin." She hoped his name hadn't come tainted with the relief she experienced at recognition of his presence. "Good day to you, sir." She bobbed a slight curtsy.

"And to you as well, ma'am. You've come to see how your mare is managing, no doubt." He moved to the next stall, opened its door, and held out an arm to indicate she was to join him. Going to his side, she saw Duchess contentedly munching hay, looking fit and comfortable. At recognition of her mistress, the bay mare raised her head and nickered a soft welcome.

"She looks well." Isabella held a hand out, and the horse came to nuzzle it. "I feared the sea voyage might be too much for her."

"I had the same trepidations about Galahad." She looked up to see him smiling down at her. "Bringing a horse across the Atlantic is a risky business."

"Galahad?"

"First knight to seek the Holy Grail. I thought it appropriate, since he came to this country on a quest as well."

"Quest?"

"A quest to be allowed to run free, to enjoy life to the fullest, not destined to break his heart, legs, or neck chasing down a defenseless fox. And your Pug…Perceval, I believe you call him. Second knight to seek the Grail, wasn't he?"

"He was. I chose the name for my dog because he's proven to be as brave as any knight errant. He once chased a nasty rat from Duchess's stall."

"A rat?"

"A very large rat." Catching a hint of humor in his response, she was quick to compensate. "You'll realize just how fearless he is once you get to know him."

"I'm sure I shall. Now…" He drew himself up. "Allow me to introduce you to Galahad. I think you might be surprised."

He led the way to the next box stall. The gelding, at the approach of its owner, came to the door to thrust his head out against the man's chest.

"Oh, my!" As she got a full view of the animal, Isabella gasped. With his black stockings, tail, and mane, gleaming red body, and white blaze down his face, Galahad was a near mirror image of Duchess.

"Yes, oh my." The man scratched the horse behind the ears. "Did you notice my astonishment when your groom brought your mount up on the deck of your uncle's ship? I could barely believe my eyes. Nearly a perfect match, wouldn't you say?"

"I concur."

"Perhaps someday you and your fine mare would do us the honor of riding out with Galahad and me."

"I'm not sure Mr. MacPherson would approve." Avoiding looking up at her companion, she patted Galahad's arched neck as he strained toward his master.

"That should not be a concern or a consideration. Mr. MacPherson knows I can behave as a gentleman. Since he doesn't enjoy riding and realizes that, given the presence of your lovely mare, you do, he's given me carte blanche to accompany you in lieu of"—he hesitated—"another servant."

"Well, then, if you have Mr. MacPherson's approval, I can see no reason not to accept your invitation. I would not, however, have named you a servant, Mr. Atkin. You seem more of"—she searched for a decent description—"a factotum and friend to Mr. MacPherson."

"You honor me with the description. On some days, I feel it applies. On others…" He shook his head.

"Mr. MacPherson is a man of many moods and humors, is he not?"

"Yes, but at heart an honest and sincere person. Since he has sanctioned my riding out with you, you may rest assured he'll take no offense."

"Very well. Some day soon, weather permitting." The prospect of galloping her mare through the freshening greenery of this new land intrigued her and raised her spirits.

"Now I must get to the reason for my visit on a working day." He stepped back and focused his attention to the gelding. "Cully…Mr. MacPherson has asked that you accompany him to church tomorrow. Afterwards he invites you on a tour of his house and grounds."

"Church?" The idea of the buckskin-clad man she'd met the previous day going to church astonished her. "Mr. MacPherson is a churchgoer?"

"The prospect surprises you?" He went into the gelding's stall to run a hand along his sleek body.

"Yes, I must admit…"

"Don't let his rustic appearance disarm you, Miss Marston. Culloden MacPherson is no heathen…even if his exterior tends to indicate that possibility." He paused to meet her gaze. "Like his father before him, he's a Calvinist to the core. While he keeps his timber business running at top capacity all week long, there's not a tap of work done on Sundays."

"Astonishing."

"I suppose it is." He came out of the stall. "Now, I must be getting back to the mill. I've accomplished my errand, and my employer isn't a man to take kindly to dallying. Shall I tell him he may collect you in time for church in the morning?"

"Of course."

"Very well." He touched his hat brim. "Thank you."

"Aren't you going to ride your horse?" she asked as he headed for the barn door. "Surely, since I cannot hear the sound of milling, the location of the enterprise must be some distance off."

"I shall be busy all day." He paused to turn back to her. "It would be unkind to leave Galahad standing tied to a tree. He'll be much more comfortable here in the stable. Good day to you, Miss Marston."

"Mr. Atkin, will you please enlighten me?" She stopped his leaving. "I don't understand this terrible animosity between Mr. MacPherson and that man MacMillan. Since I have arrived in the midst of whatever it is, I believe I have a right to know."

He hesitated. "Miss Marston, perhaps it is, as Cully said, best left as trouble between men."

"But surely you must see it cannot remain that way, not when there are wives and other women involved. Surely we have a right to know what is happening that has driven these two men to such lengths of apparent hatred."

"Very well." He drew back his shoulders. "I'll tell you with as little bias as I can."

She listened, rapt, as he told the story of rivalry between the two timber businesses, of how it had been manageable until spikes had begun to appear in trees in the area where Harry Wallace's group were cutting. When he came to describe the danger of such practices and the injuries Harry Wallace, a father of nine children, had sustained, she gasped.

"Surely no one could be so cruel, so dastardly…"

"Surely someone has been." He rubbed his chin thoughtfully. "But I will swear to you on the Bible that Cully would not do it. He might not like Harry Wallace and Brodie MacMillan, but he'd not perpetrate such a cowardly prank."

"Prank? Prank? You call this action that has nearly killed a man, that may yet be the cause of his death, a prank?"

"Crime, then, if you choose. A crime."

"Well, then, if it is indeed a crime, why has not the

local law enforcement become involved?"

"Because there is no proof. No one has seen the perpetrators in action, and no one has bragged of being responsible."

"Bragged? What kind of human being would brag of doing such a thing?"

"Miss Marston, this is a rough country. Most of the niceties and long arms of the law have not yet extended to this area. For now, it's pretty much every man for himself, and God help those who can't handle such a situation. I must be going. I'm due back at work. But first, I suggest we turn these two fine creatures out into the pasture. I'm sure your mare would be grateful after being confined in a ship for weeks. It will also give us an opportunity to see how they behave together. Can you bring Duchess out on your own, or do you prefer to wait until I let Galahad loose and return for her?"

"I'm perfectly capable of managing my mare, thank you, Mr. Atkin."

"Very well." He handed her a lead rope. "Attach this to her halter."

"Do I catch humor in your words, sir?" she cocked her head to cast him an annoyed glance.

"No, not at all. It's simply that most ladies I've met left anything aside from riding to their grooms."

"Well, not this lady." She strode into the stall and snapped the lead onto Duchess's halter.

The mare shook her head and began to prance.

"Whoa, whoa." Isabella spoke softly. "Be easy, my dear girl. You'll be free soon."

The animal quieted. With a slight smirk in Fletcher's direction, Isabella led the horse past him and out into the sunshine.

Shortly, both animals were racing across the fenced paddock, apparently enjoying the fine day and each other's company.

"They make a fine pair," Fletcher Atkin commented as he watched them frolicking in the fresh green grass.

"That they do. I'm glad."

"So am I." He looked down at her and smiled. "Now I must be getting back to the mill. I bid you good day."

****

"Mrs. O'Malley, I should like to begin learning my duties." Isabella, returned from the paddock, faced the Irishwoman.

From her place standing at a counter beneath a window, Lucinda turned from peeling potatoes, eyebrows rising.

"Now, now, dearie, there's no need to start off your stay in this new land at a full run." The Irishwoman beamed at her. "Give yourself a few days..."

"Mrs. O'Malley, please." The thought of being treated as a guest galled her. She needed something that would make her feel useful, that would show she was capable of adapting to life in this new land...something that would keep her mind from dwelling on that great buckskin-clad oaf that she'd come to this country to marry. "I need employment."

The housekeeper hesitated a moment, then pointed to a stack of clothing on the table. "There's a deal of mending to be done. I repair the outfits of the men who work at the mill. Most are bachelors who have no wives to do the chore. Perhaps you might lend a hand."

"Gladly." She took a seat at the table and grimaced

at the stench rising from unlaundered garments.

"While I mend their rags, I don't wash them." Mrs. O'Malley explained. "Those men have enough time free from work in the mill to do that chore for themselves. There's a pond and stream at their disposal. As you can tell, many prefer not to take advantage of such natural amenities. If you're willing to help, you'll have to abide the odor. The only one who sends clean clothes to be repaired is Mr. Atkin. But then, he's a gentleman."

"Mrs. O'Malley, what can you tell me about this feud between Brodie MacMillan and Mr. MacPherson?" she asked as she began to thread a needle. "Mr. Atkin told me about the spiking and how dangerous such a practice can be to lumbermen who encounter it. Why did their differences escalate to this degree?"

"The timber trade is a right competitive one, dearie." The housekeeper heaved a sigh as she took a seat across from the younger woman. "And men being men…" She let her words drift off.

"But surely…"

"Surely we'd best leave all this squabbling to the men." Mrs. O'Malley picked up a badly torn shirt. "We've got enough to occupy us without involving ourselves in their foolishness."

Two hours later Isabella folded the tenth torn garment she'd mended and placed it on top of the others. Her fingers ached from forcing the needle through the coarse materials. Her neck and shoulders pained. This needlework presented a much greater challenge than the dainty bits and pieces of fancywork she'd done at Hollybranch Hall. She was beginning to wish she'd chosen to go outdoors to work at the laundry with Lucinda. Her former maid, having finished with the vegetables, had moved on to the chore of washing clothing and bedding in a tub in the dooryard.

"Time for a pot of tea." Mrs. O'Malley stood from where she'd been working with needle and thread at the opposite side of the table. "Lucy," she called through the doorway that had been left open to let in the warmth of the sunny day. "Leave off that washing. It's time for a bit of a rest."

"Lucy?" Isabella looked over at the woman.

"Lucinda is a might too starched and stiff." Irene O'Malley bustled about with preparations for their respite. "Such doesn't sit well in this country. I'd suggest you start calling him"—she gestured to the Pug snoring contentedly near the hearth—"Percy."

"Percy?" Isabella spoke the name. To her surprise, the little dog opened his eyes, raised his head, and turned to her. His tail wiggled.

"You see? He likes it." Mrs. O'Malley turned her attention to measuring tea leaves into a pot.

"Very well." Isabella stood and went to fetch cups from the dresser. "Percy and Lucy it shall be. And I'm Isabella, not miss or mistress. I fear I cannot allow myself to be monikered anything else such as my mother called me when she was annoyed. We're starting a new way of life. Why not fit ourselves with fresh names as well?"

****

She heard the wagon rumble into the yard as Lucy was putting the last pins in her hair.

"He's here." Her companion gave Isabella's coiffure a final pat and cocked her head to one side to admire the results.

"Do you think this gown suitable, Lucy? I won't appear too…too refined or snobbish?" Isabella smoothed her skirts with a lace-gloved hand.

"The man wanted a lady wife, didn't he, and you more than measure up." Lucy stepped back to study her. "But I don't think you should take the parasol. You'll need both hands to hold fast to the seat of that crude thing he calls a wagon. Your reticule should be safe on its drawstring around your wrist."

"What would I do without you to advise me, Lucy?" Isabella stood, drew in a deep breath, and glanced at the dainty sunshade on the table. Of course it wouldn't be manageable on the rough wagon ride she fancied lay ahead. Putting it in the dust at her feet during the journey wasn't an alternative. The dirt would render it a mess by the time she arrived at the church. As she picked up her bonnet and adjusted it into place, she wondered what the day would bring. At least the weather was cooperating. Sunlight flowed in through each of the log house's east-facing windows. Combined with the fire left over from breakfast preparation burning low on the hearth, it made the rooms warm and cheerful.

"We must make haste." Lucy placed Isabella's cloak about her shoulders and picked up her own. "I do not think Mr. MacPherson is a man who enjoys waiting."

"I believe you're right. Mrs. O'Malley"—she turned to the housekeeper bustling about the kitchen as she cleared away their breakfast—"will you be joining us?"

"Not a chance, dearie." She paused and turned to

beam at her. "I'm a good Irish Catholic. I'll be attending Mass as soon as Father Flynn is again in Riverhaven."

"Very well." Isabella headed for the door. "Good morning to you. I'm not sure when we'll be returning. Mr. MacPherson has expressed a desire to show us his home and grounds after services."

"He's ordered dinner at one sharp, miss...er, Isabella." The Irishwoman surprised her with the reply.

"When?" She stopped to swing back. She hadn't thought Culloden MacPherson had been at the log house since their arrival.

"Bless you, I met him down by the barn yesterday while you were resting. He gave the instructions. Having done so, he didn't think it was necessary for him to come up to the house."

"I see. Thank you, Mrs. O'Malley." She turned back toward the door.

Definitely not the actions of a delighted bridegroom eager to again see his intended.

Going out onto the veranda, she saw him on the high seat of his work wagon, reins draped between the fingers of his large hands. He wore a black coat and trousers, knee-high boots, and a white shirt opened at the throat that lacked a neckcloth. A battered tricorn perched on his head.

As she paused on the top step, he turned to look at her. Briefly his gaze raked over her. Then with a grunt that she took to sanction approval, he returned his attention to his team.

Beside the conveyance, wearing doeskin trousers, a fine black coat, maroon vest, white shirt complete with neatly tied neckcloth, and gleaming black riding boots,

Fletcher Atkin sat astride Galahad. The horse's coat gleamed with good health and careful grooming.

"Good morning, Miss Marston." He swung to the ground. "Permit me to assist you."

He strode forward and offered his arm. With a nod, she accepted it and allowed him to lead her to the wagon. There he caught her about the waist and swung her up beside Culloden MacPherson.

"Thank you, sir."

"You are most welcome, ma'am." Stepping back with a slight bow, he cast Culloden an admonishing glance which she understood. It should have been her intended who assisted her aboard.

The man on the seat scowled down at his employee. Fletcher turned away to lift Lucy into the cargo section.

The sound of the stable door shutting drew Isabella's attention. Dressed in what at home had been his livery for driving the carriage, Horace had emerged and was shambling toward the wagon. Beside it he paused to look up at her.

"Mr. Atkin said I might accompany you to church, mistress." Looking embarrassed and even shy, he explained. "He said in this country there's no need for such as myself not to attend service with the family."

"Mr. Atkin is exactly correct." Bella smiled down at him. "Please get aboard, Horace."

She had to suppress a smile as the big man climbed into the wagon's cargo space. What would the local people think of this person dressed as a coachman, newly arrived in their midst?

She was given no further time for speculation. Without so much as a good morning to her, Culloden

MacPherson, staring straight ahead, snapped the reins over the backs of the team. She barely had time to grip the board seat to avoid being unseated by the ensuing jolt as the wagon lurched forward.

Fletcher Atkin vaulted onto his horse to follow.

****

The drive through the burgeoning countryside, aside from the squeaking of wheels, horses' plodding hooves, and the animals' occasional blowing and snorting, was a silent one. Isabella didn't mind. She strongly suspected any conversation in which she attempted to engage the man seated beside her would be abruptly concluded. She remained content to clutch the plank seat as they joggled along. On this, her initial foray into the countryside since the ignominious day of her arrival, she was content to drink in the beauty of this unspoiled new land. The verdant freshness, the clear blue sky, even the tiny budding wildflowers and blossoms along the route pleased her and filled her with enjoyment.

Finally they turned down a narrow trail where blooming wild fruit trees scraped along the sides of the wagon. Isabella clutched her bonnet with one hand, to keep it from being snatched from her head by intruding greenery, while maintaining a tight grip on the seat with the other.

"The new church is on an island," Fletcher Atkin informed her when he rode up beside the wagon as the trail widened and a short bridge came in sight. "Our minister chose the site because of its beauty and peacefulness."

Beside her, Culloden MacPherson emitted a disgruntled sound.

They crossed the bridge and emerged into a meadow, bright with newness of spring grass and surrounded by lofty pines. In its center stood a lovely little white church, its modest spire pointing upwards into the flawless blue of the morning sky. About a dozen wagons with horses harnessed to them waited in the shade of the tall trees to one side of the church. Farther back, sheltered by soughing pines, looking truly a place of peace, was a cemetery.

Culloden halted the team at the end of the line of wagons and leaped to the ground. Without so much as a backward glance or an offer to assist Isabella to alight, he strode to the horses' heads to secure them to a tree.

Again Fletcher Atkin filled the void left by his employer. He dismounted, tied Galahad to the rear of the wagon, and hastened to her side.

"Thank you, sir." Isabella, rankled by this second failure of the other man to recognize his duty, spoke sharply, loud enough for Culloden to hear as Fletcher placed her feet on the grass beside the wagon. "You are a gentleman."

"Your servant, ma'am." With a bow, Fletcher stepped back as his friend approached. With a grunt, the big man turned and would have headed for the church alone had not Fletcher laid a hand on his shoulder.

"Cully, your arm?"

"Argh!" Culloden swung back to glare at the man.

"It's the proper way to bring your intended *lady* wife into the church."

The big man drew a deep, exasperated breath, then kinked his elbow and thrust it out to her.

"I thank you, kind sir." With a curt nod, her tone reflecting cold compliance, Isabella slipped her gloved hand into the curve. "Shall we proceed?"

The churchyard was empty except for horses and wagons, the parishioners apparently already inside. Isabella attempted to pause to draw a breath before her first appearance in front of community members, but she was jerked forward by the man whose arm she held.

As they crossed the grassy expanse toward the house of worship, she barely avoided breaking into a trot to keep up with her companion's long, brisk strides. He wasn't about to give quarter for her smaller stature or dainty shoes. At the church steps, he continued his unrelenting pace, taking each riser with fierce vigor. When he paused in the foyer to pull off his tricorn, she took the opportunity to attempt to gather her dignity.

Except for a bench at the front on the right side of the aisle, the small room was filled with congregants. A woman seated opposite the empty one, chestnut curls peeking from beneath a straw bonnet, turned from settling a restless golden-haired child and saw them. She hesitated only a moment before a smile brightened her pretty face. Isabella was about to return the greeting when she heard a grunt and glanced down to see a small pig lying at the end of the pew.

Is it permissible to bring animals to service in this country? How extraordinary! Perhaps next Sunday I will bring Perceval...Percy.

When she looked up again, she saw others had caught the woman's welcoming expression and turned to see its reason. They stared. The chestnut-haired lady's reaction wasn't reflected in their looks.

Curious and cautious. Not about to accept a newcomer on face value.

"Don't you go lookin' at that lass!" Her

companion's hissed admonition startled her as he scowled toward the woman who'd smiled at her.

"Why ever not?"

"Dunnae ask daft questions, lass. Will ya look at who's sittin' beside her?"

Until then she'd seen only the back of the tall, broad-shouldered man next to the welcoming woman. Now he turned and she saw his face. Startled, she recognized the man who had accosted them on the road on the day of her arrival. Brodie MacMillan glared at her escort before turning away.

"Very well." She slanted him an annoyed glance before squaring her shoulders. "Shall we proceed, Mr. MacPherson?" She forced what she hoped was a serene smile across her face and adjusted her hand in the crook of his arm.

He glanced down at her, into her face framed by the elegant bonnet. His bellicose expression slowly relaxed into one she could only fathom as one of satisfaction.

"Aye." Drawing himself up to his full, impressive height, pushing out his chest, and squaring broad shoulders, he started up the center aisle between the two rows of benches. He stopped at the one opposite the chestnut-haired woman and her companions. It was conspicuously empty.

The MacPherson pew? The man must wield more than a modicum of respect in the community to warrant such a concession. Perhaps he is a generous contributor to the building's maintenance.

Keeping the smile on her face, she thrust out her chin, hoping she exuded grace and dignity as they proceeded between the two groups of staring parishioners.

They reached their destination to find the little pig blocking their way.

"Good mornin' ta ya, my fine lady." Culloden's response to the animal startled Isabella. She was further surprised when he bent to scratch it behind an ear.

The pig muttered appreciation and scrambled to its hooves to move aside.

She remembered Culloden MacPherson's first meeting with Perceval. Although he'd mistaken the Pug for some rare type of swine, he hadn't been unkind to the little dog. *Surely a man who cares for animals must have at least a bit of goodness in his heart.*

A sound from the left-hand pew made Isabella cast a swift look in that direction. Brodie MacMillan had swung toward Culloden, his expression dark with anger. The woman by his side placed a restraining hand on his arm, but he glared at Isabella's escort a moment longer before turning away.

Is the ill will between these two men so strong it extends even into the house of the Lord?

As Culloden was about to precede her to a seat, out of the tail of her eye she saw Fletcher Atkin touch his arm. When her companion swung on him, Fletcher indicated by a discreet jerk of his head that Isabella should go first.

With a muted scoff, Culloden MacPherson stepped aside. She moved demurely past him and seated herself well along the bench to allow space for him and their three companions.

Lowering her head in a pretense of prayer, she slipped a glance across the aisle. The woman who'd favored her with that welcoming smile caught her look and nodded. With a slight inclination of her head, Bella acknowledged the gesture.

Perhaps a friend in the making? Someone who might act as peacemaker between these two bitter factions?

"Who is that woman you've advised me to ignore? Is it Mr. MacMillan's wife?" she whispered to Culloden.

"Dinnae go makin' up to that one," he muttered. "That's Margaret Wallace, wife of the man whose family and workers are dead set on makin' false accusations against me. Ya'll be stayin' away from her."

She was about to ask more questions when a door behind the altar opened to admit a tall, broad-shouldered man with dark red hair and a wide, sun-bronzed face. His appearance startled her. Although the white surplice he wore identified him as the minister of this small church, he had more the build, stance, and outlook of a war lord, a formidable soldier. The congregation stood.

He stepped up to the podium and smiled out over the assemblage. The expression transformed her first impression. Definitely here was a man of compassion. Surely no one could look out over an audience with such kindness and concern mirrored in his countenance without having it in his heart.

"Good morning, my friends," he began. "Please be seated. We've been blessed with as lovely a spring day as the Good Lord ever saw fit to bestow. This fine weather has been beneficent in many ways. Not only has it given us an opportunity to see our newly planted crops sprout up vigorously into the sunshine, but it has also brought ships to our small community…ships laden with much needed supplies. Those vessels have also furnished three new members to our congregation. My friends, I hope you will join my family and me in welcoming Miss Isabella Marston, Miss Lucinda Welsh, and Mr. Makepeace Horace into our midst." He smiled down at the trio.

On the far end of the bench, the groom grunted. Isabella bit down on her lower lip to repress a chuckle. Horace hated his Christian name.

"In honor of these newcomers, let us open our service of worship this morning with our traditional hymn for such occasions, 'God, You Have Brought Us to This Place.' " Reverend Edward Morgan looked heavenward and began to sing, at first alone but others joined in until it appeared the entire congregation was adding voice to the hymn.

A gentle peace began to settle over Isabella. The clergyman's introduction of her and her company to the community had given a welcoming balm to her spirit.

Her serenity was not to last. Later, when Reverend Edward Morgan launched into his sermon, she caught Culloden casting a nasty glance to his left at the man in the opposite pew. Brodie MacMillan returned the look with a scowl that narrowed his eyes and furrowed his forehead.

Chapter Six

When services ended, Horace waited until those in the opposite pew had filed out before moving into the aisle. Stepping aside, he then allowed Culloden and Isabella to precede him, Lucinda, and Fletcher Atkin out of the church.

As a result of their being at the front and Horace's acquiescence, they were the last to bid farewell to the clergyman. Reverend Edward Morgan stood on the steps, shaking hands with each person as they exited the building. When Isabella, on Culloden's arm, reached the minister, the clergyman beamed down at her. He took her hand, and she dropped a small curtsy.

"My dear Miss Marston, welcome. It's always a delight to receive a new member into our midst. I hope you'll find our valley a pleasant place in which to settle and raise a family."

"Thank you, Reverend." She smiled. "If the weather continues like this, living here will be pure joy. I've come from a far less congenial climate."

"Ah, yes, the winter and spring rains of jolly old England." He chuckled. "Not something to cherish." He turned to a pretty, dark-haired woman who'd come to stand beside him holding by the hand a small child with a thatch of red curls. "Miss Marston, may I present my wife, Mary, and our daughter, Iona."

"Welcome, Miss Marston." The woman's face

beamed a warmth equal to that of her husband.

"Thank you, Mrs. Morgan." Isabella inclined her head toward the woman. "You have a sweet child." She smiled down at the little girl.

"Thank you. Shamelessly, we're quite proud of her."

"Mary, my dear." The minister turned to his wife. "You must have a tea party for Miss Marston, to introduce her to the women of the community."

"Of course. I will send you a message when I can arrange a gathering, Miss Marston."

"That's most kind. I shall look forward to it."

"Come along." Culloden jerked the arm she held. "We cannae dally here all day." He gave the clergyman's hand a quick, hard shake before urging Isabella down the steps.

"Behave yourself, Culloden MacPherson." The minister's stern remonstrance followed them. "You've a lady on your arm and in your future...if you can manage to convince her to take on such as you. Mark this well—if you don't behave as a gentleman, you'll have both me and the wrath of God to contend with."

The only reply he received was a derisive guffaw as Culloden MacPherson towed her down the church steps and across the yard toward his horses and wagon.

Trotting to keep up with the man's long strides, Isabella believed her initial assessment of the reverend had been correct. He was a warrior as well as a man of the cloth. But how? And what had brought such a person to this place?

Most of the wagons, horses, and conveyances had already left or were well on their way to the narrow bridge that connected the churchyard with the mainland. Only one, attached to a team of Clydesdales, remained beside Culloden's. It had been delayed in its departure by the loading of the number of its passengers. Brodie MacMillan sat on the high seat, reins in hand, while a tall, handsome, sandy-haired young man hoisted three young girls, the pig she'd seen in church, and the pretty chestnut-haired woman aboard. Three young lads who resembled the one helping them into the wagon jumped aboard and took places with the four on the board seats along the sides.

Fletcher Atkin helped Isabella to her seat and went to the rear of the wagon to fetch Galahad as Horace hoisted Lucy into the back. Culloden finished untying his team and vaulted up beside Isabella. She noticed the big, black horses were tossing their heads and stamping. Quite possibly, these hard-working animals chafed at the inactivity of being tied up, especially outdoors. At any rate, she'd seen enough of Culloden MacPherson's driving to be confident he could manage them.

"All aboard, Uncle Brodie." As the young man finished his task at the wagon beside them, Fletcher mounted his gelding.

"Out of my way, MacPherson!" Brodie MacMillan swung the Clydesdales abruptly about, causing them to churn up the earth with their great hooves and toss their heads as they narrowly missed colliding with Culloden's restless team. Culloden guffawed as he struggled to hold Best and Timber sufficiently under control to allow the other wagon first opportunity to cross the narrow bridge.

His efforts suddenly failed. Timber reared, while Best lunged forward. The wagon and its four passengers lurched ahead at a furious gallop toward

Brodie MacMillan's wagon. Her bonnet flying on its ribbons from her head, Isabella clutched the seat, fear paralyzing her. A collision seemed inevitable.

Chapter Seven

Suddenly, Fletcher Atkin was galloping beside them and then on to the horses' heads. Leaning in his saddle, he caught at Best's reins. And just as suddenly, seemingly out of nowhere, the clergyman, in open-necked white shirt, black pants, and riding boots and mounted on a massive chestnut horse, was grabbing Timber's lines.

"Halt, ya two great fools!" he shouted at the animals, his command colored by a Scottish accent Isabella hadn't heard previously. "Whoa!"

Seconds before the two wagons collided, the riders managed to pull Culloden's team away from the other wagon and to a cavorting stop. Horace leaped to the ground to run forward and place himself between the team's heads, holding fast to their bridles as they snorted and swung their heads in resistance.

"Air ye daft, Culloden MacPherson!" The clergyman, with the team under control, rode back to confront her companion. "Whit air ya thinkin'? Attemptin' ta intercept a wagon carryin' a woman and bairns? Man, ya could have caused a great accident, gotten people killed!"

"Do ya think I'm mad?" Culloden swung on the clergyman while Isabella fought to recover her breath. "Somethin' spooked my team. They're fair broke out in a sweat after only a few strides. Look at them!"

"'Aye, well, ya better damn well get them under control." The clergyman continued, "Brodie, get yer rig across the bridge and out of here."

"I won't be forgettin' this, MacPherson." With a glare, Brodie MacMillan clucked to his team and headed them toward the bridge. "Next time we meet, there won't be lasses and bairns between us."

"I'll be lookin' forward ta it!" Culloden shouted at him as the Wallace wagon proceeded past his cavorting team. "Whoa, Timber! Hold up there, Best!"

"You tried to murder Father, Culloden MacPherson!" the youngest of the boys in the passing wagon yelled. "We'll see you pay, my brothers and me!"

"Samuel, sit down this instant!" Margaret Wallace grasped him by an arm. "Behave yourself or I'll be taking a stick to your backside! Eppie"—she moderated her tone as she lifted the smallest girl onto her lap. The child had begun to whimper—"Mother isn't angry with you. Sam is being naughty, that's all."

Margaret Wallace cast a rueful glance back at Isabella and shook her head. *Forgive the foolishness of men* was what Isabella read into it. The bellicose expressions on the faces of all the children nevertheless made her wonder if even a woman of Margaret Wallace's strength could contain their outrage at the man they believed had crippled their father.

"Tea, sir." As Brodie MacMillan's conveyance disappeared into the trees on the far side of the bridge, Horace, still struggling to hold the horses in check, called out his discovery. "Someone fed them tea. A few of the leaves are still about their mouths."

"Tea!" Culloden's response was a snarl. "Bloody

hell, someone is out to see me dead."

"Tea?" Isabella recovered sufficiently to inquire.

"Horses fed tea leaves go mad for a while." With the team in Horace's and Reverend Morgan's hands, Fletcher rode back to explain. "They love the taste and will gobble them up."

"It will take a fair bit of time for them to settle." Culloden's face contorted with outrage as he worked the reins to assist the two men at the horses' heads struggling to control the cavorting pair.

"I suggest that the ladies ride Galahad back to the house." Fletcher dismounted. "I'll walk and lead him. It's not safe for them to continue in the wagon. Horace"—he turned to the groom—"you'll assist Mr. MacPherson in getting Best and Timber to their stable?"

"Of course, sir." The groom's broad face lent sincerity to his words.

Fletcher lifted Isabella from the wagon that jerked and rattled from the movements of the disturbed team. While she replaced her bonnet, he went to the rear and assisted Lucy to the ground.

"Miss Marston?" He stood beside Galahad, his hands cupped into stirrup shape. "May I offer you a leg up? I'm afraid you ladies will have to ride astride."

Isabella hesitated, then fitted her shoe into his palms. As he lifted her upward and she swung her leg over the horse's back, she was aware of the impropriety of her gown rising up to mid calf.

Once in place in Fletcher Atkin's saddle, she glanced down at the man and caught him staring at her ankle and the exposed section of leg.

"Your shoes"—he hastened to make an attempt at

explanation—"they're not intended for riding."

"I'll manage, sir." Isabella slipped her feet into the stirrups, attempting a haughty attitude, but she experienced a tingle of excitement at the man's interest. She adjusted her hands on the reins as Fletcher Atkin assisted Lucy to mount behind her.

****

"You must be getting weary, Mr. Atkin." Looking down at the man leading the horse, Isabella commented as they neared his homestead. It had been a largely silent trek.

"Not nearly so wearisome as an army march, Miss Marston." He avoided looking up her.

"You were in the army?" His response surprised her. "When? Where?"

"Years ago in France…although, I admit, I spent a good deal of time on horseback."

Horseback? Isabella pondered this bit of information. *Generally, from what I've heard, only officers ride. And often their rank has been purchased by their wealthy or aristocratic families because they've proven troublesome or somehow become a disgrace at home. What is your story, Fletcher Atkin?*

"There were several young people, even a child, in the wagon Mr. MacMillan was driving. Are they part of his family?" Sensing the man didn't wish to pursue the former line of conversation, she changed the subject.

"He regards them as such." Fletcher walked steadily ahead. "Actually, those children are Margaret and Harry Wallace's stepchildren. The couple took over their guardianship after their birth parents passed."

"Quite a responsibility."

"Yes, it was and continues to be. The four boys,

97

although generally good lads, have minds of their own, I've been told, not always easy to handle. And now there're two more. Not long ago, Margaret and Harry had the first offspring of their own…a pair of twin boys."

"Good heavens! So Harry Wallace, the man who has been grievously injured, is the father of nine children?"

"Correct. Although things could be worse. During his illness, Brodie will take over. I've heard he's an excellent millwright and not a bad hand at farming, either. How he manages in the role of father to that group…"

"But you've said Mr. MacMillan regards himself as a family member. Does that mean he's not a blood relative?"

"I don't believe so. His connection with Harry Wallace is rumored to have begun in the Highlands of Scotland." He glanced up at Isabella. "It's said Brodie, Harry, Reverend Morgan, and even the Reverend's wife ran as a band of outlaws back there. Now they hold clannish ties to each other. A formidable group when aroused."

He returned his attention to guiding Galahad over the roots and ruts of the trail.

Isabella was left to ponder all he had told her. This Riverhaven was seeming more and more to live up to its name.

****

"Lord bless us and save us! What happened?" Mrs. O'Malley, who'd been awaiting their arrival for the noon meal, lurched from her seat on the veranda as the trio emerged from the trees into the homestead yard.

"Where's the wagon? Where's Mr. MacPherson and that great bulk of a groom? Don't tell me there's been another run-in with that MacMillan person! Has anyone been injured…killed?" The last possibility came out as a hushed gasp.

"No one has been injured or killed, Mrs. O'Malley." Fletcher stopped his horse at the steps and reached up to help first Lucy and then Isabella from the horse. "There was some trouble with the team. We decided it best that the ladies ride home on Galahad."

"Someone fed Mr. MacPherson's horses tea," Lucy blurted indignantly as she brushed down the skirt of her gown. "We were near killed."

"Jesus, Mary, and Joseph!" Mrs. O'Malley clutched her apron. "Attempted murder, that's what it is! I'm hoping you'll be reporting the incident to the magistrate. Brodie MacMillan has to be stopped!"

"We've no proof it was him who gave the horses tea." Fletcher tied Galahad to the hitching post. "It could have been anyone. We were the last to leave the church."

"Well, I've no need for proof." Mrs. O'Malley came down the steps to put an arm around each of the young women and hustle them into the log house. "The man has to be stopped. But to more immediate needs. You two poor sweethearts look all in. A cup of hot, sweet tea will help put you to rights."

Fletcher shook his head ruefully as the trio disappeared into the house.

Thank God Irene O'Malley isn't a man. She's worse than a mother bobcat when she thinks any of those she fancies under her protection are threatened.

****

The meal, although a delicious combination of poached salmon, potatoes, and greens Isabella learned were called fiddleheads, was mainly a silent one except for Lucy's nudges and admonitions to Culloden in an effort to refine his table manners. It was only when a rhubarb dessert was served that Culloden spoke.

"I've been reflectin'. I don't believe MacMillan put that tea in my team's way. It's not his way of fightin'. I'm more inclined to think 'twas one of Harry Wallace's sons as did it. It's a near childish trick. I'm recallin' the way the youngest yelled at me as our wagons passed. People say he fair worships his stepfather."

"I find that difficult to even consider." Fletcher looked down the table at his employer. "Those boys may be a bit wild, but bringing harm to a wagon carrying women…that I cannot believe. In spite of their father's accident, which they, no doubt like their uncle, blame on us, they'd never carry out such a dastardly response. Their stepmother would be appalled, and I'm not so sure Brodie MacMillan wouldn't be tempted to take a stripe off any of them who carried out such a heinous act. If I know anything about the Fowler-Wallace-MacMillan clan, it's that they're men, not blatant cowards."

"Aye, well, ya can go about spoutin' yer faith in that bunch. but they're as clannish as if they were still back in the hills of the Highlands. They'll stick together through thick and thin, and woe betide anyone who harms one of them." Culloden stood, shoved back his chair, and strode toward the door. "We'll be walkin' ta my house. Best and Timber haven't yet cooled enough ta be safe ta drive with lasses aboard. See that yer ready ta set out within the hour."

****

As Isabella, Fletcher, Lucy, and Culloden emerged from the trail through the woods, Isabella saw it for the first time…a large, stately, three-story house with a veranda sweeping around the front and sides, so freshly painted white it gleamed in the spring sunlight. Isabella stared. From their vantage point, it certainly lived up to the description of a manor.

"Well?" His sharp word made her turn her attention to him as he stood awaiting her. "Air ya comin' or not?" He'd forged ahead of the others.

She heard Fletcher Atkin breathe what sounded like an exasperated sigh.

"Of course, Mr. MacPherson. It's a fine-looking house. Shall we proceed?"

He glanced down at her, dark eyes as cold and inscrutable as any she'd ever encountered. With a grunt, he started toward the house with his usual long, uncompromising strides. Hoping she didn't allow him to notice her difficulty with keeping pace, she followed him across the weedy, stump-infested yard and up the steps to the veranda and front door. At the latter, he grabbed the latch and pushed it open. Surprised to find such a house unlocked, she hesitated.

"Well, whit is it now?" Exasperated he looked down at her.

"You leave the house unlocked? Aren't you afraid highwaymen or footpads or any manner of outlaw might take refuge inside?"

He guffawed. "Anyone who knows me, who has an ounce of sense in his head, would niver dare trespass on anything that is mine." Narrowing his eyes, he cast her a warning glance. "Come along, come along." Culloden MacPherson stepped inside ahead of her.

She paused in a wide foyer where a broad staircase led up to an overlooking balcony.

"Perhaps I'd best undertake to describe the house." Fletcher Atkin stepped forward. "Here"—he swung open a door to the left—"is the drawing room."

Isabella walked into a large room with windows facing west, vacant except for a fieldstone hearth that showed no signs of ever having been used. Behind her, the men's boots echoed hollowly on the plank floor. The plaster walls were stark white. No embellishments lessened their austerity.

"Mr. MacPherson has been awaiting your arrival before choosing furnishings and decorations." Fletcher explained. "He believed it best."

"*Ya* believed it best." Already Culloden MacPherson was striding out of the room. "Well, come along, come along. We've not got all day."

Fletcher Atkin looked over at Isabella, gave a good-natured shrug, and bowed in indication she was to precede him from the room.

The remainder of the house consisted of a morning room on the east side with a dining parlor behind it, a library with empty shelves next to the drawing room, and at the rear, a large kitchen with wide hearth complete with cooking grates and side oven, where a fire languished. A spacious butler's pantry, lined like the library with blank shelves, graced the rear. A narrow, steep stairway at the back of the room was for the servants, Fletcher explained. Their quarters were to be on the third floor.

In the center of the kitchen, a large plank table

surrounded by chairs and benches stood littered with the leavings of a breakfast meal. Three bough mattresses lay scattered along the wall of the room. While two bore evidence of having their covers drawn into order, the third was a rumpled mass of quilts and blankets. Above each bed were pegs on which hung an assortment of masculine attire.

"Horace, Mr. MacPherson, and I sleep here...by the fire," Fletcher Atkin explained.

"And apparently eat and leave a general mess, as well." Lucy stepped forward to begin clearing the table. "What a great muddle men make when left to themselves!"

"It's the Sabbath, girl!" Culloden blocked her way to the counter as she headed in that direction, bowls and mugs in her hands. "There'll be no washin' and cleanin' done taday!"

"I don't think the good Lord expects us to live in squalor at any time, sir."

Watching, Isabella felt her breath catch as her former maid faced the big man, belligerence spouting from her outlook. This might be a new country with another set of rules governing behavior, but still, for Lucy to speak so boldly to a man as powerful and disgruntled as Culloden MacPherson...

They faced each other, brown eyes challenging dark ones.

"Argh!" After what seemed like a lengthy hiatus, Culloden stepped aside and allowed her to proceed.

Isabella believed she must have heaved a sigh of relief. When she glanced up at Fletcher Atkin standing beside her, he gave her a rueful grin.

Leaving Lucy to clean the kitchen, they proceeded

upstairs, where a master bedroom as devoid of furnishings as the rest of the house contained only a large fireplace. Several other rooms, smaller in scale, were equally empty, with no curtains or wall decorations to lessen their austerity.

"As you can see, Miss Marston, you have considerable work ahead of you." Fletcher Atkin said as they once more headed downstairs, Culloden MacPherson leading the way.

"It is a fine, large house," she replied. "Furnished, it will be lovely."

"Lovely, argh!" Culloden's response was one of annoyance. He headed for the front door as they reached the bottom of the stairs. "Fletch, collect that girl from the kitchen. I have ta check on my team."

****

"No reaching down the table!" Lucy's hand shot out to slap Culloden's as he stretched toward the plate of chicken she'd placed before Fletcher. They were seated about the supper table at Fletcher Atkin's cabin.

"Whit?" He yanked back, eyes black and hard as coals as he turned on her.

Lucinda...Lucy, no! Isabella's breath caught in her throat.

"This is Mr. Atkin's house." Lucy Welsh glowered back. "He will take a serving first, then hand it along. That's why it was placed before him. In a fine home, a footman would be serving, but since we've no such person, we must observe proper table behavior as best we can. If you have a desire ever to be a gentleman, worthy of my...friend, you have to learn what is acceptable and what is not in the way of manners."

For a moment, there was silence as those around

the table waited to see what would happen next. Finally, with a guffaw, Culloden sank back onto his chair.

"Well, get a move on, man!" he barked at Fletcher. "I'm fair starvin'. If we must wait until ya've chosen the best bits, get on with it."

Fletcher took up the platter and chose a drumstick. As he handed it on to Isabella, who sat on his right, he winked.

Relieved at the outcome of the scenario, she pursed her lips to suppress a chuckle. *Perhaps Lucy will prove a better tutor than I when it comes to civilizing Culloden MacPherson.*

When the plate finally reached him, Culloden chose a large section of breast and scraped it noisily onto his plate before casting a defiant glare at Lucy.

****

"Mr. Atkin, might I have a word?" The following morning, Captain Caleb Cameron's voice summoned Fletcher as he dismounted in front of Angus Harper's store. The magistrate was striding toward him.

"At your service, Captain." Fletcher tied Galahad to the hitching post and turned to him with what he intended to be an agreeable expression, although he suspected there was no pleasant reason behind the request.

"My office would offer more privacy." The man jerked his head to indicate the passersby who'd either slackened their pace or outright stopped to witness the meeting.

Fletcher understood. *By now, most everyone in this valley will have heard of the confrontation in the churchyard yesterday and are curious as cats to learn more.*

"Agreed. Lead the way."

Once inside the magistrate's office at the end of the street, with its attached jail cells, Caleb took a seat behind the scarred desk and indicated Fletcher was to take the chair in front of it. Pulling off his hat, Fletcher complied.

"Now, Fletch, what's this I hear about Cully MacPherson and Brodie MacMillan acting like a couple of fools after services yesterday? I'd already left with my wife when it happened, but I've had reports."

"From whom?" Fletcher had thought the two groups were the last to leave the churchyard. "Never from Reverend Morgan. From what I know of the man, he'd be the last to involve the law in any minor skirmish."

"Duncan Green and his wife were still back at the church. They're custodians, charged with making sure all is well before and after services. They witnessed the entire event. Bright and early this morning, Mrs. Green had her husband drive her into town to report the incident."

"I didn't see any other wagons. I thought we were the last to leave."

"They tie their horse behind the church. You couldn't have seen it. Now tell me exactly what occurred."

"It was an unfortunate happening." Fletcher looked down at his hat and turned it by its brim in his hands. "Someone's misguided idea of a prank, feeding tea to Cully's horses."

"A misguided prank that could have resulted in serious injury or death to two women, never mind the other man you had with you and Cully."

"I know, I know, Cal." He returned his focus to the magistrate's face. "What are you planning to do about it?"

"There's little I can do. From what I've been told, you and your group were nearly the last to leave the church. Anyone could have fed tea to Cully's team. The best I can do is rely on you to keep a wary eye on the situation. You appear to have a clear head in the matter. I know Harry Wallace would do the same on the other side, but right now, recovering from that accident at the mill, he's not in any condition to do more than struggle to get back on his feet. He doesn't need any more trouble. I have a gut feeling his wife warned all involved in the incident not to breathe a word to him. She knows how he'd react and that it wouldn't be in his best interests at the moment."

"Definitely. I'll do my best to keep the peace, Cal." He started to rise, but the captain stopped him.

"Hold there a minute, Fletch. What about this bride-to-be who has come to marry Cully? Is she the kind of woman who might be able to handle him?"

"I don't know." Fletcher sank back down on his chair. "She's definitely a refined young woman, and that's what Cully was seeking. So far as I can observe, she hasn't flinched away from any of the conditions she's met, surprising as they must be to her. As you may already know, Cully has political aspirations, which he sees as requiring him to have a lady wife. Whether she's capable of sharing a life with a frontiersman such as Culloden MacPherson and helping him achieve his ambitions remains to be seen."

"I have hopes that her arrival will put an end to this

timber war."

"That she'd be much like your own wife?" Aware of the spirit of the Captain's wife, Ann, Fletcher grinned over at the magistrate.

"Just what are you implying, Mr. Atkin?" Caleb Cameron stood to tower over the other man, annoyance emanating from his expression.

"Nothing, nothing at all, Cal, but it's well known your Ann stood beside you during your privateering days, strong and brave as the best seaman on the deck of the *Lady Ghost*. It's rumored she even wielded a belaying pin more than once in battle."

"Aye, that she did." Relaxing, the captain sank back down onto his chair. "Saved me from prison or possibly worse. Are you telling me there's not a great deal of hope this newly arrived lady will be able to handle Cully MacPherson?"

"I implied that only time will tell." He got to his feet.

"I understand she brought a maid servant and a coachman with her. What of them?"

"The coachman is a fine, big fellow, excellent with horses and more than willing to work in our mill when farm chores allow." Fletcher headed for the door. "The maid servant...well, now, there's a firebrand if ever there was one. Do you know she took Cully to task about the squalor in his house and actually had the temerity to begin to clean it right under his nose...on the Sabbath."

"Cleaning on a Sunday...with the man present?" The captain followed him, his tone incredulous. "Knowing Cully's religious views, I can only imagine the row that precipitated. I'm assuming he ordered her to cease and get out of his house."

"He did order her to stop, but it made no impression. She kept right on. I fear she might have a bit of your Ann's nature."

He exited the magistrate's office to the sound of the man's guffaw.

He returned to Galahad, mounted, and headed back to the mill. He understood Captain Cameron's trepidations. The men who worked for both Culloden MacPherson and Harry Wallace were tough woodsmen, not about to back down from any physical confrontation that arose between the two timber companies. There could, indeed, be a timber war, and he wasn't in any way sure Isabella Marston would have any power to stop it.

****

Isabella stood looking at her mare contentedly munching hay in her stall. She longed to go for a canter on the beautiful animal, but with Horace working in the mill, she had no one to saddle the horse or bear herself the required accompaniment. Forgetting about the groom's absence, she'd dressed in her riding habit the moment Lucinda had headed off to clean Culloden's manor house and Mrs. O'Malley left to check on her own cabin in the village. Now she wondered how she could have been so lacking in foresight. She'd never taken a horse from its stall, let alone put its saddle and bridle in place.

"I must learn." She drew a deep breath as she spoke to the mare and opened the door to her stall. "You and I are friends. I'm sure you'll bear with my fumbling."

She caught the animal by the halter and led her out

into the walkway. She saw crossties and remembered how she'd often found Duchess tied in them back in the stable at Hollybranch Hall when she'd hurried inside, too eager to wait for Horace to lead the animal out to the mounting block. Holding the mare by her halter, she reached for one of the dangling ropes. When she had it fastened in place, she reached for the other and repeated the process.

"There." Hands on her hips, she stood back to survey her handiwork. "That wasn't all that difficult. Now to get your saddle in place."

Squaring her shoulders, she strode across the barn to where her saddle and its pad rested over a sawhorse against the back wall. She gathered them up and walked over to the mare. There she let the saddle fall to the floor and threw the pad over Duchess's back. So far, so good. She picked up the saddle, drew a deep breath, and swung it upward toward the mare's back. It hit below its intended mark, rebounding to hit her mid-chest.

Losing her balance, she toppled backwards. She dropped on her bottom with a thump that made her expel a gasp, the saddle on top of her.

"Having difficulty, ma'am?" His voice made her turn to see Fletcher Atkin advancing toward her. "Allow me." He lifted the piece of equipment from her with an ease that impressed her.

Heat flushed up her neck. What an absolutely unladylike position in which to be found. The man most definitely had to be suppressing laughter.

Holding the saddle over one arm, he held down his other hand to assist her to her feet.

"Thank you, sir." Mustering what dignity she could, she accepted his offer.

"I take it you wish to go riding."

"Yes." She brushed straw and chaff from the back of her green velvet skirt.

"Allow me to assist." He threw the saddle onto the pad and began to fasten the girth. "If you'll permit, I'll ride along with you. You know I have Mr. MacPherson's permission to accompany you. Galahad is saddled outside. I just completed an errand to the village. I'm sure he'd appreciate a canter in the countryside with this pretty lady."

He jerked his head in Duchess's direction, but Isabella believed she caught a double meaning.

"Thank you, Mr. Atkin. I'd enjoy having company."

Chapter Eight

As they rode down a rough trail along the river, Isabella cast what she hoped was a furtive glance at her companion. Although dressed in the rough clothing of a mill worker, he exuded the qualities of a gentleman. Furthermore, it was obvious he was a skilled rider. He handled Galahad with a light but firm hand that kept the animal in check. She also observed he was surreptitiously watching Duchess. Did he fear the mare, new to the rugged terrain and forest-lined trail, would become skittish? Did he doubt her ability to manage if such became the case?

The idea annoyed her. What did he take her for? Just because she'd had that unseemly incident in the stable, there was no reason to think she wasn't a competent rider. In an effort to dispel any thought he might have in this regard, she urged Duchess into a brisk trot over the rutted road.

"Have a care, Miss Marston!" He urged Galahad abreast of her and put a gloved hand over hers on the reins. "This trail is far from a bridle path. It's not safe to urge a horse to more than a walk. You must allow your mount to pick her way carefully. If you've a mind for more speed, we'll soon come out to a meadow where you can allow her to trot and even canter. But not here." He brought both horses under his control and halted the pair.

As the animals stopped, his hand tightened over hers. The action sent a surprising sensation rushing through her. Startled, she looked over at him. The expression in his deep blue eyes astonished her. For a moment, they remained gazing at each other.

"Well." He was the first to break the spell as he removed his hand and turned his attention to the trail ahead. "Shall we proceed?"

"Mr. Atkin, before we continue, may I ask a question?"

"Of course." He turned to her.

"What can you tell me of Mr. MacPherson's past…his family, early life? He's not a garrulous man, as you must be well aware. I'm convinced it would be next to impossible for me to learn of it from him."

"I know little myself." Fletcher Atkin shifted in his saddle. "His father was a Scotsman, his mother a native woman. She died when Cully was very young. His father, a fur trader, took the child with him on his journeys west each year. When Cully was eighteen, his father died of a fever. For the next few years, he followed his father's work but came to see the timber trade as being far more lucrative. He settled in this valley and, for a time, worked for various lumber concerns before starting out on his own. His endeavors flourished. The rest"—he shrugged—"is obvious."

"His maternal parentage probably explains his penchant for the clothing he favors."

"Buckskins. Yes, perhaps. Now we should be getting back. I have duties to attend to."

He started to turn Galahad away, but she stopped him again. "And what about you, Mr. Atkin? You have the manners of a gentleman, yet here you are working for the likes of Culloden MacPherson. What is your story?"

"Not one that concerns you, Miss Marston." He swung his horse about. "And definitely not one you'd enjoy hearing."

As she followed him down the trail, questions burned in her mind. Questions not about her intended but about her riding companion. What was so dark about his past he couldn't confide it to her?

****

The day was a glory of sunshine and soft breezes. Isabella, weeding in the vegetable garden beyond the barn, was happy in her chore. It reminded her of what were some of her few enjoyable hours at Hollybranch Hall when she'd managed to steal away to work in the kitchen garden. She'd discovered the rows of sprouting plants the previous day, recognized that the plot needed tending, and decided to make it one of her tasks.

Inside the log house, Mrs. O'Malley and Lucy were content with their work of cooking, mending, and cleaning, but she had been disinclined to join them and miss out on the wonderful weather and what was for her a pleasurable pastime. Even Percy was enjoying the morning. Dozing on a patch of grass at the end of the drills, he was snuffling Pug snores.

The warmth of the earth beneath her hands suddenly inspired her. Did she dare follow her instincts? Why not? She'd come to this new country seeking freedom from senseless rules. Hunkering down, she loosened the laces of her half boots. Shortly, she'd released them and pulled them, together with her stockings, from her feet.

Ah, what pleasure, what a joyous sensation!

Squiggling her toes into the soft, warm earth, she tossed her footwear aside and stood. Drawing in a deep breath, she threw back her head and closed her eyes, savoring the moment.

"Good morning, Miss Marston." Her eyes flew open to see Fletcher Atkin standing at the end of the garden. He was smiling at her.

"G—good morning, sir." Instantly aware of the impropriety of her appearance, she stuttered. Standing before him in her oldest gown, barefoot, and with hair straggling from beneath an ancient sunbonnet, she knew color was flooding up her neck to suffuse her face. "I was seeing to the garden."

"Yes. Thank you." He squatted at the end of a drill of carrots to pat Percy. The Pug, coming fully awake, wriggled his tail. "I have little time to attend to it myself, and I fear its attention is more than Mrs. O'Malley should be expected to manage. Although Cully and I buy most of our winter's produce from local farmers, we both enjoy fresh vegetables in season. Thus this small effort."

"I've always enjoyed a garden." His pleasant, unassuming manner reassuring her, she found she could engage in conversation. She brushed dirt from her gown and pushed an errant curl back under her sunbonnet. "And fresh vegetables."

"Then I trust caring for this small patch isn't too arduous a chore?"

"Not at all. Mr. Atkin, may I ask what brings you here at this time of day? I would have thought you engaged at the mill."

"Normally such would be the case. This morning, however, Cully…Mr. MacPherson has advised me to accompany you into the village to select furnishings for his…your house. It appears a representative of the Lieutenant Governor will be visiting in under a month, and he wants to have the place outfitted in honor of his visit. Cully has also learned there's a ship currently at the wharf that carries a cargo of fine furniture destined for the plantations in the Caribbean. He would like you to have the opportunity of making a selection from among its wares."

"But I don't see how I can possibly…"

"Miss Marston, I remind you of your arrangement with Mr. MacPherson." The man she'd come to think of as her supporter spoke with sudden cold austerity. "The advertisement to which you replied in the affirmative stated he was seeking a lady. Your acceptance implied that you were prepared to fill the position. Now he's expecting you, as his intended, to take on a reasonable duty as the future mistress of his home. Are you determined to renege on your part of the arrangement?"

"Of course not." Indignation shadowed by disappointment in the man standing before her made her words snap out. "Very well." She squared her shoulders. "If that is his desire. You'll excuse me while I change." Stooping, she picked up her shoes and stockings.

"Perhaps into a riding habit? I thought we'd take the horses…if that's agreeable with you."

"Very well."

"Excellent. I'll get them ready."

****

"You've made some fine choices, ma'am." The ship's captain's words reflected his pleasure as Isabella paused with Fletcher Atkin at the top of the gangplank before leaving his ship. "Those bureaus, chairs, tables, cutlery, and cloth for curtains and the like were made to grace the finest of homes."

And you got top dollar for them. The thought raced across Fletcher's mind as he returned his money pouch to his waistcoat pocket. *But I mustn't get parsimonious. Cully is hell-bent on impressing that government official and instructed me to spare no expense in allowing Miss Isabella to outfit his house in preparation.*

"But will not my purchases run you short on merchandise when you reach the Caribbean, sir?" Isabella looked over at the ship's master.

"Ma'am, I'm a trader. I take my profits where I find them. Today it's in Riverhaven, New Brunswick. Rest assured your purchases have not inconvenienced me in the least."

"I'm glad to hear it. I bid you good day, Captain, with many thanks." She took Fletcher's arm and smiled up at him. "Shall we go, Mr. Atkin?"

As he guided her down the gangplank, her hand at his elbow, Fletcher Atkin was filled with a rushing wish that she'd been shopping for his household, not Culloden MacPherson's.

****

On the wharf he was assisting her to mount Duchess when a voice, thick with a Scottish accent, made them both turn to face the man Isabella recognized as Brodie MacMillan.

"Hie there, Atkin." He had halted, standing boldly a few feet away, hands on his hips, feet planted shoulder-width apart. "I've just received a right cardin' out from our esteemed magistrate about that incident in the churchyard this past Sabbath. While Captain Cameron didn't outright accuse me of meddlin' with your horses, he came close. It appears my reputation is destined to make me suspect in any untoward goin's on hereabouts. Nevertheless, I'd be beholden if you'd inform that great buckskin-clad beastie that I dunnae make war on women. Feedin' tea to a team pullin' a wagon with such passengers would be attempted murder…in the same realm of spikin' trees."

A chill washed over Isabella as she saw the man's right hand go to rest on the hilt of the sword in a scabbard at his side.

"Brodie." Her escort faced him with a calm that amazed her. "We're all civilized people. There's no reason this dispute cannot be settled equitably."

"Don't go tryin' to sweeten me up, Atkin. Just deliver my message." He glanced at Isabella. "My apologies, lass. This is a battle between men and will not further involve our women."

He bowed to her, swung about, and swaggered away.

Fletcher watched him go. "I'm sorry you had to witness Brodie MacMillan's unseemly behavior," he said, turning back to her, ready to assist her onto the mounting block. "He's correct in declaring that his past reputation for trouble often brands him wrongly. Still, he can be a loose cannon at times and a dangerous man when aroused to anger."

"I understand he's married. It must have taken quite a woman to catch his likes. Mrs. O'Malley told me people once believed his wife to be a witch. It's only since she saved the village from a dreadful disease with her healing skills that they've accepted her even to a small degree."

"Mrs. O'Malley gossips too much."

"And you womanize too much, Atkin." The sneering words made both turn to see two burly men leering at them. "Isn't that whore Molly at the tavern enough for you?" the one who'd spoken continued. "Or do you fancy something fresh and new? You'd best be careful. Cully MacPherson might not take kindly to you sampling his wares before he's had his first taste."

"Mind your mouth, Tom Bracken." Fletcher Atkin's jaw hardened and jerked, his hands knotting into fists as he swung to face the pair of big bearded men.

"Mr. Atkin, we must go." Her heart thudding, she touched his arm. These ugly oafs were deliberately goading her companion into a fight...a fight in which he was outnumbered.

"That's right, Atkin. Run away. Take her back to Cully MacPherson and pray he's in a forgiving mood."

As Fletcher made a lunge forward, Isabella grabbed his arm with all her strength.

"No, Mr. Atkin! Let us go! Now!" Fletcher paused, glaring at the provoking pair, then looked down at Isabella.

Is my face as white and terrified as I imagine? She remained clinging to his arm, knowing her strength alone couldn't hold him back but hoping her obvious fear might.

He hesitated again. Finally, taking her arm, he helped her aboard Duchess, his fingers tightening unnecessarily hard over her elbow. Relieved the danger of an outright confrontation appeared to have been averted, she avoided flinching. The moment he was mounted on Galahad, she kicked her mare into a run, giving him little choice but to follow her.

"Ride hard, Fletcher. And pray Cully MacPherson doesn't decide to break your neck!" The mocking yell followed them.

****

Side by side they galloped out of town, only slowing their pace when they reached the cover of the trees along the trail to his homestead. As they brought their horses to a trot, then a walk, and finally to a stop, Isabella recognized Fletcher's anger had lessened but slightly.

"Miss Marston," he said as they stood their horses together, his expression tense. "I must apologize for Tom Bracken and Clem Reid. They're troublemakers of the first water. I thank you for not allowing me to be driven into a senseless fist fight. Even if I had managed to acquit myself decently, it would simply have lent credence to their outrageous accusations in front of witnesses."

"Scurrilous as their allegations were, I'm hoping Mr. MacPherson never hears of them." Looking down at her hands, she fingered her reins. "Do you think he'd believe your denial of them if he did?"

"He would. He and I trust each other. He wouldn't have suggested I accompany you when you wish to ride if he didn't. Now, it's getting late." He touched his heels to Galahad's sides. "We'd best be getting on. And Miss Marston?" Turning back to her, he halted again.

"Yes?"

"The less said about this incident, the better. While Cully has faith in me, he could very easily decide to take his anger out on those two blackhearts. And that, as we both know, would accomplish nothing."

****

"The cloth is too heavy." Isabella threw aside the garment she was attempting to mend. "The needle hurts my fingers. Fancy work was never like this."

The encounter earlier in the day with the two louts identified as Tom Bracken and Clem Reid had left her nerves raw and chafed. Was this a country where women were constantly called upon to act as peacemakers? If so, she wasn't sure she could do it on a regular basis.

"You must learn." Seated beside her at the log house's table, Lucy handed the trousers back to her. "The men who work at the mill need their clothing repaired. There is no seamstress hereabouts who will come in to do the mending."

"But surely that couple in the village, the ones Mr. Atkin told us make clothing for men and women…"

"*Make*, yes. They no more repair rents and holes than a blacksmith will shovel manure from behind horses. We must learn to do for ourselves, miss."

"I suppose." Isabella drew a deep breath. "But my hands are raw. I need a change. I'm going out to work in the garden. Come along, Percy. We'll take a bit of air."

The Pug at her heels, she headed for the garden.

A half hour later, contentedly thinning a drill of turnips, she was humming an old ditty she'd learned in the nursery when a great roar erupted from the end of the garden nearest the woods. Glancing up, she froze.

A huge black bear lumbered toward her. Isabella froze. Her heart seemed to seize in her chest.

From where he'd been lying at the far end of the

121

drill, Percy leaped up. Growling, the little dog braced and faced the black monster.

With a mighty roar the creature rose on its hind legs, brandishing claws and teeth. The Pug lunged.

"Percy, no!" She screamed, but it was too late.

Dog and bear met. Roaring its annoyance, with a great swish of its massive paw, the bear slapped the Pug aside. Blood spurted from a wound in his neck, but Percy stumbled upright to lunge again. This time he succeeded in sinking his teeth into one of the animal's hind legs. The bear snarled and spun about. Again, it slapped the Pug aside, only this time with greater force. Percy flew through the air to land motionless in the tall grass beside the garden.

Swinging its massive head from side to side and slavering, the creature dropped on all fours and lumbered toward Isabella. She turned to run but tripped and fell headlong among the sprouting vegetables. Scrambling desperately to get to her feet, she screamed.

She was on her knees when gunfire rent the air. The bear roared. Out of the corner of her eye, she saw it pause, then turn and lope back into the forest.

"Are you injured?" A hand was taking her arm, drawing her to her feet. Fletcher stood beside her, smoking pistol in hand.

She shook her head. Words deserted her. Her knees had turned to jelly, her stomach to a roiling mass. She slumped against him.

"Miss!" Lucy burst around the corner of the cabin, holding up her skirts as she ran. Mrs. O'Malley bustled along behind her. "What happened? We heard a gunshot!"

"There was a bear," Fletcher Atkin explained. "It's

gone now."

"Perceval...Percy!" Isabella turned toward where the little dog lay, bloody and unmoving in a patch of grass beside the garden. "Oh, dear God, Percy!"

Lurching drunkenly, she staggered to her dog and dropped to her knees. Fletcher Atkin followed to hunker down beside her. He placed a hand on the little animal's side before turning to her.

"Isabella...Miss Marston, it will be best if you go into the cabin." His voice was soft, gentle with caring, his eyes reflecting painful sadness as he looked over at her. "I'll take care of what needs to be done here."

"No!" Isabella yanked away from the consoling hand he placed on her arm. "He's not dead! Look, he's breathing."

"Miss, miss." Lucy knelt by her side opposite Fletcher. "It's for the best. You don't want him to suffer."

"There must be something we can do!" Desperation seized her. "He came all this way with me, he was as seasick as I! I won't give up on him. I won't!"

"There is one possibility." Fletcher Atkin wet his lips.

"Yes?" A small ray of hope dawned as she looked over at the man.

"Brodie MacMillan's wife...she's reputed to be a healer of amazing powers. I'll ride out to their home and ask if she is willing to treat Percy."

"But you're at war with those people. You'd be in danger." Astonished by his offer, she stared at the man.

"Not war...yet." A sardonic expression enveloped his countenance as he got to his feet. "Brodie

MacMillan and his friends are not ready to do murder. I'll be quite safe."

"Then, please, by all means, go!" Isabella looked up at him.

He hesitated. Their gazes met and locked.

Good God, what...? Something...something...

Thunderstruck, Isabella forced her attention back to the injured Pug. Her emotions whirled.

Moments later, hoofbeats pounding past the house caused Isabella look up from where she was kneeling beside the Pug ensconced in quilts by the hearth. Something inside lurched with a small ray of hope. Fletcher Atkin was going for the healer and riding hard.

Another emotion followed fast on its heels. In spite of the man's words to the contrary, he was riding into an unstable situation.

God, keep him safe.

The prayer came from her in an imploring rush. Inappropriate as the thought was, that moment beside the garden had made her realize Fletcher Atkin had become something amazing, something wonderful in her life. Something that could never be.

****

Both he and his horse drenched with sweat, Fletcher Atkin galloped into the dooryard of Brodie MacMillan's homestead on top of the hill above the Fowler-Wallace mills. In the valley below, he could see men swarming about as they labored in the business. As he swung to the ground, he thought he glimpsed Brodie MacMillan among them. He hastened to lead Galahad out of sight around the corner of the house. If he didn't have to meet the big Scotsman before he could state the reason for his visit to Louisa, all the better. Later, no matter what her husband said, from what Fletcher knew of Louisa MacMillan's reputation for helping the sick and suffering, she'd ride to help Percy.

Leaving his gelding tied to a veranda post, he bounded up the steps and knocked loudly on the plank door.

"Mrs. MacMillan, it's Fletcher Atkin. There's been an accident at my farm…a bear attack. We need your help."

"Bear attack?" The door opened and the woman stood before him, her lovely face wrinkled with concern. "One of the women…a man…?"

"No." Suddenly he felt at a loss. "A dog. Miss Marston's Pug."

"Badly?" She gave no quarter to any lack of importance that his mission concerned an animal.

"I'm afraid so. Miss Marston and the ladies have done all they can, but I fear…"

"Give me a moment." Leaving the door open, she strode into a curtained doorway at the back. "I'll change into my riding clothes."

"Thank you." He peered inside at the neat, cozy room with its wide hearth and comfortable chairs before it, at the table with a bouquet of wildflowers in its center, at the cushions and pillows on a divan. More than a log house such as his, this was a home.

And suddenly he saw her…Isabella Marston in the white dress embroidered with tiny blue flowers, bending over the hearth, preparing his supper. When she straightened, turned to smile at him, and held out a welcoming hand, he was entranced in the moment.

"Mr. Atkin, would you saddle my horse? The white mare? She's quite affable. You should have no trouble."

Louisa MacMillan's voice from behind the curtain brought him back to the moment. "It will save time. We can be on our way more quickly."

"Yes...yes, of course." He turned and headed for the stable.

Damn it, man, are you losing your mind? She's Cully's fiancée.

****

In the stable he found the white mare in a box stall. In the attached enclosure, a beautiful red filly with a white blaze down her face pranced and whickered impatiently at his entrance. So this was the progeny of Brodie MacMillan's stallion, the great horse reputedly murdered by Cassandra Carmody when the woman had tried to burn Louisa alive. In spite of the need for haste, he took a moment to study the young mare.

"You're a wild beauty, that's for sure." He reached to touch her, but she whirled away, half rearing and squealing. "A beauty, indeed, but it will take someone special, someone who shares your spirit, to bring you to heel. I think Brodie MacMillan probably is just that soul."

He went into the docile mare's stall and led her out to be saddled.

****

The sound of hoofbeats aroused Isabella in her position by the little dog.

"A rider...on a great white horse." Lucy went to the window.

"That will be the healing woman, thank the good Lord." Mrs. O'Malley stood from where she'd been trying to concentrate on mending a shirt. She bustled to the door, and flung it open. "Mrs. MacMillan, come in, and welcome!"

The person who strode inside amazed Isabella. The woman wore trousers and knee-high boots, with a shirt and leather jerkin and a broad-brimmed hat. She carried a black leather valise. A long queue of golden-red curls hung over her shoulder. With that glorious mane and a face of delicate beauty, Louisa MacMillan resembled an angel from one of the paintings Isabella had seen back in the Old Country. Surely, if anyone could save Percy, it was this ethereal creature.

"Miss Marston?" she addressed Isabella. "Your dog has been mauled by a bear, I understand?" She wasted no time. She dropped the bag onto the table and knelt by the dog on the hearth.

"Thank you for coming." Isabella hunkered down beside her as Louisa MacMillan made a quick appraisal of the patient. "I feared that because Percy is a dog you might refuse."

"I'm always willing to try to help any suffering creature." She stood and turned to the housekeeper. "Mrs. O'Malley, I'll have to commandeer your table. I'll also need heated water and cloth torn into strips. Miss Marston, it will be best if you and your friend go into your bedroom and pull the curtain. Or, better still, take a walk outside."

"No!" Resentment rose in Isabella. "I wish to stay with Percy. I wish…"

"What you wish matters little at this time." Louisa MacMillan's commanding tone startled Isabella. "I need but one pair of hands to assist me, and experienced ones, at that. Mrs. O'Malley has helped me with wounded woodsmen. She's not about to fall over in a swoon at any of my procedures."

"Fall over in a swoon!" Indignation coursed through Isabella. "I'll have you know that back at my home in England I've seen calves borne, I've…"

"All well and good, but a surgical procedure is a very different matter." The green-eyed gaze met Isabella's angry one with unflinching determination.

"I'm staying." Isabella drew back her shoulders, crossed her arms on her chest, and planted her feet.

"Very well." The healer opened her valise to draw out a leather apron. "Take a seat. At least if you lose consciousness, you'll have but a short distance to fall."

Isabella hesitated before taking a chair at the head of the table. Willing herself to be strong, to prove herself capable of dealing with emergencies in this new country, her stomach roiling in nervous anticipation, she watched as Mrs. O'Malley wiped the table clean.

****

Later, with Percy again ensconced in a quilt before the fire burning low on the hearth, the table scrubbed free of all traces of the medical procedure that had recently taken place on its planks, Isabella looked across at the woman who'd battled to save her dog's life.

"Thank you most sincerely, Mrs. MacMillan," she said, a cup of hot, sweet tea in her hand. Plates of bread and cheese, courtesy of Lucy, graced the table, but Isabella had little appetite.

"No more than I'm sure you'd do for any creature it was in your power to help." Louisa MacMillan, sitting opposite, also savoring a cup of the brew, smiled over at her. "You did well assisting to get laudanum into the little dog. Now I'd suggest you hold your beverage in both hands. I wouldn't want to have to treat you for a burn."

"Yes…yes, of course." Isabella took her advice. Her hand was trembling, making small waves in the liquid. "How embarrassing."

"I assume this is the first surgery you've witnessed?"

Isabella nodded.

"Then you did very well indeed. The first time I assisted my husband in a medical procedure such as the one performed here today, I became quite giddy."

"Mr. MacMillan is a healer as well?" Surprised, Isabella looked across the table at her.

"My first husband, Dr. Neil Abbot." She stood. "I was a widow when I married Brodie MacMillan. Now I must be going. Thank you for the bread and cheese, Mrs. O'Malley. You brew a lovely cup of tea. I'm well fortified for my ride back to our homestead."

"I have no coin with which to pay you for your services, Mrs. MacMillan." Isabella got to her feet as well. "But I will inform Mr. MacPherson of your generous work this day. I'm sure he'll see you're fittingly compensated."

"That isn't necessary, Miss Marston." She picked up her black bag from a bench. "I'm not a true physician. It would be quite wrong for me to expect or accept payment. Seeing a person or creature survive and regain their health is more than enough recompense."

"Horace has seen to your mare, Mrs. MacMillan," Mrs. O'Malley called after her as the healer pulled open the door. "The animal has been fed and watered. She should be fit as a fiddle to carry you back to your home. You won't find anyone in the barn at the moment. His mission accomplished, the man has gone back to the mill. I'm afraid you'll have to be saddling the creature on your own."

"Please thank Horace for me." She gathered up her supplies. "Don't concern yourself about my getting Snow ready to ride. I do it most of the time."

"Mrs. MacMillan." The mention of the horse brought another thought to Isabella's mind. "What of Mr. Fletcher? He didn't accompany you."

"You're understandably concerned about him." Smiling, Louisa swung back to her. "I feel confident he's well. Although Mr. Atkin refused to remain at our homestead to rest himself and his mount, even though my husband was from home, he did advise me he planned to cool the animal down on his journey back to Riverhaven. He'll pass through the village on his way here. There, I've no doubt, he'll have paused to water, rest, and feed his horse. Miss Marston"—she continued, her expression becoming serious—"although both Mr. MacPherson and my husband can misbehave on occasion, I assure you neither is a cruel man. No animal or person under their care will ever suffer if they can prevent it. Mr. Atkin will be quite safe."

"Thank you." The woman's words strengthened an opinion Isabella had been coming to believe. Spoken by this strong, wise woman, they were welcome reinforcement.

"Good day to you, ladies. If you have any further concerns about Sir Percy, please feel welcome to summon me." She favored them with another smile before exiting the log house.

"A remarkable woman," Isabella said.

"She'd have to be, to handle the likes of that

renegade Brodie MacMillan." Shaking her head, Mrs. O'Malley bustled about, clearing away the remains of their meal. "A goodly number of these lumbermen need a strong hand on the reins to keep them in check. Louisa MacMillan is such a one. Aside from her work as a healer, she also writes stories, I'm told…stories that are published back in the Old Country."

"She does? How remarkable. Percy appears to be resting comfortably now. I believe I'll go and see Mrs. MacMillan on her way." Intrigued by this last bit of information, Isabella made for the door.

In the barn, she found Louisa adjusting a surprising saddle onto her mare's back.

"You ride astride?"

"Yes, I am able to go faster and easier this way." She pulled the girth tight. "When I came to this country and began to accompany my doctor husband on some of his rounds, it just came naturally to ride astride…and in clothing to suit the situation."

"I rode sidesaddle back home in England. Your method appears more practical. Is there a saddler in the village? I believe I may purchase an apparatus such as yours. That is"—she continued more slowly as she recalled her lack of financial means—"if I can somehow manage the cost."

"Your intended is a man of means." Louisa reached for a bridle. "I'm sure he can afford a saddle."

"My intended, yes." The words came out slowly.

"You sound unsure." The bridle in place on her mare, the woman turned to her, eyebrows rising slightly.

"I…" Isabella struggled to find words. "That is…"

"My dear Miss Marston, are you having second

thoughts about your choice?" Louisa MacMillan faced her squarely.

"I…" Isabella hated the way her words were stumbling, yet she felt a great need to confide her uncertainties to someone, someone not connected with Culloden MacPherson. "That is, Mrs. MacMillan, may I speak frankly and confidentially to you?"

"Of course." She leaned against her mare's shoulder, prepared to listen.

"As you may be aware, I accepted Mr. MacPherson's proposal by mail. He was a virtual stranger to me when I arrived in this country. I had no way of knowing, from his letters…"

"That he was a frontiersman? That he is a bit, shall we say, rough around the edges?"

"Yes, yes, that's it exactly. I'm sure he's a fine, decent man in his own way, but…"

"But you've not been able to resolve taking him as a husband?"

"Disgraceful, isn't it? I give a man to understand he will be getting a woman ready and willing to become his wife, and now…"

"My dear girl, it's natural. I'd advise you to take your time before committing to the man. Marriage is for life. If you're not truly at least fond of your choice, it can be a long and miserable existence."

"Thank you for listening and not condemning my fickleness. I'm most grateful for your thoughts on the matter."

"Not at all. I appreciate your confidence in sharing your concerns with me. Now"—she led the white mare out of the barn with Isabella following—"I must be getting home. My husband will shortly be returning from his work in the mill and expecting a meal. Please do not hesitate to call on me whenever you feel in need of my services."

"Mrs. MacMillan." Isabella stopped the woman again as she prepared to mount.

"Yes?" She turned back.

"Mrs. O'Malley has told me you're a writer."

"Well, yes, you could say that I am, although I will never be entering the ranks of great literary authors. I write romances, light tales with happy endings." She smiled, a bit embarrassedly, Isabella thought. "Why do you ask?"

"I..." Isabella found it difficult to proceed. "I've made attempts at writing. I write life experiences mostly...sketches of my impressions of the world around me. I don't know what value they would have to others. My mother and sisters disparaged them as a waste of time and paper."

"Your work sounds interesting." The woman rubbed her mare's neck and smiled at Isabella. "Have you written anything about your decision to come to this country, your voyage, your thoughts on arrival, your plans for the future?"

"Not yet. Why do you ask?"

"I can see your writings as being of value to prospective emigrants. So often land speculators give glowing reports to people considering a move to America, accounts designed to take their money without giving them an honest version of what coming out to this country is likely to entail. An unbiased description and an ongoing story of how you settle in could prove invaluable. In fact"—she gathered up her reins and swung into the saddle—"write a sample, and

I'll be happy to offer my opinion. Although I'm not an editor, if I see merit in it, I will ship it off to my publisher in London and get his opinion. Now I must go. Good day to you, Miss Marston. I'll look forward to reading your efforts."

She put her heels to the mare's sides and galloped out of the yard. Isabella stared after her. *A remarkable woman.* Hope made her spirits rise. An opportunity to have her writings considered by a genuine author! She turned and strolled slowly and thoughtfully back to the house. Now if only Percy would mend...

Chapter Nine

When Horace and Culloden arrived for supper that evening, the latter stopped short as he saw the dog lying on the hearth.

"Bloody hell, whit happened?"

Isabella explained. He listened intently as she described the incident.

"Brave wee heart." The lumberman's words, soft with Scottish inflection, amazed Isabella. "Ye might be a strange-lookin' beastie, but ya've the courage of a lion."

In response to the gentle words, Percy opened one eye and feebly moved his tail. Then, with a sigh, he drifted back into oblivion.

"It's God's own fortune that Fletch arrived when he did." Culloden went to take his place at the table.

"Yes." Isabella, already seated on the right hand bench, agreed. "Indeed. Especially since we weren't expecting him."

"He was sent to tell ya all the trimmin's for the house have arrived and find out when ya would begin settin' them up." He squared broad shoulders and looked at her, lord and master in outlook.

"I've seen your wagon passing through the yard and along the road to your house several times, Mr. MacPherson, with a number of cargoes. I am willing to begin work at the manor as soon as I know Percy is out of danger."

"Aye, it's what I would expect. But dunnae drag your feet about it. Sir Henry Brandish and his lady wife are due shortly. I plan ta entertain them in a style befittin' such folk."

As Horace and Mrs. O'Malley took places at the table and Lucy went to the sideboard for the first plate of food, he continued, "Has Fletch returned?"

"Not to our knowledge, sir." Lucy placed a platter of meat in front of him. "In his absence, I'll ask you to begin the serving."

"Bloody hell, where is the lad?" The words were a mutter as Culloden helped himself to a generous several slices and passed the plate on to Isabella.

"Perhaps resting his horse in the village?" Isabella volunteered, taking a helping and handing it to Horace.

"Or at the tavern," Culloden growled as he snatched a bowl of potatoes from Lucy.

"And what would be the crime in that?" Lucy placed her hands on her hips and cast him a belittling look. "The man has this day saved Isabella from a bear, rescued poor little Percy, and ridden like the devil was behind him to get help. Surely you can't go denying him a few ales."

"It's no' the ales that is concernin' me." Scowling, he dumped four large potatoes onto his plate before handing the container to Isabella. "And it's none of yer business whit is."

"Blimey!" Lucy went back to the sideboard for a bowl of carrots. "That bear seems a right friendly fellow compared with you, Culloden MacPherson."

****

"Another ale, if you please, Molly." Fletcher Atkin

raised his empty tankard in the direction of the bar.

"Right you are, Mr. Atkin." The buxom barmaid cast him a flirtatious glance.

Molly is more than willing. She's made it obvious on more than one occasion. Why not take advantage? I'm unattached, I've made no vow to live as a monk, and I cannot afford to purchase a bride as Cully has…nor would I want to.

He had no desire to go back to his homestead, at least not for some time. Even though he'd found Louisa MacMillan at the cabin she shared with her husband and had managed to tell her the problem without encountering the man, he feared the healer, even with her reputed magic powers, had not been able to save the severely mauled Pug. He didn't fancy himself a coward, but at the moment, facing Isabella, those beautiful eyes full of pain, was more than he could bear.

Be honest, man. The real reason you don't want to go back to your house is because of that vision at the MacMillan house…the vision of you sharing such a home with your best friend's future wife. Admit it. You've been attracted to her from the first time you laid eyes on her on the deck of her uncle's ship. Even fresh from the tortures of seasickness, she appeared too beautiful for a man to resist. And getting to know her just made her more so. You've got to put an end to any and all fantasies regarding Miss Isabella Marston.

As Molly placed a full tankard in front of him, he felt her arm about his shoulders. Leaning close to his ear, she whispered, "My room is at the top of the stairs…in a couple of hours?"

He looked up at her, hesitated, then nodded. A night with a tavern tart was just what he needed to

137

make him realize a gentle woman like Isabella wasn't in his future. With a sly smirk, Molly moved away, sashaying back behind the bar with a cat-in-the-cream expression on her face.

Well, Molly has finally succeeded. Why I haven't given in before is a mystery. She's not a bad-looking girl.

He took a long draw on his ale and acknowledged the reason. He'd had women such as Molly back in the Old Country, women who warmed men's beds for a bit of coin. And other women as well. Women who simply enjoyed a roll in the hay with a decent-looking man of aristocratic birth, but who weren't about to cast their lot permanently with a penniless second son bound for service either in the army or the church.

Such assignations now appeared shoddy and empty. What he wanted—what he needed—was a wife and a home and children. Waking up in the morning in a soiled, sweaty bed, a rude bedraggled woman beside him, generally the conditions of such fornication, held no charm. The physical need they'd fulfilled left him filled with disgust and self loathing. Still he had needs…

Now if it were Isabella…

Good God, man, stop it! Just stop it!

Much as he wanted to deny it, Tom Bracken and Clem Reid's false accusations had only served to make him more aware of what he truly felt for the woman. Today her wide green eyes had looked straight into his soul and forever lodged a feeling there he couldn't shake.

And kneeling beside that little dog, tears about to spill down her cheeks…

Hopeless, hopeless, hopeless. Although it had been his, Fletcher Atkin's, letter that had enticed her to come to this country, she belonged to Cully. He had no one to blame but himself for his present unhappiness and unrest. He'd deceived the woman with his words. Now he was paying the price.

"Mr. Atkin." Looking up, Fletcher saw Tom Bracken standing beside his table. "My mate and I were wondering if you'd fancy a small game of cards." He indicated Clem Reid behind him. "I've heard you were once quite a player."

"Once is the correct word, Bracken. No longer." He made a move to rise. "My horse is rested. I'll be leaving."

Molly's charms will have to wait for another time. I don't want this pair goading me into something I've sworn never to do again.

"Ah, come now, man." Tom Bracken slapped him on the back in a spirit of bonhomie. "What's your hurry? You've got no one at home waiting for you...have you?" The last came out as a smirking innuendo. "That is, not unless you and Cully MacPherson's little lady really have something going on."

"Mind your mouth, Bracken. The lady is not here today to restrain me." On his feet, Fletcher seized the big man by his shirt front.

"Fine, fine. Take it easy. Guess that woman's got you so tied up you haven't got the guts to engage in a game of chance. Or maybe you've lost your touch."

"Break out the cards!" Incensed, Fletcher released the man and dropped back onto his chair. He drained his tankard in a single swill. "Molly, another drink. This time, make it whisky…good scotch whisky…and bring the bottle."

****

"Ya daft bastard!" Culloden MacPherson, his face the color of a ripe tomato, confronted Fletcher in the kitchen of the manor house. "Gamblin' again! After ya swore up and down you'd never touch another card!"

"I know, I know." Fletcher, his shirt soaked with sweat, wet his dry lips and hung his head.

"I can't imagine ya havin' the wherewithal ta keep at it all night. Ta my knowledge, ya've no great savin's, not enough ta keep ya at it until dawn."

"I borrowed a bit." He looked away from his friend, out the window into the breaking dawn.

"From who? I'll not have ya indebted ta anyone, not as long as ya stay in my employ."

"From Duncan MacDougal." Shame coursed through him as he remembered his imploring the magistrate's deputy to stand him one more hand.

"Ah, Jesus!" The big man turned away in disgust. Going to a sideboard, he planted his hands on it and stared out the window above it. When he turned back, Fletcher saw outrage still reflected, but now it was tempered with a cold calculation he recognized.

"I thought ya were sharp when it came ta cards, that ya could cheat yourself out of most situations." He glowered at Fletcher. "Whit happened this time?"

"I determined to play a straight game." Fletcher knew his response sounded hollow and weak. "But those other bastards, Tom Bracken and Clem Reid, were cheating like professionals. Bracken, from what I saw, has had lots of experience."

"And ya weren't clever enough ta outmaneuver

him?" Culloden sucked in a deep breath. "Well, now all we can do is fix the business as best possible. I fair feel like bustin' ya square in the chops, but that won't improve the situation. Instead, I'll ride in and square things with MacDougal. I'll chust be takin' yer horse. The team is needed at the mill. I'm assumin' his royal highness Sir Galahad is tethered outside?"

"No." Fletcher stood, crossed the room and reached up to the shelf for a cup. At the hearth, he poured steaming tea into it. "I walked home." He took a mouthful of the hot drink and flinched. "I lost him."

"Lost...? But surely the beast is clever enough ta find his way home. Oh, bloody hell! Lost! Ya mean ya gambled him away!"

"On the agreement that I would bring the amount owing to Tom Bracken today and retrieve him. I'd never lose him for good."

"Aye, and just where were ya expectin' ta find that kind of wealth?"

Fletcher didn't speak.

"Well, don't think it will be comin' from me, my fine laddie. Ya promised never ta gamble again when I bailed you the last time. Now, get a bit of food into yer belly and head off to the mill. I don't pay ya ta sit around nursin' an achin' head, a sick gut, and a whole lot of regret. I'm hopin' losin' your prized beast will have dashed some sense into yer thick skull."

Culloden strode out of the manor, slamming the kitchen door behind him. Fletcher flinched. He hadn't drunk a great deal while he played, but after that last hand, after he'd lost Galahad, he'd ordered a fresh bottle and guzzled it down like water.

"I'd best be off myself." From where he'd been

sitting silently at the far end of the table, Horace stood and replaced his mug of tea on its corner.

"Horace." Fletcher stopped the man with a voice so gruff he barely recognized it as his own. "The dog…the Pug. Did it survive?"

The man hesitated. He looked down at him with what Fletcher could only interpret as disappointment shaded with contempt.

"When I left your homestead after tending the stock last evening, the little beggar was lapping up a meat broth as if he was hollow."

"Good, very good." Rubbing his temples, Fletcher stood.

"It was your riding for that healing woman that saved him, but you could have done better…later." Horace followed Culloden MacPherson out of the house.

"Then yesterday wasn't a total disaster." Fletcher spoke aloud when he was alone. Pulling his soiled shirt over his head, he headed for the wash basin near the door.

God, I stink. Stupid and filthy. What would Miss Isabella Marston think if she could see you now, Fletcher Atkin? He splashed water over his face and chest. *And just what makes you think she'd give a damn?*

****

"He lost his horse…Mr. Fletcher lost Galahad?" Isabella stared at the former groom. "In a game of cards?"

"Aye." Horace went back to feeding the chickens in their corner of the barn. "The men at the mill said they weren't all that surprised. Seems Mr. Culloden bailed him out from gambling debts with folks on the ship that brought him to this country. They were taking reparations out on his body on the wharf when Mr. Culloden came along and stopped it. The story goes that Mr. Culloden paid off Mr. Fletcher's debts. The agreement was, as I understand it"—Horace paused to lean on the pitchfork—"that Mr. Fletcher was never again to engage in games of chance."

"And now he's broken that agreement." Isabella paused in rubbing a brush over Duchess's flank. "What will become of him now that he's proven untrustworthy?"

"Mr. Culloden could dismiss him." Horace shrugged as he returned to his work. "But that doesn't seem about to happen. Just sent him off back to work with a flea in his ear. Fact is, the men at the mill tell me the place has never shown such a profit as since Mr. Fletcher took over managing the finances. I don't think a canny Scot like Culloden MacPherson is about to give all that up over Mr. Fletcher taking a slip off the wagon." Horace chuckled. "From the look of him, Mr. Fletcher is being punished enough today, what with how the liquor has left him feeling amid the noise of the saws."

"Mr. Atkin was inebriated?"

"At some time in the night, very much so." Horace sprinkled grain before the clucking hens. "This morning he's bearing the results."

A gambler and a drunkard. Something inside Isabella shriveled. How could she ever have imagined herself even slightly charmed by his good looks and fine manners? Culloden MacPherson might lack manners and dress in animal skins, but he was an

143

upright man, a man whom she believed, from what she'd observed, was honest and, in a basic manner, decent.

Perhaps those qualities should be enough. Perhaps fine manners, proper dress, and a handsome countenance weren't the most important qualities to expect in a future husband.

****

A ruckus from the barn later in the morning made Isabella pause in weeding the garden and turn toward the noise. The chickens were squawking as if being attacked, wings beating madly. She scrambled to her feet just as Lucy lurched out of the building, Fletcher Atkin's rooster fighting for his freedom under her arm. The young woman's face was red, her hair a mad tangle. A bloody scratch extended down one cheek.

"No one attacks Lucinda Welsh and lives to crow about it!" she cried as she headed for the block used for chopping firewood. "You'll pay with your neck, my fine lad!"

"No, he won't." Culloden MacPherson appeared around the corner of the house. He was mounted on Galahad. Dismounting and leaving the gelding ground-tied, he advanced toward her, hands extended. "Give Lord Featherstone here."

"I most certainly will not!" The denial exploded from Lucy as she drew the bird away from him. "Look at what he's done to my dress! And I'm sure I've got a great wound down my face!"

"Go ahead, then. Kill the creature." Isabella was surprised to see the big man cross his arms on his chest and step back. "But ya'll have no chicks this year. My friend paid right dear fer that bird that he might

144

continue his flock of fowl. Ya'll also have ta learn ta get along without birds fer the pot and eggs fer cookin'."

Isabella wiped her hands on her apron and watched the small drama unfolding.

Lucy hesitated. Considering, Isabella guessed. Her friend did like roast chicken and fresh eggs.

"Very well, take the ugly bugger." She thrust the bird at the man. "But the next time he comes after me, I'll have a cudgel, and he'll get a famous knock on his proud head."

With a grunt, he took the bird. As if realizing he was safe, Lord Featherstone settled quietly under Culloden's arm as the man headed into the barn. Lucy watched him go, then put a hand to her tangled hair and smoothed her gown. A cackle and a flutter erupted as the rooster was returned to the chicken coop.

Culloden came out of the barn and strode up to Lucy. Pausing close in front of her, he reached out to remove a feather from her disheveled locks. For a moment the pair stood gazing into each other's eyes. Then, to Isabella's amazement, he took Lucy by an arm and led her to the water trough by the stable door. He dipped his hand into the water and proceeded to wash the blood from her face. When he'd finished, his fingers lingered on her cheek.

"You'd best get on inta the house, lass," he said finally, dropping his tone to one softer than Isabella had ever heard him use as he let his hand fall to his side. "Get Mrs. O'Malley ta clean that scratch up right and proper."

"Yes." Lucy's acquiescence was soft as she gazed up at the man who'd washed her wound. Isabella could barely believe this was the same Lucinda Welsh who'd sent many a stable lad packing with a spewing of curse words and a boot in a vulnerable location.

"Mr. MacPherson." Isabella decided to approach Culloden as he stood watching Lucy vanish around the corner of the house.

"Aye?" Apparently startled by her presence, he jerked away from his perusal to turn to her.

"Horace has been telling me about Mr. Atkin's...adventures of last night."

"Gossip has been spreadin', as usual, like wildfire." His brow furrowed until she was reminded of a thundercloud as he loomed over her. "Mr. Atkin's behavior is of no concern ta anyone other than himself and me."

"Perhaps, but I understood he lost his horse...Galahad...in a game of chance. Now you appear in possession of the animal."

"Aye, well, he's a fine beastie. When I learned who had won him, I couldnae countenance that bit of trash Tom Bracken havin' such a bonnie creature."

"So you bought him back."

"Aye." He picked up the horse's reins and started toward the barn. "But, rest assured, he is now my animal. Mr. Atkin will not be enjoyin' him until he's purchased him back through the sweat of his brow."

Isabella watched as he led Galahad into the stable. She wondered if the man named Tom Bracken had made any remarks to Culloden MacPherson about herself and Fletcher keeping company. On reflection, she doubted it. While the two men together might feel safe taunting Fletcher Atkin, she doubted they'd similarly annoy the big mill owner. She believed he could be a dangerous man in a fight and one not to be held back by gentlemanly manners. Furthermore, she felt, if such accusations had been made, Culloden would have had no compunction about confronting her with them.

She brought herself out of her thoughts as she remembered the purpose of Lucy's trip to the barn. Squaring her shoulders, she marched into the building. Culloden was involved in rubbing down Galahad, but he glanced over at her as she entered.

"Eggs," she gave as her explanation. "Mrs. O'Malley needs eggs for her baking."

"Aye." He gave her a wary look before returning to his task.

He's not about to fetch them. But then, what did I expect? He hasn't a gentlemanly bone in his body. Probably gathering eggs is regarded as a woman's task. Well, I'll show him I'm up to it. And no nasty bird named Lord Featherstone will stop me.

She went to the door of the chicken coop and peered inside. The rooster sat on a roost in a corner above the other birds, head held high. When Isabella lifted the latch to enter, he eyed her with a bellicose stare.

It's only a bird, Isabella Marston. Don't allow the nasty creature to make you look less than capable of carrying out such a simple duty as egg collection.

Stepping inside, she bent to pick up the basket Lucy must have dropped in her battle with the rooster, all the time keeping a furtive eye on Lord Featherstone. When the bird made no move to attack, she straightened, put her shoulders back and her chin out, and headed for the nests.

You're the mistress of the manor…or soon will be. Act like one.

She proceeded to gather eggs, even thrusting a few disgruntled hens aside to complete the task. Stepping out of the coop, basket over her arm, she carefully latched the door and heaved a breath of relief. She looked over to Galahad's stall, curious to see what Culloden MacPherson had thought of her bravado. He'd finished grooming the gelding and had paused to replace the brushes on a shelf.

If Isabella had been expecting praise or acknowledgement for her completed task, she was disappointed. He grunted and strode out of the barn.

Not an easy man to impress. But why should I care? He's as near to a savage as any living being I've ever met. His heart is probably as hard and black as a lump of coal.

Annoyance chafing her, she headed out of the barn. She was nearing the log house when she recalled his treatment of Lucy after her encounter with Lord Featherstone. The man was capable of concern for others but perhaps only when he felt it was needed. Successfully completing what for him must have seemed a mundane task deserved no special acknowledgement.

Carrying her basket of eggs, she headed for the house. Culloden MacPherson might not see fit to note her courage in facing down that nasty bird, but she, Isabella Marston, would give herself an imaginary medal for it.

As Isabella entered, Mrs. O'Malley turned from where she was tending to Lucy's scratched face. The young woman sat at the table, and the look of surprise on both women's countenances compensated for Culloden MacPherson's lack of appreciation.

"You needed eggs?" She placed the basket before them, feeling smug.

"Did Mr. MacPherson collect them?" Mrs. O'Malley asked, wonder in her words. "He's never done such a thing…"

"No, I did." Isabella swaggered to the cupboard and took down a cup. Going to the hearth, she poured tea into it with hands that were suddenly shaky. At the table, she sat down in the chair designated for Culloden MacPherson. "Tomorrow I believe I'll milk the cow."

****

"Are you certain sure you don't wish to come into the village with us?" Lucy asked her for the second time as she tied her bonnet beneath her chin.

"Quite certain." Isabella looked up from where she was seated at the table, quill in hand. "I have letters to my family to finish. Horace has volunteered to see that they get to the ship that is leaving for England tomorrow."

"Very well. Good morning to you." Lucy followed Mrs. O'Malley out of the house and into the yard, where Culloden MacPherson waited with his wagon and team. Isabella stood and followed them. As the two women approached the conveyance, the man vaulted to the ground. When they reached him, his hands shot out to encircle Lucy's waist and hoist her to the driver's seat.

Well! More than he's ever done for me.

His action astonished Isabella, much as the incident in the barnyard with Lord Featherstone the previous day. Was he developing a soft spot for her former

149

maid? If so, it would make establishing Lucy into the manor house as her companion much easier. That is, if she, Isabella, decided to marry the mill owner. Slowly and thoughtfully she returned to her letter.

She was near its completion when a soft knock made her turn toward the door, which she'd left open to let in the warmth of the day. Turning, she saw Fletcher Atkin framed in the entrance. Percy, who'd been resting in his nest of blankets by the hearth, struggled to his paws and staggered over to greet the man.

"Good day to you, Sir Percy." He hunkered down to greet the little dog. "You look well on the mend."

"That he is, thanks to your riding to fetch Mrs. MacMillan." Isabella laid aside her quill to smile at him. She observed that although the man was clean, neatly dressed, and freshly shaven, his face was gaunt and he looked paler than she'd ever seen him appear. His night of debauchery had taken its toll.

"His valor had to be rewarded as best possible." He stood but remained in the doorway.

"Come in, please."

"I wasn't sure I'd be welcome." He entered but remained standing by the table. "I'm certain you've heard of my misconduct of the other evening."

"This is your house, Mr. Atkin. I could hardly ban you from it."

"I suppose you cannot. Still, I wouldn't wish to force my unwanted company upon you."

"You most definitely are not unwanted. I admit I was distressed to hear of the unfortunate events in the village yesterday, but I am not your keeper...as Mr. MacPherson apparently is. Please sit."

"Yes, I suppose in a way he is." He took a chair at

the table end opposite where she sat. "May we change the topic? I've disturbed you. I see you're writing a letter."

"Something I've put off as long as I could. Aside from the shortage of paper and ink and the eccentricities of this quill, it's no easy chore writing to such as my mother and sisters. I'm battling to include every positive aspect of my arrival and settling in on this single sheet. I must make it seem I've made a prudent determination in coming to this country. They're all too ready to brand me foolish and brash."

"Seem? You're having doubts?"

"I must admit, I didn't expect someone like Mr. MacPherson. From the letters…"

"The letters I wrote."

"Yes, I guessed as much."

"I'm sorry I misled you. I didn't expect any lady of quality to accept such an adventurous challenge."

"You haven't met my dear mama and my three darling sisters. They are enough to make anyone take a chance on any form of escape."

"Aha. And your father?"

"Papa is wonderful." A reminiscent smile tipped her lips. "He understood my decision, and he actually said he'd come with me if he didn't have the estate to manage."

"You're fortunate to have such a parent." He shifted on the chair.

"Your father…?"

"Was only too glad to be rid of me." He cast her a rueful look. "As you may have guessed after yesterday's debauchery, I'm the black sheep of the family. First he shipped me off to the army, then here."

"Your mother?"

"Died years ago."

"I'm sorry."

"Life goes on." He shrugged and stood. "I came to see how the Pug was doing. I'd best be getting back to the mill. Cully is determined to wring penance from me by working me as hard as he can. It's no more than I deserve. Good day to you, Miss Marston. I'm delighted to see Sir Percy doing so well." He paused before continuing. "Cully…Mr. MacPherson has told me about the incident involving my rooster and Miss Lucy…and yourself. It took courage on your part to go into that chicken coop so soon after witnessing the results of Lord Featherstone's wrath. I'm impressed."

"He's only a bird." Isabella had to struggle to hide the pleasure his acknowledgement of her task gave as she pretended to pass it off lightly.

"Yes, indeed, but I know him well. If he's not shown who is in charge, he can be nasty. Obviously you were able to take command, and he recognized it. Now I must be going."

He gave her a brief nod and went out.

"Good day to you as well, Mr. Atkin," she called after him. "I thank you for your concern."

After Fletcher Atkin had gone, she finished her letter, folded the paper, and used a bit of candle wax to seal it. Laying it aside, she decided it was time for an experiment she'd been contemplating ever since she'd ridden Galahad with Lucy home from church…an experiment that had become definite possibility after she'd seen Louisa MacMillan riding her white horse. Her heart beating with excitement, she went into her bedroom and donned her riding habit.

"You stay here, Percy," she told the Pug, who looked up at her from his place by the hearth as she passed him a few moments later. "I'm about to do something new."

She hastened out of the house and around to the barn. Inside, she strode to the sawhorse where Fletcher stored his saddle and its cloth. If Culloden MacPherson's decision to withhold Galahad from his foreman held true, Mr. Atkin wouldn't be needing it for some time. Taking both, she headed into her mare's stall.

Later, as she led Duchess out into the sunshine of the dooryard, she swiped a damp curl back from her forehead. It had been a challenge, getting the pad, saddle, and bridle each in place.

"Now, my fine lady, let us see how you deal with your mistress riding astride." She put her foot in the stirrup, bounced a few times to give momentum to her mounting, and scrambled aboard.

Duchess shook her head but showed no other signs of concern at this new situation. Turning the mare away from the house and down a trail into the forest, Isabella urged her to a trot.

Absolutely delightful.

The trail emerged into a meadow sprouting a fine crop of hay. A stream ran through its center. A gush of delight flooding through her veins, Isabella drew a deep breath of the fresh, clean air. She touched her heels to the mare's sides and headed at a canter around the perimeter of the field. Hair loosened from its queue blew back from her face. Her skills as a rider came to the fore, and as she reached the stream, only slightly slackening her pace for the horse's safety, she plunged through it. Cold water splashed up her legs above her boots, its touch stimulating to her uninhibited pleasure.

She was rounding the far corner of the meadow, heading back toward the trail, when she saw him. About to ride through the stream, she halted to wait. She needed time to find words to explain her behavior, to excuse her pilfering of his saddle.

"Good morning, Miss Marston." Mounted bareback on Galahad, Fletcher Atkin touched his hat brim as he drew rein beside her. "You've been taking in the pleasures of the day, I see."

"That I have, sir. I hope you'll excuse my borrowing your saddle. After I saw Mrs. MacMillan riding astride, I was intrigued to try the experience."

"And you assumed I'd not be needing it for some time?"

"Yet here you are, boldly riding the mount you've been forbidden."

"Only because, on entering the stable to visit him—something Cully hasn't prohibited—I saw Duchess and my saddle were missing. Miss Marston, I really must caution you again. It's not safe for a young woman to ride alone in this country."

"You mean there are bears and other surly creatures inhabiting these fields and forests?"

"Yes, and unpleasant humans. The man who cheated Galahad away from me, Tom Bracken together with his friend Clem Reid, is a prime example. You've met the pair. You must recognize they're both troublemakers."

"Do you consider them criminally dangerous?" Isabella asked.

"They're a couple of unprincipled vagabonds,

mercenaries willing to do anything for a price. You must exercise caution." He abruptly changed the subject. "How are you enjoying riding astride?"

"Wonderful! So much more convenient than crooking a limb around a hook. I planned to have your gear back in place before you discovered it missing." She concentrated on rubbing Duchess's neck.

"But the beauties of the day and our countryside and the joy of the ride made you tardy?"

"As good a smattering of reasons as any. I do beg your pardon for absconding with your saddle."

"Please feel at liberty to use it. I won't be needing it any time soon."

"I'm sorry Mr. MacPherson saw fit to punish you in such a fashion. Being deprived of riding one's favorite mount is indeed harsh."

"Perhaps, but it's a penalty of my own making. I swore off gambling when I went to work for Cully."

"Were you a serious gambler, Mr. Atkin?" She faced him squarely.

"I'm afraid I was. And not always a very ethical one." He rubbed Galahad's shoulder, avoiding her eyes. "But losing this fine animal has shown me what can result from unrestricted wagering. This time when I swore to Cully never to touch cards again, I meant it. Now I suggest we both head back to my house. I have to return to work at the mill before Cully sees fit to heap more punishment on my head. Miss Marston..." He looked over at her, the intensity in his blue eyes making her breath catch in her throat.

"Yes?"

"You..."

"Yes?"

"You ride very well." He turned away and nudged his horse back into motion.

What had he been about to say? Something in his manner declared he hadn't planned to comment on her equestrian skills.

"I was delighted to see Sir Percy doing so well," he continued conversationally as they continued on their way.

"Yes, he is." Her mare moved easily in step with his gelding. "Mrs. MacMillan appears to have worked a miracle."

"Ah, yes, Mrs. MacMillan." He drew a breath. "An amazing woman. Her husband may be something of a rogue, but he's someone I'd like to call friend one day. Brodie MacMillan is a man who would make a fiercely loyal and boon companion."

"But he and Mr. MacPherson are at serious odds."

"Sad but true. Therefore I'll probably never have the chance to become better acquainted with Mr. MacMillan."

"Perhaps that's as well." She cast him a sly smile.

"Why do you say that?"

"Apparently you are a pair of rogues…each in his own way."

She urged her horse to a slow canter and felt a surge of delight when he pursued her.

When they arrived at the stable yard, Isabella made a move to swing to the ground, but he was quickly beside Duchess to lift her down. His strong hands placed her carefully beside her mount.

"Thank you, Mr. Atkin." Isabella looked up at him.

"You are most welcome, my lady," he replied. "You go on up to the house. I'll take care of the horses."

Turning away, she walked with a spritely step toward the house. She had to suppress the desire to skip that threatened to enter her strides. Her ride with Fletcher Atkin had left her feeling exuberant and happy. And when he'd stammered into remarks about Percy's health, she'd gotten the distinct feeling that wasn't what he'd started out to say.

Had it been something more personal, something that might have changed their relationship forever into a more intimate one? She wished for a brief moment...before guilt overcame her.

Stop it, Isabella Marston. Culloden MacPherson is the man you've come to this country to marry, not his foreman. You have no right to go building fantasies around Fletcher Atkin.

In an effort to put such disturbing thoughts aside, she went into her bedroom and pulled open the third drawer in the dresser. She'd confined her use of this piece of furniture to the topmost two after she'd discovered Fletcher had left some of his clothing in the lower pair.

She hesitated. She had no right to go rummaging through his personal effects, but Louisa MacMillan's comfortable-looking attire had given her an idea.

She reached inside and pulled out a pair of trousers. They were old and shabby. Surely he wouldn't mind... She dug deeper and found a white shirt worn thin.

She carried the articles into the kitchen, fetched her sewing basket, and set to work.

****

Images of Isabella Marston, glowing from a

vigorous ride, tangled curls framing her face, breast heaving above the cut of her riding habit, haunted Fletcher Atkin as he rubbed down her mare.

And, bloody hell, what he'd almost said on their ride home! Stumbling out the weak remark about her riding ability to conceal the thoughts that had made him halt beside her, to prevent the inappropriate words that had nearly blurted from his mouth... The woman was his friend's intended, for God's sake, the fiancée of the man who'd saved his life, who'd gotten Galahad back and paid his debts. What kind of villain would he have to be to make advances to her?

Resolved to put thoughts of the woman from his mind, he finished his task, ran an affectionate hand over the mare's neck, and left her stall. He had his own horse to rub down and chores waiting at the mill. Work was the best remedy for hopeless meanderings. His actions of the previous night had confirmed the fact that he wasn't fit for any decent woman.

Chapter Ten

"What is this?" The next day Isabella looked at the saddle over a stand outside Duchess's stall.

"I picked it up in the village." Fletcher came out of his horse's stall where he'd been brushing Galahad. "But more to the point, what is this?"

He stared at her wearing a pair of his old trousers and shirt, altered to fit her slim form.

"I hope you don't mind." A hot blush suffused her neck and face. "Riding astride in a gown, even a riding habit, is just too cumbersome. Mrs. MacMillan's attire looked much more suitable. I thought, perhaps, since these garments appeared somewhat old and since you hadn't thought them sufficiently necessary to take them with you…"

"Of course I don't mind." He was staring. "But I can only imagine Mrs. O'Malley's reaction when she saw you dressed in them." A grin began to spread across his face.

"At first she was…disturbed." Isabella searched for a word to gently describe the housekeeper's outburst of chagrin. "But when I reminded her that Louisa MacMillan rode in such clothing and in such a manner, she calmed…even though she did mutter remarks to the effect that Mrs. MacMillan was once a suspected witch and she didn't want me being tarred with the same brush because of unseemly attire. It appears I finished my alterations just in time." She gestured at the saddle.

"It's old and worn, but the girth is strong, and it has a few more years' wear in it. It will prevent your absconding with mine again." She caught the jesting in his words.

"You bought it for me?" She turned to him, green eyes widening.

"Bartered." He went back to his task. "I had an extra bridle the village saddler admired."

"I don't know when or even if I will be able to repay you."

"Not mentioning it to Cully will be sufficient." His hand paused in its task, and he looked over the horse's back toward her. "If he notices, tell him it was among the belongings you brought from England, perhaps with an eye to Horace accompanying on your rides? I'm already in enough trouble with the man. I've no desire to get into a donnybrook with him over an ancient saddle."

Isabella hesitated. Concealing from her intended a gift from another man couldn't be right. Yet she did long to enjoy that weathered saddle. Actually, what harm could it do? Fletcher Atkin was a gentleman, a man who'd proven to be a respectful friend.

She nodded. "Very well."

"Do you want me to put it on Duchess and saddle Galahad? I'm assuming from your attire you planned to go riding."

"Thank you, yes, but I thought you'd been forbidden your horse until you'd repaid Mr. MacPherson."

"True, but when I tell him you were dead set on riding, he'll understand I couldn't allow you to go alone." He turned to begin to ready the horses. "It will give me an opportunity to exercise Galahad. As you no doubt have come to understand, Cully doesn't enjoying riding."

Shortly he led both horses into the dooryard. After tossing Galahad's reins around a fence rail, he came to assist Isabella aboard.

"I think I can manage." She put her left foot into the stirrup, but suddenly his hand was on her bottom, thrusting her upward. Startled, she landed in the saddle and looked down at him.

"Not perhaps the most gentlemanly gesture, but it got you seated quickly, didn't it?" He looked up at her, blue eyes twinkling mischievously.

"It certainly did." His words gave her a brash sense of unconstraint. She laughed.

This is why I came here…to be free…and happy.

As he swung into his saddle and they trotted their horses out of the dooryard, she realized the man riding by her side was becoming a major part of that feeling. Nothing could be more wrong.

They rode in silence until they came to the brook. Splashing their horses through the shallow water, their gazes met, and Isabella felt a flutter in her heart. When they reached the far bank, they halted, and Fletcher dismounted to help her down.

"Isabella," he said, his hand covering hers as he took Duchess's reins. Her name came out soft and sensuous, his expression one that made her breath catch in her throat as she looked up at him.

And suddenly she was in his arms and he was kissing her, kissing her as she'd never imagined a man would kiss a woman. She whirled into a place of magic, a place that held only her and Fletcher Atkin. Her arms went about his neck, she melted against him, against the damp cotton of his shirt.

"Dear God!" He jerked away from her with a violence that made her stagger. Rubbing his hands through his hair, he strode off a few steps before whirling back to face her. When he did, the raw emotions mirrored in his face astonished her, frightening her with their violence.

"Isabella, forgive me. Sweet Jesus, what was I thinking? You're my best friend's fiancée. My God!"

"Fletcher..." She reached out a hand, his name imploring, begging.

"No, Isabella." He drew in a breath that raised his shoulders. "Don't tempt me. Don't make me a greater traitor than I already have proven to be." He moved to stand squarely in front of her, his expression desperately serious. "I must never let anything like this happen again. I'll be eternally grateful if you will blot it from your mind. You do understand, don't you?"

She swallowed hard and nodded, even as her thoughts denied the possibility.

They rode back to his homestead in silence, but Isabella's mind was far from quiet. The actions of the man riding beside her had upset her world, had sent her thoughts and emotions tumbling into a wild melee.

At the stable door, they dismounted and he took the horses' reins to lead them inside. Isabella turned away. She could bear no more time alone with the man now that, by her actions, she'd admitted how she felt about him.

That night she lay sleepless for hours in the bed that was his. As she mentally relived the wonder of that sudden, unexpected kiss, she realized it had changed her life, had opened up an entire new world to her. A world of exalting, sensuous freedom that she'd never known existed. A world where an amazing man had forced her to reevaluate her entire future...and her relationship with him and his best friend.

****

The sun shone down, warm and soothing. A gentle breeze kept uncomfortable heat and insects at bay. Barefoot and wearing a tattered sunbonnet and a shabby cotton gown, Isabella worked at the task of thinning turnips and carrots in the vegetable garden. Tender green sprouts were popping up in need of space and nutrition to continue their growth.

Her thoughts were interrupted as the farm wagon rattled into the dooryard with Fletcher Atkin driving. He'd taken Mrs. O'Malley and Lucinda shopping in the village. Isabella had begged off, saying the garden needed her care. She couldn't bear to be near him and continue to deny her feelings. Brushing earth from her hands, she hastened to join them.

"What have you purchased?" she asked, peering at the bags and casks in the cargo space.

"Tea, sugar, salt." With a grunt, Mrs. O'Malley let Fletcher assist her to the ground. "And even though Culloden MacPherson disapproves, flour and oatmeal produced at the Wallace-Fowler grist mill. There isn't much choice, seeing as how they have the only grinding facility in the county."

"Lucy, what is that package you're clutching?" Isabella asked as her former maid jumped down, not waiting for their driver's assistance.

"Shirts for that great barbarian who insists on

wearing animal skins instead of proper clothing." Lucy held her head high as she marched toward the log house. "It's high time he wore something that can be properly laundered."

Isabella glanced at Fletcher. He gave her a resigned shrug.

"I told her she had scant to no hope of getting Cully into cotton clothing on a daily basis," he said. "But she insisted. It will be interesting to see what happens."

He headed for the rear of the wagon and began unloading its contents. Trying to stop the butterflies that refused to stop fluttering inside her due to the man's nearness, she turned away from the sight of his tall, broad-shouldered form.

Isabella never knew how Lucy accomplished the feat, but the following day Culloden MacPherson, a deep scowl emphasizing his mood, arrived for supper wearing a cotton shirt. Glancing at Lucy, Isabella saw a self-satisfied smirk on her friend's face.

Later, when she asked her friend how she'd managed it, Lucy tossed her head and gave her sly smile.

"You just have to know how to manage the creature, Isabella," she replied. "Nothing to it once you've mastered the task."

Lucy's dominion over the man was to reveal itself once again the following morning.

Carried by a mill laborer on his way back to work at Culloden's mill, the invitation to tea at the minister's house arrived the following morning.

"We're all invited." Delighted, Isabella read the short message. "Oh, my, this very afternoon."

"We'll be needing the team and wagon," Mrs. O'Malley said. "Though convincing Mr. MacPherson to relinquish them for even a few hours on a working day for what he'll no doubt consider an unnecessary journey won't be easy."

"Leave it to me." Lucy stood from her place at the table and flounced to the sideboard, head held high. "As soon as we've eaten, I'll see to it."

Lucy proved as good as her promise. Shortly after they'd finished a light repast, she dressed in her most fetching gown, plopped her sunbonnet on her head, and set off down the trail to Culloden's mill. Within an hour she was back, sitting proudly beside Fletcher Atkin, who drove Culloden's team harnessed to his wagon.

Mrs. O'Malley and Isabella, waiting on the veranda, hastened down the steps. Fletcher handed the reins to Lucy and jumped to the ground to assist them aboard.

"You ladies could be headed for the Queen's garden party," he said, looking at the housekeeper in her best gown and Isabella in a fine muslin one. Both wore sunbonnets, although Isabella's with its tasteful trimming of ribbons and lace far outstripped those of the other two women. "You're looking most fetching, ladies," he continued, but his eyes were on Isabella.

Oh, God, Fletcher, don't look at me like that. Don't give me any more pain and longing than you already have.

Lucy had scrambled into the back by the time Isabella and the Irishwoman had arrived at the conveyance. Fletcher assisted Mrs. O'Malley into the rear before lifting Isabella to the front. His hands lingered on her waist a few moments longer than necessary after he'd seated her, his eyes looking into hers with what she read as regret and…yes, desire.

No, Fletcher, please!

He climbed up beside her, took the reins, and threaded them through his fingers. As the wagon lurched forward, Mrs. O'Malley and Lucy fell into conversation, leaving the couple in front free to share words.

"Was Mr. MacPherson very loath to relinquish the team?" Isabella asked, glancing at the man as he headed the horses down the trail. She had to aim for general conversation to keep her mind from more intimate thoughts.

"A lot less than I would have thought." Grinning, he cast her a quick glance that made her heart flutter before returning his attention to driving. "Lucy seems to have a way of handling him."

"She certainly does. Will you be waiting for us?"

"I've been given strict instructions to wait one hour, no more. Cully says that should give you ample time for tea, cakes, and gossip. In the meantime, I'll visit with the reverend. This fine day will probably find him mowing his meadow. I'll lend a hand."

"Reverend Morgan is a farmer?"

"In this country, a man frequently has to wear many hats in order to survive. The reverend and his wife have a small farm attached to the manse lot. His wife often works in the field with him." He slanted her a sideways look. "Such is the lot of women in this country."

They were silent for a few moments, the tittle-tattle of the two women in the rear, the creaking of the wagon, and the sounds of the horses filling the void.

"Do you think I'm overdressed?" she asked suddenly. "It's the one I would have worn to tea back home. Lucy advised me against wearing it. She said I mustn't appear pretentious if I want to be accepted."

"I think you look wonderful." Startling her with his response, he turned his full attention on her as the horses continued to plod along. "The perfect lady."

"Such as Culloden MacPherson was seeking when he advertised for a lady wife?" The ironic tone in her voice startled her.

Where had that come from?

"Yes." He swung his concentration back to the team. "Most definitely, yes."

****

At the manse, Isabella, Lucy, and Mrs. O'Malley were met at the door by a smiling minister's wife.

"Come in, come in." Mary Morgan's delight at their arrival shone from her pretty face. "I'm happy to see you. The others are in the parlor. Please, follow me."

She led the way through a door to their right. Seated around the room were several ladies, all in what Isabella guessed were their best gowns and bonnets. As she entered, all eyes turned on her. Their expressions as they gave a head-to-toe consideration of the newcomer made Isabella realize Lucy had been right. She should have worn something less elegant.

"Now." Mary Morgan took her and Lucy each by an arm and began to lead them around the circle of women. "I'll introduce you. Mrs. O'Malley, of course, has met all of these ladies previously. This is Mrs. Ann Cameron, Captain Cameron's wife—Captain Cameron, as you may know is our magistrate—and beside her is

Mrs. Virginia MacDougal—we call her Ginny—Duncan MacDougal's wife. Her husband is the captain's lieutenant. Next to them, Mrs. Lillian Gardiner and Mrs. Hazel Green and Mrs. Green's daughter Morag. And last but certainly not least, Mrs. Margaret Wallace."

"It's a pleasure to meet you." With an effort to include all of her new acquaintances, Isabella looked around and bobbed a slight curtsy, Lucy following her example a bit awkwardly. Smiles, even if some were a trifle cautious, greeted her with three exceptions. The expressions on the faces of Lillian Gardiner and Hazel Green appeared stiff and calculating. Beside that pair, the young woman Morag sat, head down, only glancing up briefly to acknowledge the introduction. Isabella couldn't help being impressed by Morag's dark-haired beauty, but her shyness made her less than the attractive young woman she could be.

Perhaps Mrs. Gardiner and Mrs. Green disapprove of mail-order brides and have impressed this opinion on this pretty young woman?

"Now to the business of the day." Mary indicated seats for the three new arrivals. Taking her seat at the serving table on one side of the room, she began to pour tea into cups.

As the afternoon progressed, Isabella found herself enjoying the companionship of most of the women. Only Lillian Gardiner and Hazel Green held themselves apart, seemingly content to gossip between themselves and cast appraising glances at Isabella and Lucy.

Understandable, I suppose. Isabella turned away from them. *I doubt many women would cross the Atlantic to marry a man such as Culloden*

MacPherson...that is, if they had any idea of the man's true self.

The minister's wife interrupted her thoughts with a smile and a proffered plate. "I'm only slowly learning to bake, but I believe these are edible."

"Thank you, I'm sure they're delicious." She took one onto her saucer. "I haven't yet tried my hand at the process but, with Mrs. O'Malley's help, I'm willing to make an attempt. By the way," she lowered her voice below the level of the other women's cacophony, remembering what Culloden had said about Louisa MacMillan being regarded as a witch by some residents. "Where is Mrs. MacMillan? Perhaps she doesn't have time to attend such occasions? I understand she's a very busy woman."

"Louisa insisted Margaret come while she stayed with Mr. Wallace. He's still not well enough to be left alone in the care of his young stepdaughters. She declared Margaret needed a few hours away from the heavy responsibilities she's had to assume since her husband's misfortune."

"It was a terrible accident, I understand." Isabella kept her tone low to carry on the conversation with Mary Morgan.

"That it was." For the first time, Isabella caught a Highland lilt in the minister's wife's voice. "Whoever spiked those trees is a criminal of the first water." Her normally gentle tone had taken on a cold bitterness. "They deserve to be punished to the full extent of the law."

"Mrs. Morgan, you don't think Mr. MacPherson was in any way involved?" Isabella experienced a sudden need to defend the man. "Although I've known him only briefly, I can't imagine him doing anything so heinous."

"Nor can I, Miss Marston...Isabella. Still, the animosity between him and Brodie MacMillan hangs like a great, dark cloud over this valley. We must all pray that it may be brought to a peaceful resolution." She stood to reach for the teapot. "Perhaps, in the end, it will be up to us women to settle the matter." With a significant glance at Isabella, she moved away to replenish cups. "Who's for more tea?"

What can Mary Morgan possibly mean? How can women stop the likes of Brodie MacMillan and Culloden MacPherson?

Looking across the room, her gaze met Margaret Wallace's. The woman smiled at her and raised her tea cup in a salute. After a surprised hesitation at the form of address, Isabella replied in like manner. She remembered Mrs. O'Malley having told her Margaret Wallace had worked in the village tavern before marrying. The gesture was likely second nature to her.

At least she and I don't have to be enemies.

Across the room, Lillian Gardiner, catching their exchange, guffawed. Raising her voice, she spoke loudly to command the attention of the room.

"Here we sit, enjoying tea and scones, while a great evil inhabits our valley. I think what occurred in the churchyard last Sunday was disgraceful, utterly disgraceful. My friend Mrs. Green was a witness and described the incident to me in detail. Whoever fed tea leaves to Culloden MacPherson's team must be brought to account for attempted murder."

"No worse than whoever spiked trees on my husband's patch." Margaret Wallace took the bait, her eyes bright with anger.

"Furthermore, it appears our magistrate and his deputy have done little to bring an end to these acts of lawlessness." Undeterred, Lillian Gardiner cast a haughty glance at Ann Cameron and Ginny MacDougal.

"Our husbands have done their best to quell the disputes." Ann Cameron spoke calmly but distinctly. "Without evidence to substantiate who is responsible, there's little they can do."

Isabella saw her place a placating hand over Ginny MacDougal's as the woman by her side made to rise, her expression bellicose. Duncan MacDougal's wife appeared a firebrand with a spirit not unlike Lucy's.

"Ladies, ladies, enough." Mary Morgan began to hand around small cakes. "This is not the time or place for such discussions. Whatever will Miss Marston and Miss Welsh think if we leave them with the impression of quarreling over afternoon tea?"

"I fear we must be going." Isabella glanced out a window to see Fletcher approaching with the wagon and team. "Mr. MacPherson can spare his horses only briefly." She stood, with Mrs. O'Malley and Lucy following her example. "Mrs. Morgan, ladies, it's been a lovely afternoon, and I thank you."

She was in the vestibule with Mrs. O'Malley and Lucy when Lillian Gardiner caught up with the group and grasped Isabella's arm. The woman held her back from her companions and Mary Morgan, who was accompanying her guests to the door.

"A word in your ear, Miss Marston," she hissed.

"Yes?" Surprised, Isabella turned to her.

"In private, if you please." Her eyes danced

171

maliciously.

"You may speak in the dining parlor." Mary Morgan indicated the door opposite the one they'd left.

Still astonished but curious to know what the woman could have to say to her, Isabella allowed herself to be drawn into the room. With the door closed firmly behind them, Lillian Gardiner clutched her arm in a grip that made her flinch.

"Mind yourself around that Fletcher Atkin." The woman leaned close, her expression one of nasty intent. "He's a drunkard, a gambler, and, worst of all, a shameless womanizer. He's got the gift of gab to seduce and the fine looks to carry out his ungodly actions."

"How would you know all this?" Something inside Isabella coiled and brought a roil of nausea into her stomach. "He's seldom in the village, he attends church…"

"It's general knowledge, my fine lady." Lillian Gardiner stepped back to glare at her contemptuously. "Recently he was seen leaving the tavern at dawn, drunk and disheveled, after a night of debauchery. The tavern wench Molly Butler wasted no time spreading the news that the great gentleman Fletcher Atkin had warmed her bed most successfully during the night."

"That's a vile accusation. I'll listen to no more." Whirling away from the glowering woman, Isabella pulled open the door.

"Very well. But never say you haven't been warned."

By the time Isabella reached the wagon, Lucy and Mrs. O'Malley were already seated in the back and chatting. Fletcher waited beside the conveyance, ready to assist her to the driver's seat.

"You and Mrs. Morgan were having a few parting words?" he asked as his hands encircled her waist and he hoisted her aboard.

"No." She waited until he was seated beside her and had put the team into motion. She felt confident Mrs. O'Malley and Lucy were too lost in their discussion of the afternoon to give attention to them, but she was trembling inside and out. "Mrs. Gardiner was having a few parting words."

"Aha. About me, no doubt."

"That sounds a knowledgeable response. How can you possibly know…?"

"I'm acquainted with Mrs. Gardiner…and more intimately with her friend Mrs. Green." He flapped the reins over the team's backs to urge them to a quicker pace. "I will venture to guess that she was warning you against me, that she regards me as the local lothario. Or perhaps she branded me a gambler and drunkard. Possibly all three?"

He shot her a questioning glance.

"Yes."

"I suspected as much." He guffawed.

"What reason would she have for making such accusations? Surely…"

"Surely Lillian Gardiner and Hazel Green are sour old troublemakers." The harshness of his words and tone startled Isabella. "Mrs. Green guards that daughter of hers as if she were a precious jewel. No man in the valley is good enough for Miss Morag. I once made the mistake of asking that young lady to a church supper. When I went to collect her, her mother took a broom to me. Chased me all the way back to this wagon, beating me about the shoulders."

Isabella stifled a chuckle. In spite of the hurt Lillian Gardiner's accusations had caused, the image of this tall, powerful man being driven off by a small, sour woman amused her.

"You find it humorous?" Frowning, Fletcher turned to her.

"I'm sorry, but yes, I do."

"A ridiculous scenario, I agree. But perhaps it's as well Nasty Lillian has told you of my sins. It will help you to realize the value in an upright if roughshod man like Cully."

He flapped the reins over the backs of the team to send them into a trot.

****

Isabella stood back, cocked her head to one side, and frowned.

"More to the left, Horace, if you please," she directed, shoving a stray curl back from her forehead. "That armoire should be midway along the wall."

In her oldest cotton gown, a kerchief tied about her head, Isabella together with Lucy and Horace was setting the furnishings in place in Culloden MacPherson's manor house. It had proven more of a task than she had anticipated. Now, with most of the pieces settled and the house cleaned top to bottom, she was weary. She drew a deep breath, deriving a sense of pride from the completed work. For someone with scant experience in household management, she thought she had accomplished the details well, and she congratulated herself on a job decently done.

She thought of Mrs. O'Malley, back at the log house busily putting the finishing touches on curtains and bed and table linens. Within the hour Fletcher Atkin would be driving the Irishwoman and Lucy into the village to select necessary items of food and drink in anticipation of Sir Henry Brandish's arrival. Since he was bringing his wife Charlotte, Isabella felt it was doubly important that the household be in excellent standing. Women noticed so much more than men in these matters.

"It all looks very well, Isabella." Lucy came to stand beside her and survey the guest bedroom. "Once the bedcovers are in place, it will be more than worthy of Sir Henry what's-his-name and his lady."

"Thank you, Lucy. It's no more than Mr. MacPherson expected of me when he invited me to come to this country."

"He does expect more." Lucy looked at her knowingly.

"Well, yes, but I was referring to these matters…setting up his house and such."

"Isabella, it's not my place to pry, but…"

"Yes?"

"Are you having second thoughts about marrying Culloden…Mr. MacPherson?"

"Why do you ask such a question?" Isabella started at her friend's question.

"Because"—Lucy turned away, her usual brashness stumbling—"I'm sorry. It is none of my business. Let us get on with our work."

Isabella paused to stare after her friend as Lucy returned to placing a chair before a dressing table. *What is happening here?*

****

"I see no need for this infernal scrubbin'!"

Culloden sat, knees to his chest, in the wash tub before the hearth in the kitchen of the manor house. "I wash my hands, face, chest, and nether parts every day."

"Yes, but your neck and back have been sadly neglected." Fletcher went to the hearth to fetch another bucket of warm water.

"Aye, aye, and now ye've near scrubbed the hide off of them."

"If you want to impress Sir Henry Brandish as a man looking decent enough to head this province, you have to be clean and well groomed. Anyway, we're near done. We have to finish before the ladies arrive to begin preparing the meal. Just one more bucket of rinse, and…"

Culloden yowled and leaped to his feet when Fletcher dumped the bucket over him.

"Oh, my!"

Both men swung toward the door to see Lucy and Mrs. O'Malley framed in it. For an instant both stared before Mrs. O'Malley clamped a hand over Lucy's eyes.

"Get yourself decent, Culloden MacPherson!" the Irishwoman snapped. "Shame on you, parading yourself around naked before an innocent young girl!"

"I wasn't…" Culloden began to defend himself as Fletcher tossed him a length of drying linen.

"Too late for explanations, Cully." Fletcher grinned. "You've just bared more than your soul to the ladies."

****

"Careful, careful, laddie! I'm no' a sheep that needs shearin'."

Culloden MacPherson, a length of toweling linen

about his shoulders, cautioned Fletcher as his friend trimmed his hair and beard. The pair were in the master bedroom of his manor house, preparing for Sir Henry's visit that evening.

"You can't go about looking like a forest creature." Fletcher ran a brush through his friend's dark hair and stepped back to consider his handiwork. "If you're hoping for a government appointment, you have to appear worthy of the part. Now, take a look." He held out a looking glass.

"Man, ye've fair scalped me!"

"Hardly. You still have the most hair and beard a man can display and look civilized."

"Well, if ya say so. Ya'd know, I suppose." Yanking the cloth from his shoulders, Culloden stood and drew a deep breath. "But, damn it all, it was yer idea ta strip me naked and wash me that led ta my current shame. I don't know as how I'll ever be able ta look that young lass in the eye again."

"From her expression, though I glimpsed it for only a moment, I'd say she did more than look you in the face." Fletcher chuckled. "And was not displeased with what she saw."

"That's a daft thing ta stay. And right unfair ta the lass."

"You don't seem as disturbed that Mrs. O'Malley was also a witness?"

"She's a widow. I doubt she saw anything that would surprise her. Bollocks! I knew all this scrubbin' would come ta a bad end."

"Take it easy. You'll pop the buttons on that waistcoat or maybe split your trousers. Remember these garments were made to fit snugly and don't stretch like buckskin." Fletcher brushed a few stray hairs from the shoulders of the dark coat Culloden wore.

"Damn tailor!" Culloden strode across the room to stare into a cheval mirror. "I'll never be able ta get out o' these bloody pants if I have ta have a quick piss."

"Then plan to relieve yourself before the necessity becomes too great. And remember 'piss' is not an acceptable word."

"Verrae well, verrae well. I'm headin' down ta the kitchen ta see what the lass has on the fire in the way of a meal fer his Royal Pain in the Arseness."

Shaking his head, Fletcher followed. The evening ahead promised to be a disaster of major proportions.

****

"Whit is it yer cookin', lass?" Culloden strode into the kitchen and paused, sniffing the air. "Smells right tolerable."

Lucy and Mrs. O'Malley turned from where they'd been tending pots hanging over the fire. Both women froze, mouths gaping open.

"Well, whit is it?" Culloden advanced toward the hearth. "I'll chust be tastin'…"

He reached to take a spoon from Lucy's hand. She snapped back to animation and slapped him away. "Don't be daft! You'll get spots on your clothes."

"Argh!" He gave up and headed out of the room. "Fletch, come inta the front room…drawing room or whatever ya choose ta call it. I'm needin' a wee dram."

"Looks fine, doesn't he?" Before he followed his friend, Fletcher winked at the women.

"He does clean up real nice," Lucy murmured, her eyes shining.

Chapter Eleven

"Bugger all!"

Back at Fletcher Atkin's homestead, Isabella struggled to pin her hair into a coiffure suitable for a dinner and evening such as had been planned for Sir Henry Brandish and his wife. Staring into the mirror, she gave her efforts a final pat and heaved a resigned sigh. Without Lucy's help, it was the best she could manage and therefore would have to do. At any rate, her gown, her best white muslin with tiny blue flowers embroidered over it, was suitable.

She felt the corners of her mouth twitch upward as she recalled her expletive. Maybe she was learning how to cope with this way of life. At least she'd adopted some of its more colorful language.

The sound of a wagon in the dooryard drew her attention. Horace must have arrived to fetch her. Gathering up her shawl, she hurried into the kitchen.

"Come along, Percy," she said, picking up the Pug from his usual place by the hearth. "I can't abide leaving you alone for an entire evening. You'll stay in the kitchen at the manor house until I'm ready to return."

Outside, Horace helped her and the little dog to the wagon seat. Once they were comfortable, he climbed aboard and clucked to the team.

"You look right fetchin', miss," the groom

surprised her by commenting once they were underway.

"Thank you, Horace." She smiled. Apparently the man was relaxing into the ways of this new country. Back in England, such a comment to someone regarded as his mistress would have been deemed entirely inappropriate.

"Mr. Culloden looks well, also." He glanced at her with such a look she was left wondering what change Fletcher Atkin had managed to make in the mill owner.

She didn't have long to wait to find out. At the manor, the man himself, with Fletcher following, came out to meet her.

"It's about time," Culloden greeted her. "The guests have arrived and are preenin' themselves in that room ya prepared for them." He held up hands to lift her to the ground, but she sat staring at him.

Fletcher had to be a wizard. The man looking up at her, offering assistance, freed of masses of hair and well dressed, was as handsome as…well, almost as handsome as Fletcher Atkin.

"Don't just stand there gawkin'." Impatiently, Culloden shook his waiting hands. "Dinner will be spoilin'."

Moved into action, she accepted his help. In short order, both she and Percy were on the ground.

"Well, well!" Culloden crooked his arm to her. "Let's get a move on."

As she accepted his offer and they moved toward the manor, he muttered, "Ya do look right bonnie. Thank ya."

Good God! Some of the manners Fletcher and Lucy have struggled to impress on the man must have stuck. Maybe the evening will go well after all.

****

Isabella watched anxiously as they took their places around the dining parlor table. This evening with Sir Henry Brandish and his wife Lady Charlotte would surely be a test of all that she, Lucy, and Fletcher Atkin had struggled to teach the mill owner. Fletcher had effected an amazing physical transformation in his friend, but what of manners and polite conversation? So far Culloden, with subtle glances and even a few prods from Lucy, had managed their procedure into the room and to their seating arrangements without any major flaws.

Isabella wondered, as she watched her friend in the neat maid's uniform she'd revived from her former position in England, if Lucy would be able to keep the man in check during the entire course of the meal. Several times she caught her friend furtively prodding Culloden in the back to alert him to a faux pas as, in the process of serving, she passed behind his chair. Afterwards, when the ladies left the men to port and cigars, she realized the evening would be out of Lucy's control. Hopefully Fletcher would be able to avert any major gaffes for the remainder of the evening.

As the meal progressed, Isabella found she was relaxing. She marveled at Lucy's skill in managing the man dressed in formal wear, even if he did give an occasional pull at his neckcloth and scratch the front of his waistcoat.

Isabella glanced up the table to where Fletcher Atkin sat watching and saying little as events unfolded. Catching Isabella's look, he glanced in her direction, gave a conspiratorial smile and an almost imperceptible shrug. Seemingly content to let Lucy orchestrate the evening, he was remaining mostly silent.

Shortly after the meal had drawn to a close and the ladies had adjourned to the drawing room, Lady Charlotte stifled a yawn and turned to Isabella as Lucy served coffee.

"I really must beg to be excused, Miss Marston." She drew herself up and looked down her long nose at Lucy. "We've had an arduous journey today. I trust my maid has eaten in the kitchen and been shown to my room?"

"Of course, ma'am." Lucy bobbed politely.

"Then I'll retire." The woman started to leave the room but paused at the doorway. "I must say, Miss Marston, you've been most fortunate to find such well trained help here in the colonies." She indicated Lucy. "My maid utterly refused to come with me from England. I'm forced to deal with a girl absolutely lacking in manners and ability."

"I'm sorry to hear that, Lady Charlotte. Perhaps given time she'll improve."

"Perhaps, but"—she faced Lucy—"if you ever wish to change positions, to be employed in the relative grace and convenience of this province's capital, my door will be open to you."

"Thank you, ma'am." Again Lucy acknowledged the woman's words politely, but Isabella could sense the resentment bubbling beneath it in her friend's dark eyes.

Lucy was enjoying her new life free of servitude and wasn't about to go to work for this belittling aristocrat.

Fearing an outburst of her friend's resentment, Isabella stepped quickly into the void.

"Lucinda and I have been together a goodly number of years, my lady. We've formed a special bond."

"Don't be deceived, my dear. I thought my former maid was loyal to me, but the moment such a slight difficulty arose in our relationship, she left me."

Can this foolish woman seriously believe crossing the Atlantic, leaving all that is safe and familiar behind, heading to an entirely new way of life, is only a "slight difficulty"?

"I must be leaving, as well." Stifling an inappropriate reply, Isabella adjusted her gloves. "My groom will be waiting. I stay with my chaperone in a house about a quarter mile away."

"Most correct that you don't live in this house with Mr. MacPherson until you're properly married. Come along, girl. I'll need you to light the way to my room." She addressed the final remark to Lucy.

Isabella repressed a snicker as Lucy picked up a candle and led Lady Charlotte out into the foyer, walking in imitation of the woman's stiff-backed strides.

****

"That was a fine dinner, Mr. MacPherson. My compliments to your cook."

"Thank ya, sir. She does not a bad job...for an Irishwoman." Still seated at the dining table with Fletcher and Sir Henry, Culloden poured port from the bottle in the three glasses Lucy had placed beside him before leaving with the ladies. "Even if she makes a fair bust of preparin' a haggis."

Fletcher shot his employer an admonishing glance, but either Culloden missed it or chose not to take notice. "Next time you visit, I'll have Mrs. MacNeil, a village woman, make one for ya and yer lady." He handed around the drinks.

Cully, for God's sake! No Englishman, short of a starving one, would ever consider eating a haggis. Hold your tongue, man, hold your damn Scotsman's tongue! Fletcher shot the man another warning look accompanied by a subtle head shake, but Culloden paid him no heed. *It's a hell of a thing, that we had to leave the ladies...Lucy in particular. She's the only person who seems capable of handling Cully.*

"A rare treat, I'm sure." Sir Henry Brandish swirled the liquid in his glass and watched it move.

"Aye, aye. Now to a matter that has been interestin' me of late, yer lordship...the namin' of a new governor fer this province."

Bloody hell! The man has absolutely no diplomatic skills. His chances of being named governor are scant at best...in a few minutes they'll be nonexistent if he keeps on in this blunt manner.

"We've heard rumors, Sir Henry." In an effort at damage control, Fletcher spoke. "Of course, that event could be several years away..."

"Or not." Cully appeared hell-bent on charging ahead. "I've always been a man ta look ta the future, Sir Henry, ta prepare fer it, not sit on the sidelines pickin' my nose."

Sweet Jesus! Fletcher felt like dropping his head into his hands in despair.

"What are you thinking, Mr. MacPherson?" Lord Brandish didn't appear in the least disturbed by the man's crude words, but Fletcher guessed that his lordship, like most aristocrats, had been well schooled in not letting his feelings show.

"I'm thinkin' what this province needs is a man who knows it inside and out, who's built his life here...not some damned red-coated military man with his chest sportin' a daft rainbow of foolish ribbons who wouldn't know a white pine from a red, who hasn't any idea o' the true wealth New Brunswick has ta offer, its value ta the empire, who thinks the only way ta deal with the natives is ta murder them."

Good God, man, can you dig yourself any deeper into this man's poor opinion? Don't you recall I told you Sir Henry was a much decorated military man himself?

"You're a Scotsman, sir, I believe." Sir Henry appeared as untouched by Culloden's denouncements as a rock on a hillside by a summer storm, but Fletcher saw the lines about his mouth tighten ever so slightly.

"Aye, that I am."

"Highlander, I'm inclined to believe from your accent?"

"My father was."

"And may I assume you're suggesting yourself as the next lieutenant governor of this fine colony?"

"That I am, sir. I stand ready and willin' ta serve. In fact"—he stood and went to help himself to more port—"I have Mr. Atkin trained up ta be able ta take over my business here in Riverhaven while I'm in Fredericton attendin' ta government concerns."

"I see." Sir Henry cleared his throat and shifted in his chair. "You've given this serious consideration."

"That I have."

"And investigated the history and requirements of the position?"

"Aye." Culloden turned suspicious eyes on the man. "Sir, I'm gettin' the feelin' that yer leadin' up ta something that won't fill my gut with joy?"

"If, as you say, you've looked into the past of the office, you'll note the office is generally filled by an Englishman, frequently one of a distinguished military or aristocratic background." Sir Henry settled more comfortably into his chair and cleared his throat. "I'm sure you can appreciate the King's reluctance to appoint anyone else to such a position. Given the Highlanders' history of defiance to the Crown, I think it unlikely His Majesty would look favorably on your application."

He paused before continuing. "Furthermore, this community, this Riverhaven, has lived up to its name, if what I've heard is true. It's offered refuge for any number of rebels and rogues, particularly Highland outlaws. I hardly see anyone from such a place being a serious candidate for the office. Your colleague Mr. Fletcher would be a more viable person to put forward for such an office...even though, as I've said, having residence in this village, he would be a dark horse. Why, Mr. MacPherson, your name alone would raise eyebrows if presented for such an office. The treasonous rebellion of Highlanders that culminated at Culloden Moor has not been forgotten."

Culloden had listened without comment throughout the official's comments, his face deepening into redness with each disparaging remark. At the final sentence, he rose to his feet with a great bellow that reminded Fletcher of an enraged bull.

"The name MacPherson is a proud and honorable one, I'll have you know."

"Perhaps, in the Highlands." Sir Henry raised his

empty glass, and Fletcher hastened to replenish it. "But your Christian name, sir...Culloden. Surely it raises only images of a most nefarious uprising against the Crown. And"—he continued after his drink had been renewed—"a crushing defeat of a treasonous cause."

Fletcher's breath caught in his throat. *Sweet Jesus!* He braced his feet, ready to attempt to prevent his friend from throttling the official. Physically he doubted he could, but he would have to try. Attacking a representative of the King could most definitely be viewed as treason.

"My father named me Culloden ta honor the memory o' those brave Highlanders who died on that moor that day." Culloden drew himself up to his impressive height, dark eyes flashing. "If my people hadn't lacked proper weapons and artillery, hadn't been half-starved and weary to the bone from weeks of hard marchin' and fightin', the outcome would have been far different, I can assure ya. My grandfather died there."

"I cannot image that ragtag army of Jacobites presenting more than a mere skirmish to the well-trained troops of the British army. Our troops mowed them down in a matter of a few hours."

"So that's how ya see it, is it, ya fat pompous ass?" Culloden advanced across the room to glare down at his guest.

"Sir." The man stood to confront his host. "That *is* exactly how I see it, and I'm sure it is the same way others in a position to offer you the post of lieutenant governor will view it. Old sins cast long shadows, Mr. MacPherson."

I have to admire the portly old chap, facing up to Cully. Most wouldn't dare. Still...

"Then ya've been the guest of my hospitality long enough and fer the last time." Culloden's fists knotted at his sides, dark eyes hard as coals. "If it weren't for the fact that ya have your lady accompanyin' ya, I'd kick yer fat arse out inta the rain this verrae moment. As it is, I'll give ya until dawn tomorrow to be on yer way." He flung his glass into the fire burning on the hearth. It crashed, its liquid contents sending up an alcohol-scented flare.

"Mr. Atkin, I'll be beholden ta ye if ye'll see this fool ta his sleepin' quarters," he flung back over his shoulder as he strode toward the door. "And make damn sure him and his lady are on their way back ta Fredericton at first light."

****

"Cully, you damned fool!" Fletcher found Culloden slouched in a chair at the kitchen table, a tankard in his hand, a bottle of whisky in front of him. The man had removed his coat and vest, pulled off his neckcloth, and opened his shirt down over his chest.

"Dunnae go ta reproachin' me, laddie! Ya heard what the pompous ass said. Bollocks! On his worst day, a Scotsman is better than any English flunky with a red face and a paunch like a pregnant pig!"

Repressing a chuckle, Fletcher went to a cupboard to fetch a mug. He joined his friend at the table, helped himself to whisky, and took a seat opposite him.

"Cully, it's that kind of thinking and language that will keep you from a governing position in this province. You have to learn diplomacy, how to cater to the whims and fancies..."

"Ta become a blessed milksop ta such as Henry Brandish? Niver!"

"Then you must content yourself to remain exactly what you are…a successful, wealthy timber baron. Perhaps someday your riches alone will earn you a place in government."

"Argh!" Culloden reached for the bottle and splashed more whisky into his tankard. "Well, then, if that's the lay of the land, I won't be needin' that fancy piece for a wife. Ya can ride over ta yer house tomorrow and tell her ta pack her belongin's ta be ready ta return ta England when her uncle returns."

"Are you mad?" Fletcher was on his feet, glowering down at his friend. "She's not a bit of goods you can order and then return when you decide you don't need it! Isabella Marston has come out to this country on good faith…good faith that you will be a man of your word and marry her."

"A man of *yer* words, ye'll recall, laddie. Ya lured her here with yer fancy writing. Now ya can send her back with more of them. Any road, I wasn't satisfied from the first time I saw her neck-ed. She's fair skinny as a rake."

"You saw her naked?" Astonishment and anger made him choke out the words. "How…when…?"

"On the day she and her great circus arrived. I was takin' the last of her belongin's inta her bedroom at yer house. How was I ta know she'd stripped neck-ed out of her wet clothing?"

"Sweet Jesus!" Fletcher leaned back in his chair, astounded. "I hope you apologized?"

"I dunnae recollect…bein' fair as surprised as she was."

"Well"—Fletcher regained his equilibrium—"I'm assuming Mrs. O'Malley saw to any necessary explanations and apologies."

"I dunnae know." He took another swig from his tankard. "It little matters, scrawny piece that Miss Isabella Marston is. Seein' her unclothed was a stroke of luck. Now that friend of hers, the one that was her maidservant, now there's a bonny lass with meat on her bones."

"I'd have thought you'd be more sympathetic. As I recall, you were more than slightly embarrassed when Miss Lucy Welsh saw you rising out of your bath this morning."

"Argh!" Culloden quaffed the last of his whisky and stood. "I'm sure I came as no surprise ta that one."

****

"Miss Marston?"

Isabella looked up from weeding the garden to see Fletcher Atkin standing at the end of the drill of carrots.

"Yes?" She turned on her knees to face him, surprised that he'd omitted his usual proper greeting of wishing her good day. He was as handsome as ever, bringing an all too familiar quiver to her innards.

"Miss Marston, might we speak...privately?" He cast a glance toward the log house, from which issued the voices of Lucy and Mrs. O'Malley in a heated discussion about dinner plans.

"Of course." She brushed earth from her hands before taking the one he held down to help her to her feet.

"Perhaps we might walk?" He indicated the trail that led to a small stream beyond the homestead.

"If you wish." She shook out her apron before falling into step beside him. The sun glared down, hot and merciless. Aware that her hair was straggling from its queue, that her sunbonnet was an old, ragged one, that her feet were bare, and that her dress clung to her body with perspiration, she was glad when they reached the shelter of the tree-shadowed path.

I must look a fright. Still, Mr. Atkin's expression tells me he's worried about something more than my dowdy appearance.

"Will you please take a seat?" Once they were out of hearing distance of the log house, he indicated a log.

"Mr. Atkin, I have a troubled feeling you've unpleasant news to relate." Squinting up at him in a ray of sunlight that had forced its way through the branches, she accepted the proffered resting place.

"Yes." He heaved a sigh and sat down beside her. Clasping his hands between his spread knees, he rubbed them together, focusing on them.

"Then I believe it's best you get right to it." She turned to him. "Hesitating never helps."

"Last evening, after we men left you ladies, things did not go well between Sir Henry and Culloden." Glancing sideways, he met her gaze.

"I admit I had apprehensions concerning how Mr. MacPherson would conduct himself without Lucy to oversee his behavior." She frowned. "Was it very terrible?"

"He and Cully nearly came to blows." Fletcher returned his focus to his hands. "When Cully put forward his hope to become lieutenant governor of the province, Sir Henry informed him that, being a Highlander from such a notorious community as Riverhaven, Cully had little possibility of ever achieving such an office. Sir Henry went on to disparage Highlanders in general and demean their

191

efforts in the historic battle on Culloden Moor."

"Oh, my." Isabella shifted into a more comfortable position and drew a deep breath.

"Miss Marston." He paused.

Casting him a sideways glance, Isabella saw him wet his lips and draw a breath. "Yes?"

"Mr. MacPherson therefore feels he is no longer in need of a lady wife. He has given me leave to arrange for your transportation back to England…you and your entourage."

"Good God!" Dumbstruck, she stared at the man. "Back to England! Surely he can't be serious. Surely he realizes he cannot return me like so much unwanted goods! Surely…surely"—her words began to falter—"he must be aware of how I would be regarded under such a condition."

"Mr. MacPherson is prepared to make you a most generous recompense." His words came out flat and dry.

"Recompense! Recompense? What could possibly compensate for rejection…humiliation…disgrace!" She bolted to her feet, hands clenched at her sides. "Does he not realize that no decent man would have me after he's paid to bring me to this country and then found me unacceptable? Does he not realize that there would be gossip of the most heinous kind?"

"Miss Marston, I'm sorry. I've tried to talk to him, to explain how polite society might regard this decision, but…" He stood, his expression compassionate, distressed.

"The man is a great oaf! A man without the slightest idea of propriety! Well, you can tell him for me he won't so easily be rid of me! If I'm to be regarded as a discarded woman, I'll face my future here in this country, here in Riverhaven where everyone can see what a great, unprincipled creature he is!"

She turned and stumbled back up the path down which they'd come, the pain in her soul numbing her to the prick of pebbles and pine needles beneath her feet, and even to the occasional stubbing of her toes on roots.

"Miss Marston!" His voice calling her name echoed in her fevered brain as she staggered forward.

At the homestead, she burst into the stable and leaned panting against the wall. She couldn't face Lucy and Mrs. O'Malley with this dreadful disgrace. She needed time to compose herself, to think of the least humiliating manner in which to inform them. Finally she moved deeper into the barn and pulled open the door of Duchess's stall.

"What are we to do?" She put a hand to the mare's soft cheek. "I thought I was the one who had the option of either marrying Culloden MacPherson or refusing him. I never thought…"

She couldn't go on. Shock still holding her in its grip, she rested her forehead against the mare's neck and closed her eyes.

You've told Fletcher Atkin that you're going to stay here, to show the community exactly how very little honor Culloden MacPherson has in his soul. Those words were a wild, spontaneous outburst, the result of shock, not rational thought. Is that really what you want to do? Do you have the strength to do it? Would it be preferable to go back to the reprimands and jeers of my mother and sisters? You have to decide. Think, think, Isabella Marston.

But cogent thoughts wouldn't come. She was still

in the throes of shock and disbelief.

****

"What has happened, child?" Mrs. O'Malley dropped her mending on the table to stare at Isabella as she entered the log house. "You're white as a sheet. Here"—she stood and went to put an arm about her—"sit. I'll fetch you a nice cup of tea."

"Water will do as well, thank you, Mrs. O'Malley," Isabella replied as the woman thrust her into a chair at the table.

"Of course, child." The Irishwoman hastened to the pump while Lucy, who'd been seated on a bench, put aside her mending to gaze at her friend.

"Isabella, what is it?" Lucy asked, her own face becoming tense with concern. "You look as if you've seen a ghost."

"Seeing a phantom would have been much better. Thank you, Mrs. O'Malley." Isabella took the mug of cold water and drank before continuing. "It seems Mr. MacPherson had a great row with Sir Henry last evening…as we ladies surmised. Now…" She took another drink.

"Now?" Lucy slid closer along the bench to sit beside her friend.

"Sir Henry told Mr. MacPherson that he had next to no chance of obtaining public office in Fredericton. As a result"—she took another drink—"Mr. MacPherson has decided he no long requires a lady wife and that I"—she looked at Lucinda—"that you, Horace, Percy, Duchess, and I are to be returned to England."

"Jesus, Mary, and Joseph!" Mrs. O'Malley froze as she was about to resume her seat at the table. "Has the man gone mad? Surely he can't be serious. Did he tell you so himself?"

"No, he wasn't gentleman enough." Isabella squared her shoulders. "He sent Mr. Atkin to deliver the message."

"We'll just see about that!" Lucy was on her feet, grasping her shawl from its peg by the door.

"No, no, Lucy, please!" Isabella swung on her seat. "The man has made up his mind. I doubt that even you can force him to change it."

"I'm not talking about changing his mind! I'm talking about giving him a great piece of mine!"

Before Isabella could protest further, Lucy was gone.

****

Out of the tail of his eye, Fletcher Atkin caught a flash of a woman's dress. Pausing in his task of piling boards in the mill yard, he turned to see Lucy Welsh striding toward the operation with all the determination of a soldier marching into battle. He moved out of the line of workers to watch.

She burst into the mill where, above the whine of saws and clash of machinery, Culloden MacPherson was shouting orders to his men. As he strode about, naked to the waist in the heat, his broad chest glistened with sweat. Unaware of Lucy's approach because of the racket, he flinched when she grabbed his arm.

He swung to stare down at her. In response, she jerked her head toward the trees beyond the mill yard. When he didn't move in response, she gave his bare arm a yank in that direction. Although Fletcher was well aware his friend could have cast her off like a fly, Culloden MacPherson acquiesced. Appearing to drag him, Lucy Welsh marched the big man into the trees.

Fletcher couldn't resist. Leaving his work, he furtively followed the couple. Once they were in the woods and paused, Fletcher took up a hidden vantage point and listened and watched.

"You great oaf!" Lucy struck Culloden a blow with the flat of her hands on the chest. "You great, dumb oaf! Who do you think you are, planning to ship Isabella back to England like some castoff! Are you so ignorant that you don't know how she'll be regarded, how you've ruined any chance she might have had of a decent marriage? I could…"

She didn't get to finish. To Fletcher's utter astonishment, Culloden grasped her into his arms and into a kiss—a kiss that only for a moment did the woman struggle against before relaxing into his embrace, her arms going about his neck.

Dear God! Was this maybe a part of the reason for Cully's decision not to marry Isabella? Had he had feelings all along for Lucy? Had the fiasco with Sir Henry simply given him an excuse not to continue a relationship with Isabella? Could it be possible Culloden MacPherson was in love with Lucy Welsh? The questions ricocheted around in Fletcher's head.

Easing away into the trees, he left the couple alone. He went back to his chore of piling lumber, more thoughts than he cared to entertain rumbling around in his mind.

****

"Miss Marston, I'm wondering…will you go riding with me?"

Isabella turned from where she'd been packing her belongings to see Fletcher Atkin, hat in hand, standing

196

in the bedroom doorway.

"It is a fine day, with a breeze to keep the flies at bay…and the horses could use the exercise."

"Mr. Fletcher, I'm packing. Lucy and I are moving to Mrs. O'Malley's house in the village. In fact, Lucy and Mrs. O'Malley have already gone down there to prepare the place for us. As you can understand, our lives are rather in a turmoil at the moment. I don't think…"

"All the more reason for you to take a breath of fresh air. There's no reason for haste in vacating this house. I'm quite comfortable living with Cully and Horace at the manor. Furthermore, I may have a solution to your problems. Please?" He smiled, blue eyes asking a boon she found difficult to decline. Furthermore, he'd said something about a remedy to her current untenable circumstances.

"Perhaps you're right." She heaved a sigh. "Very well. I'll change into riding attire."

"Excellent." The word was bright with pleasure. "I'll saddle Duchess. Galahad is already prepared. Cully has lifted his restraints on my riding him. He's been in a more affable frame of mind of late." He gave a nod and turned away, booted footsteps announcing his retreat to the door.

****

"Miss Marston, I wish to speak to you on a matter of some importance."

Fletcher Atkin's words and tone made her turn sharply to face him. They'd paused their horses and dismounted by a brook.

"Yes, of course."

"Miss Marston…Isabella." He startled her by

dropping on one knee before her and taking her gloved hand in his. "I have admired you from the first moment I saw you arriving on your uncle's ship, but you were spoken for, bound to be a lady of wealth and importance in this valley. It would have been wrong, in fact contemptible, for me to have expressed my regard at that time, as you were ostensibly affianced to my friend and employer. Now…"

"Mr. Atkin, what…?" She stared down into his earnest expression.

"Isabella, I'm asking you to marry me."

She blinked, then stared down at him. Words deserted her.

"I know my proposal must come as a surprise." He was hurrying ahead. "But as I've said, I've long held you in high regard and thought that if it were not for your promise to wed my friend, I'd have been delighted to court you from the moment of your arrival. Now that Cully has freed you of all former obligations, I'm in a position to follow my heart's desire."

"Mr. Atkin, this is most kind and generous of you." Coming out of shock, Isabella found she could speak what she tried to make a rational and kindly response. "You've so carefully and considerately phrased your proposal that a rejected bride such as myself could only feel honored. You deserve much better than Culloden MacPherson's castoff. Therefore, please, I beg you, try not to be hurt by my refusal." She withdrew her hand from his and, unable to look any longer into his sincere blue eyes, turned away.

"Refusal?" He stumbled to his feet, clutching his hat in his left hand. "But surely…that day when we kissed…I thought…"

"Surely?" She swung back to him, ashamed of the tears that brimmed in her eyes, an anger she couldn't control tainting her response. "Surely you thought that, given my inappropriate response to your advances, and having been rejected by one man, I'd be more than willing to accept the next offer that came my way?"

"No, no!" He caught her by her shoulders. "I hoped. Hoped, nothing more. I've watched you working about my homestead. I believed you'd come to enjoy life there. I thought you might like to stay... permanently. It's not the grand manor or wealth Cully has to offer, but I share in the profits of his business to the extent that I make a more than livable wage."

"Mr. Atkin, I'm sorry." Regaining control of her emotions, Isabella blinked back the tears and smiled at him. "I shouldn't have accused you of taking advantage of the situation. I also apologize for unduly encouraging you. I most sincerely appreciate your proposal, but I must decline. Having met Culloden MacPherson, I realized I couldn't marry for wealth and position. And I shan't marry you for convenience."

"Isabella"—his hands dropped to his sides, and he drew a deep breath before continuing—"you know it was I who wrote those letters that convinced you to come to this country. It was I who allowed you the impression that you would be finding a literate man when you arrived. I'm responsible for your current situation."

"How can I hold you responsible when it was my own fierce desire to escape the untenable circumstances under which I was living in England that incited me to accept Mr. MacPherson's proposal? No, Mr. Atkin, I will never hold you in any way responsible for all that has transpired."

They stood facing each other, only the sounds of bird song from the trees above their heads breaking the silence of the summer's day. Something deep and poignant hung in the air between them.

Finally he spoke. "Very well. Perhaps we should be getting back. Rain is threatening."

He turned to gather up the horses' reins. Something inside Isabella sank. Had she just made a dreadful mistake? She hadn't wanted to marry Culloden MacPherson. Her reaction on his repudiation of his marriage proposal had been one of shock, not disappointment.

In fact, after the first blow from his decision had subsided, she'd come to regard it as a giant relief, a godsend. Still, marrying Fletcher Atkin on the rebound, no matter how she felt about him, no matter how he swept her off her feet with each glance, each touch, each word…it wasn't right. She couldn't mitigate the feeling that he'd felt obliged to ask for her hand out of guilt, out of a sense of duty to one whom he considered he'd seriously wronged.

****

"You refused him?" Her eyes round with astonishment, Lucy stared at her friend as they sat at tea later that morning. Lucy had been sketching images on bits of paper. "You refused Mr. Atkin? Why?"

"Lucy, surely you must see how inappropriate it would be." Isabella fingered her cup. "Everyone believes me Culloden MacPherson's intended. To suddenly announce my engagement to his best friend, his foreman, would raise more than a few eyebrows. I could never be respected in this valley."

"But as word of Mr. MacPherson's rejection…" Lucy rushed on.

"Worse still. People would say I was an opportunist, willing to marry any man who offered. Lucy, surely you must understand."

"Well, child, that's as it may be, but I must stand with Lucy in not comprehending." Mrs. O'Malley gathered herself up and went to fetch the teapot. "Marriage isn't always as the result of a great love affair. Some of the best of them have been based on mutual respect and a desire to work together toward a better life. I married Mr. O'Malley two days after I met him, the idea of romance never entering my head. I was newly arrived in this country, with nary a penny to my name. He was a woodsman, big and gruff and"—her expression became wistful as she stared off into space, teapot in hand—"and kind."

She cleared her throat before refilling cups and continuing. "We became close, close as two people can be."

"What happened?" Isabella asked softly.

"An accident." The Irishwoman drew a deep breath as she replaced the pot on the hearth and returned to her seat. "A tree fell on him. We'd been married only a few months, but they were wonderful days." Her eyes filled with tears and took on a dreaming look. "That big Irishman will live in my heart forever."

"I'm sorry." Isabella's response was sincere. "I had no idea."

"Ah, well, dearie, life goes on." She blinked and picked up her cup. "I'm just happy I married him as I did. Without him in my life, there would have been forever a great void."

"Well, enough talk of men and romance." Lucy stood to carry her cup to the sideboard. "I must collect the eggs. That nasty Lord Featherstone had better not get in my way. This time Culloden MacPherson won't be around to save his precious neck."

She picked up a basket and went out.

Isabella reached across the table and pulled Lucy's sketches to her. The woman was a talented natural artist, Isabella recognized, remembering the fine likeness Lucy had made to send to Culloden with Isabella's letter of acceptance. She flipped through several drawings of the cabin, their surroundings, and even one of Percy, but when she came to the final one, she stared, mesmerized.

It was a likeness of Culloden MacPherson standing in profile, looking out toward the forest.

Clad in buckskins, he sported the revised hair and beard of the day of the dinner for Sir Henry and Lady Charlotte. Isabella was astounded. The man cut a magnificent image of a handsome, bold frontiersman. Lucy's rendering left her speechless.

"What is it, child?" Mrs. O'Malley paused in removing a plate of bread and butter from the table.

"Have you seen this?" She extended the drawing toward the housekeeper.

"Oh, aye, yes." Mrs. O'Malley glanced at it in passing. "She's made him look right handsome, hasn't she?"

"Mrs. O'Malley, has Lucy developed a liking for Mr. MacPherson?"

"How can you ask such a thing! He's...or he was...your intended. Lucy Welsh is a young woman of honor. She'd never..."

"Not deliberately, perhaps, but romances do develop whether we choose them or not. I wouldn't be offended or hurt if Lucy were to express an interest in the man. Or"—she continued, remembering the scene in the barnyard with Lord Featherstone—"he in her. Mrs. O'Malley"—she stood and began to pace up and down the kitchen—"we've all noticed how Lucy has the ability to make Mr. MacPherson do her bidding. I believe she'd make him a fine wife."

When Lucy returned with a basketful of eggs, Isabella and Mrs. O'Malley were seated at the table, waiting for her.

"What?" Lucy glanced from one to the other. "You look smug as two cats who've just enjoyed a big jug of cream."

"We believe you've fallen in love with Culloden MacPherson." Isabella held up the pad bearing his likeness. "Furthermore, we believe you'd make him the perfect wife."

"Me!" Lucy plunked her basket down so hard Isabella wondered if any of the eggs would survive. "Me, marry that great pain in the behind! That great oaf!"

"Lucy, this portrait was drawn with passion, defined through eyes of love." Isabella was not about to be deterred. "Furthermore"—she moderated her tone—"you'll make him a far better wife than I ever could. He listens to you, obeys you, even if at times a trifle reluctantly. You're the woman who can refine him, guide him into becoming the kind of man who might one day hold an important office in this province."

"Oh, and what of me?" Lucy put her hands on her hips and faced the pair defiantly. "I'm no fine lady he could sport about on his arm in such circumstances."

"You can be." Isabella wasn't about to be put off. "You know the ways of a lady of the house. You could very easily play the part."

"You're both daft." Lucy picked up her basket and proceeded to the sideboard. Working the hand pump vigorously, she splashed water into a bowl to begin washing the eggs.

As Isabella watched, she saw stiff defiance relax from her friend's back and shoulders. She winked at Mrs. O'Malley, and the Irishwoman nodded with a conspiratorial smile. They'd most definitely set an idea churning in Lucy Welsh's head.

Chapter Twelve

"May I ask your intentions, sir?" Fletcher ventured to ask as the two men walked away from the mill late that afternoon. They were returning to the manor.

"My intentions about whit?" Without missing a step, Culloden continued to stride along beside his foreman.

"Your intentions regarding Miss Lucy Welsh."

The statement brought Culloden to an abrupt halt. He swung on his companion.

"Whit air ya talkin' about?"

"I saw you in the trees by the mill this morning. I hope I didn't witness a mere dalliance. The young lady deserves better."

"So now yer a bloody voyeur! Is there nothin' ya won't stoop ta? I ought ta knock you from here ta the river for spyin' on me and accusin' me of triflin' with the affections of such a fine lass."

Fletcher steeled himself for a blow. He knew of Culloden's sharp, quick temper.

"Then, I ask once again, what are your intentions?" When Culloden remained glaring at him, hands knotted into fists, Fletcher pressed his query.

"I...I don't know." For the first time since he'd known Culloden MacPherson, Fletcher Atkin saw the man stumble for words.

"Are you in love with her?"

"Love…whit's that? If ya mean does she fair drive me mad with her orders"—he paused—"if ya mean that I wake up at night in a hot sweat thinkin' about her, if ya mean that I'd kill any man who laid an evil hand on her, if ya mean she makes my innards turn ta jelly and my nether parts stiffen like a dog on the point, if ya mean I think her the finest woman I've ever laid eyes on, aye, if that's love, then I do."

"I agree. You'd best ask her to marry you before your innards and nether parts get into more of a muddle."

"Air ya tauntin' me, laddie? Because if ya air…"

"Never. I'm simply offering what I see as good advice."

"And ya be seein' nothin' untaward about it so soon after decidin' against the other one?"

"If, by 'the other one' you mean Miss Marston, no, I do not. Not if you're absolutely certain you do not wish to marry her."

"Between ya and me, Fletch, I didn't want ta wed the lass from the first minute I clapped eyes on her aboard that ship. It was the other one, Lucy, who caught my attention—and, in spite of her bossin' me about, has been the lass for me ever since."

"And yet you let Miss Marston think you were still her future husband."

"I fair didn't know how ta go about tellin' the lass. She'd come all that way and all. And I was right determined I needed her as my wife if I wanted ta become governor of this province."

"But when you discovered that wasn't likely to happen, you felt justified in casting Miss Marston aside. I find that not only despicable, Cully, but also cowardly."

"Aye, aye, that it was." They paused, and the big man hung his head. "But I saw it as a way out…a way of endin' our arrangement without makin' it seem it was the lass herself I no longer wanted ta marry, that my reason for breakin' off our arrangement was only because I no longer needed her. I thought"—he looked up at his companion, and Fletcher saw honest regret in his expression—"the best I could do was ta ship her back home with a fat purse. I'm no' versed in the ways of society in the Old Country, Fletch. I didn't realize how she could be regarded on her return."

They continued on their way in silence. When they were nearing the manor, Culloden again spoke.

"I have a feelin' ya've got a wee confession of yer own, laddie." He glanced at his companion. "A confession regardin' Miss Marston."

"There is nothing between Miss Marston and myself."

"No? Well, then, I must be half blind. Ya've been lookin' at her with all but yer tongue hangin' out whenever ya thought I wasn't lookin'. In fact, I was holdin' out a hope ya'd declare yer intentions taward her…take her off my hands, as it were."

"Forget that idea, Cully. The lady has made it clear she's not about to redeem any possible modicum of her self respect by taking up with the likes of me."

"Fletch, yer a good man. Aw, ya had a bit of backslide a short while ago, but with a good woman like Miss Marston ta guide ya, ya'd do chust fine. Yer far more suited ta her than I ever was, what with ya bein' a gentleman ta the manor born, as it were."

"If you must know, I asked the lady to marry me,

and she turned me down flat." Fletcher snapped out the words. "Now will you leave off troubling me about the woman?"

"And when was this?" Culloden stopped short and swung on him. "Not while she was still my intended, I hope."

"Of course not. You know me better than that, Cully. Later, after you…"

"After I decided to send her back to England." Culloden snorted. "Even I can understand why she refused you at that point. She's a clever woman, too clever to accept a proposal fostered from guilt."

"Guilt?" The two men stood facing each other.

"I'm right certain that it wasn't long after Miss Isabella Marston arrived in this country that she figured out it wasn't me what wrote that advertisement and acceptance. So ya feel ya lured her under false pretenses and because ya did, yer in no small way responsible for the present unpleasantness she's in. Wait a bit, then ask her again. Dunnae give up, laddie." Culloden slapped him on a shoulder and started walking again. "Like my old pa used to say, 'If at first ya dunnae succeed, try, try again.' "

****

"Mistress, a word."

With a start, Isabella looked up from where she'd been writing at the table in Mrs. O'Malley's house to see Culloden MacPherson in the doorway.

"You might have knocked, Mr. MacPherson." She couldn't contain the rebuke. "Gentlemen do not barge into a home unannounced."

"Aye, aye"—he advanced inside—"but, as ya air well aware, I'm no' a gentleman."

"What brings you, sir?" She fought to banish the awkwardness of this first meeting after his reneging on their marriage agreement.

"My lad Fletcher Atkin tells me he's offered his hand in marriage and that ya've refused him." He moved to stand beside the table and look down at her, large and overpowering.

"He was being kind." She wet her lips and fought the feeling of having a giant looming over her. "Or perhaps"—a sudden thought hit her—"he was sent on your orders, to absolve you of blame or guilt by taking your place as bridegroom."

"Whit do ya take me fer, lass?" The scowl that engulfed Culloden MacPherson's countenance made her want to flee, to get as far away from this overpowering man as possible.

"You seem to have a way of getting what you wish." Forcing herself to hold her ground, she looked up at him. "Perhaps you promised to give Mr. Fletcher back his horse if he married me."

"Bloody hell, woman!" The explosion made her heart jump to what she fancied was the back of her throat. "Whit do ya think of the man, that he'd make such a bargain for a beast! I'll have ya know Fletcher Atkin is a good lad, one of the best. I'll not have ya spoutin' such ideas!"

"You're right." Isabella, realizing she'd gone too far and didn't mean the words spoken in fear and haste, stood to face the outraged man. "He offered me marriage out of the kindness of his heart. Fortunately, I turned him down. He deserves better. I apologize."

"Aye, well, that ya should." He reached inside his buckskin shirt and drew out a hide pouch. It clanked

209

when he dropped it on the table in front of her.

"What is that?" She stared at it.

"A small recompense fer the trouble I've caused ta ya. Do with it as ya will."

She hesitated before picking it up and opening it gingerly. Gold coins winked up her.

"Mr. MacPherson, this isn't necessary..." she began.

"Ah, but it is, lass." His tone had softened to the gentle Highland lilt similar to that of Brodie MacMillan. It was a beguiling inflection as he looked at her, dark eyes sincere. "I've brought ya ta this country with the plan of marryin'. Now I've changed my mind through no fault of yers. Indeed, ya've fulfilled yer end of the deal up ta this point right well, what with furnishin' my house and arrangin' a fine dinner for that pompous ass Sir Henry. I've no fault ta find with ya on those scores. As a result, I owe ya." He paused to draw deep breath before continuing. "Mr. Fletcher has informed me that yer returnin' ta England might not be such a fine idea. Therefore, I offer this token. It will allow ya ta stay in this country or move on ta another, as ya wish." He turned to leave. "My apologies for any pain I may have caused."

"Mr. MacPherson, wait." She stepped around the table to follow him to the door. "Thank you. Actually, I believe your breaking our engagement is for the best. We are ill suited. We would only have brought each other unhappiness."

"Aye, aye." He glanced back over his shoulder at her. "I wish ya all the best, lass. Yer a good woman."

He went out.

****

"Good morning, Miss Marston." Fletcher paused at the edge of the small vegetable garden behind Mrs. O'Malley's small house in the village, where Isabella knelt pulling weeds. He carried a wrapped package beneath his arm.

"Good morning, Mr. Atkin." Pushing a wisp of hair from her forehead, she swiveled sufficiently to face him. "Another fine morning, is it not?"

She'd grown tanned by the sun, filled out in all the right places with good food and freedom from the illness caused by a tossing ship. If he'd thought she was pretty when she arrived, weary and bedraggled from the voyage, he believed her now downright beautiful, even with a smudge of earth on the flawless complexion of her cheek.

She got to her feet, brushing dirt from her worn gown. It had been two weeks since his proposal, two weeks since she and Lucy had moved out of his log house and into Mrs. O'Malley's small residence in the village. "What brings you?"

"Not another unwelcome proposal of marriage, I assure you." Although he felt a rush of embarrassment, he caught the apprehension in her tone and hastened to reassure her. Hunkering down, he patted Percy, who'd gotten to his paws with a welcoming wiggle of his tail at the man's arrival.

"Mr. Atkin, please…" He saw a blush moving into her cheeks.

"Let us put that behind us and move on. I came simply to see if I can be of service, if there are any supplies I may fetch for you, any wood that needs chopping…anything that may require a man's attention."

"Thank you, that's most kind. Horace sees to such matters for us."

"Excellent. I've also come to bring this to you and Miss Lucy." He proffered the package.

She hesitated, then moved to accept it.

"Perhaps you'd best go inside before opening it. The contents may spill."

"Very well. Please. Come with me."

With Percy prancing at their heels, they went into the cabin. Fletcher watched apprehensively as she laid it on the table and untied the twine holding the burlap shut. Perhaps she'd think him too forward, too presumptive.

Sheets of paper, pencils, a bottle of ink, and a metal pen were revealed. Isabella stared down at the collection for a moment before raising surprised eyes to Fletcher.

"I recall your mentioning that paper and other writing materials were scarce, on the day I came upon you writing a letter to your family." He hoped his rushing ahead with the explanation didn't sound as awkward as a schoolboy offering a daisy to his first childhood love. "Therefore…"

"Mr. Atkin, how thoughtful." She sat down to admire the gift, and relief flooded through him. "But this"—she held up the metal-nibbed pen—"this must have been costly. How…?"

"How, after I've recently indebted myself to Cully, after I've been forced to relinquish Galahad into his care, could I afford to buy a loaf of bread, never mind writing materials? Don't distress yourself over that matter, Miss Marston. The MacPherson mill has had a highly profitable year. As a shareholder, I've benefited.

Actually"—he moved closer to the table—"these things come from both Cully and me."

"Mr. Fletcher, I cannot tell you how much your gift means to me and will mean to Lucy when she becomes aware of it." She looked up at him, eyes glowing. "It means I can do more than simply write letters to my family, and Lucy can sketch on more than scraps of paper. How could you possibly know…?"

"I met Mrs. MacMillan in the village a few days ago. She informed me of your desire to write about your experiences in this country. I already knew of Lucy's talent, given the portrait she drew to accompany your acceptance of Cully's proposal. An artist such as she's shown herself to be does not easily abandon her talent."

"Thank you, thank you." She stood, her eyes so bright it put stars to shame. His entire being longed to reach out, draw her into his arms, to kiss her…

"You're most welcome." He managed to stifle the urge with an effort that gave him physical agony. "Now I must be going. I hope you'll enjoy our small offering."

"Mr. Atkin, although I hesitate to ask, after this wonderful gift…"

"Yes?"

"Do you know of any gainful employment I may undertake? Mrs. O'Malley, although she comes back here each evening, continues to be your housekeeper by day, and Lucy is now working as housekeeper for Mr. MacPherson. I am the only member of this household who is not employed. As you probably know, Mr. MacPherson has been most generous in offering me recompense. The fact is, I wish to be gainfully employed, not sitting about like a lady of leisure."

"But your writing will…"

"Perhaps, but not for a very long time, if ever. First I must compose my thoughts, then submit them for Mrs. MacMillan's approval. Quite possibly, she'll suggest changes. Later the stories must be shipped to London on speculation. If I ever see recompense for them, it won't be until next spring, at the very earliest. In the meantime…"

"I'm sure Mrs. O'Malley and Lucy are quite satisfied with your maintaining this cabin and its grounds. As you can see, the garden has been in desperate need of tending, and I'm sure Mrs. O'Malley has been forced to leave many other domestic chores undone while she was working for me. She'll be appreciative of your help. Furthermore, an artist needs time to create. You must allow yourself the freedom to do so."

"Artist?" She blushed. "I hardly fancy myself as such."

"Perhaps not presently, but once you see your work in print, once you realize your words are being read and appreciated by others far away…"

"Mr. Fletcher, have a care. You'll be filling my head with grandiose ideas much beyond my reach. Having my writing published is but a dream, as yet a long way from reality."

"Ah, yes, but where would we be without our dreams?" As he spoke the words, he tried not to think about the impossibility of his own. "Mrs. O'Malley and Lucy will understand."

"Mrs. O'Malley and Lucy have both been most kind in accepting my lack of paid employment." She rubbed the dirt from her hands, looking down at them. "But"—she glanced up again, meeting his gaze—"I am not comfortable with my situation. Please, I will be obliged, if you come upon someone in need of any service that I might be capable of providing, that you will mention my name."

"Of course." He replaced his hat and turned away. "But keep alive your plans to write."

****

As she watched Fletcher Atkin walk away, a wave of regret washed over Isabella. He was a fine man, a kind man, a gentleman, most remarkably of all, a man ready to bear with and encourage her wild dream of becoming a writer. Marrying him would have been more than a viable alternative to facing an uncertain future alone. But a marriage proposed out of guilt and pity? Hardly what she wanted. And there were those rumblings of his past…gambler, drunkard, and worst of all, reputed womanizer.

Nevertheless, something, a flutter in her heart, also told her she was not without being attracted to him. An embarrassed feeling tempered with wonderful memories of erotic sensations suffused her as she recalled that kiss and the astonishing, arousing sensations the man had caused to overcome her. She slid her hands down the front of her faded cotton gown and wondered if that had been a hint of what was termed love.

Never mind mulling over what never will be. I want to try to live on my own. In this new land, all things could be possible, even a woman surviving without a man.

With Percy at her heels, she went back outside to

the small veranda at the front of Mrs. O'Malley's cottage and sat down on a bench along its back wall. She leaned back against the logs that composed the building's front, closed her eyes, and ran her thoughts over all that she had learned since coming to Riverhaven. Surely somewhere amid those impressions lay a clue to future endeavors.

Percy nudged her leg, asking to be picked up. Lost in thought, she bent and took the Pug into her arms. He still had hair missing from his shoulder where Louisa MacMillan had shaved it away to mend his wound. Looking down at it, she recalled the woman and her competence in treating the little dog. A strong woman, a brave woman. Mrs. O'Malley had told of how Louisa, as a widow, had lived alone on a wilderness homestead for a time before meeting Brodie. Louisa Abbot had survived, treated the sick and injured, and still managed to write enough stories to pay for any provisions she might need.

Louisa MacMillan! Of course! I must talk to her, learn how she managed.

"Percy, you'll have to stay here." She stood and carried the Pug indoors. "I'm going to Mr. Fletcher's homestead to fetch Duchess. Then I'll find someone in this village who can tell me how to find Louisa's home."

Inside, she changed hastily into her riding habit of trousers and shirt and gathered up a collection of the few writings she'd managed to compose since her arrival and some she'd brought with her from England. She wrote a quick note to Mrs. O'Malley and Lucy, to explain where she'd gone. Leaving it on the table, she rushed out the door, a swirl of air into the cabin marking her exit.

****

"Mr. MacMillan, may I have a word?" Isabella stopped to stand beside the man leaning on the bar in the Riverhaven tavern.

He started and swung on her, handsome face reflecting his surprise.

"Mr. MacMillan, will you step outside that we might speak privately?" Glancing about, she lowered her voice, acutely aware of the stares of the men watching them. It had taken all her courage to enter the establishment. She didn't know how long that bravado would hold.

"Mistress Marston, is it not?" The big Scotsman drew himself up and faced her, tankard in one hand, the other on the hilt of his sword.

"Yes. Please. I'd be most grateful if you'd spare me a moment."

Good God, please, please agree. I can't carry on much longer in this place, under the leers of these men.

"Do you come on your intended's business?" A scowl furrowed his forehead. "If so, you can go back to him and tell him I'll no' deal with women. He's to be man enough to come himself."

"I come only on my own behalf." Her words were barely above a whisper, her voice beginning to tremble. "Please, Mr. MacMillan. A word. I shall be most grateful."

He stared down at her for a moment. Perhaps he saw sincerity and desperation in her expression. She couldn't be sure. All she knew was that he quaffed the rest of his ale, put a hand beneath her elbow, and guided her through the gaping men out into the fresh air.

"Now," he said when they'd gone several yards away from the tavern entrance. "Whit is the purpose of your visit, if not on behalf of your lord and master?"

"He's not my lord and master...nor ever will be." Looking up into the man's keen blue eyes, she knew nothing short of the absolute truth would satisfy him. "Mr. MacPherson has decided against marrying me."

"Whit! Tell me my ears deceive me! Not even Culloden MacPherson would be such a great cur as to entice a young lass to this country with promises of matrimony and then withdraw his offer." He stared down at her, eyes wide.

"He has decided he no longer requires such as myself to be his wife." She struggled to keep her voice steady. "Therefore he has freed me of all obligation to him."

"Freed you of obligation...to him! Bloody hell, no man with an ounce of honor in his soul would do such a thing!"

"Mr. MacMillan, please." She glanced right and left, hoping no one heard his outburst. "I shall be most grateful if you will lower your tone. The fact is not yet general knowledge."

"Oh, aye." Lowering his voice, he glanced about at passersby showing interest in this unusual meeting. "But I've a good mind to ride out to his bloody mill and beat the tar out of him."

"That's most kind, Mr. MacMillan." Isabella was regaining her equilibrium and able to smile at the big Scotsman's idea of vengeance. "But that would do little to remedy my situation. If you are sincere in wanting to assist me, I'd be most obliged if you'd either guide me to visit your wife or give me directions to your home. I wish to consult with her."

"Not ill, are ye, lassie?" Concern that touched her deeply was reflected in his words. This might be a rogue, a wild man, but he had a compassionate heart.

"No, indeed not. I simply want to ask her how she made her way in this country when she was widowed, how she managed to make a living by her writing. She once mentioned she might be able to assist me in finding a publisher for some of my own work."

"I'm certain sure she'll be happy to help you." Enthusiasm entered his words. "If you'll stay here for a bit, I'll take you out to our homestead myself. At the moment, I'm awaitin' the arrival of a ship that has been spotted comin' up the river. It's carryin' a batch of supplies that we're in dire need of at the mill and farm. Where might I find you in an hour or two?"

"I'm staying at Mrs. O'Malley's house at the edge of the village. Do you know where it is?"

"Aye, that I do. I'll meet you there shortly, and we'll head down that road over yonder." He indicated a trail leading into the forest, touched his cap, and turned and strode off down the street.

Isabella watched him go. A fine figure of a man, as Lucy would have described him, Brodie MacMillan was also capable of unfettered empathy.

She went to the hitching rail where she'd left Duchess tied. She'd ridden the mare to the tavern in hopes of leaving for the Fowler-Wallace settlement immediately. Now she'd have to wait.

She was leading the animal down the street when she saw the wagon approaching. Loaded with sawn lumber, the big conveyance was driven by Culloden

MacPherson, Fletcher Atkin at his side. A fierce desire to avoid the two men who'd forever changed her life overwhelmed her. She was plotting out a new future without them and wasn't about to let either of them disrupt her plans.

Scrambling onto Duchess, she swung the startled mare about, clapped her heels to her sides, and set her racing out of the village and down the rutted road Brodie MacMillan had indicated as leading to his home. With that loaded wagon, they couldn't possibly follow her. She'd stay hidden out in the forest until it was time to meet Brodie MacMillan.

She kept Duchess to a gallop until they were at a distance down the trail that she deemed safe from the men and their plodding team. Stopping the mare, she contemplated her next move. Did this trail lead anywhere other than to the Fowler-Wallace businesses? Thus far she'd seen no branching roads that would cause her to make any decisions.

She had no idea how long it would take to unload the wagon and settle business with the ship's captain. Returning to the village, even a couple of hours later, meant she could still encounter Culloden MacPherson and Fletcher Atkin. She urged Duchess forward. She'd attempt to find Louisa MacMillan's house on her own. If her trek threatened to become complicated, she had only to retrace her way back to the village.

****

"Where is she?" Fletcher Atkin prided himself on being a man who kept his temper in most circumstances, but as he confronted Brodie MacMillan on the Riverhaven dock, the power deserted him.

"Where is who?" The Scotsman turned from

watching the unloading of the recently docked vessel.

"Isabella Marston. Don't try to tell me you haven't seen her. Jonah Parson was in the tavern when she came to find you. He said you left the building together. Now I'm giving you one more opportunity to tell me what became of her before I resort to physical means to extract the truth from you."

"Aye, aye, the old sinner spoke the truth." A bellicose expression suffusing his countenance, Brodie sucked in a deep breath. "And we did leave together. The lassie wanted a wee word—and small wonder, after the way Culloden MacPherson treated her. As his right-hand man, Atkin, I include you in that infamy. A pair of genuine bastards, I'd say."

"I'm not about to argue with you over my employer's decisions. At the moment, all that concerns me is the whereabouts of Miss Marston. We saw her ride out of the village but were unable to pursue her, with a wagon loaded with lumber."

"She's disappeared?"

"Yes, and I can only hope you and your clannish bunch have had no hand in it."

"Sweet Jesus, Atkin, what do you take us for? We've women of our own…and children, too, for that matter. They're no part of our differences."

"Do you deny that you or one of your family fed tea to Cully's team at the church?"

"Fed tea to the bastard's team…with two women his passengers in his wagon? Whit do you take us for?"

"For people out to avenge the grievous injuries inflicted on Harry Wallace supposedly as the result of Cully's actions."

"Aye, well, the man deserves to be punished, and

severely so, for such a dastardly act, but none of my family or friends would ever lower themselves to doing anything so heinous as feedin' horses tea, and in a churchyard, for God's sake!"

"We'll argue that incident out another time. At the moment, all I'm concerned about is the whereabouts of Miss Marston."

"Aye, aye, I understand your concern." Brodie MacMillan backed off. "All I know is that the lass asked to talk to my wife, to be directed to our home. I couldn't allow her to ride there alone. I told her to wait until I'd seen to the unloadin' of this ship's cargo, and then I'd take her with me to visit Louisa. I was to meet her at the O'Malley house. Now you're tellin' me she's not to be found?"

"She took off down the trail out of the village. Cully and I tried to follow her, but encumbered with a load, we couldn't overtake her. We gave up when we came to a point where the trail was freshly churned up with hoof prints...as if several horses had cavorted about, with no further marks down the road. The riders headed into the trees. We couldn't follow with the wagon."

"Lookin' as if someone intercepted her." Brodie's words were thoughtful for a moment before he rejoined, "Well, it wasn't any of our folks."

"It better not have been." Fletcher Atkin, angry to the bone, moved to glare into his face. "Because if I find out that it was, and you're lying…"

Without continuing with his threat, he turned and strode off down the street.

****

"They took her!" Culloden MacPherson's face

knotted with rage. "Took her ta spite me!"

"MacMillan swears it wasn't any of their doing." Fletcher Atkin tried to appease his companion as the mill owner drove the team back toward the homestead. "I'm inclined to believe him. Neither he nor Harry Wallace would take advantage of women."

"You think so, do ya?" Culloden flapped the reins over the team's backs to urge them into a faster trot. "Brodie MacMillan and Harry Wallace were highwaymen back in the Old Country. Oh, they might try ta put a pretty name on it—fightin' fer Scotland and the like—but they're still what they once were, outlaws carin' nothing fer law and order. And what about that gaggle of stepsons Wallace has? Hotheads, all four o' them, from what I've heard. They're young and probably not as steeped in honor as that bastard Brodie MacMillan purports ta be. As soon as we get ta yer homestead, I'm orderin' ya ta saddle that beast of yers and go back ta where the tracks end. There has ta be broken branches, trampled grass, something ta indicate which way she was taken."

"And what of you? Have you so much deserted her that you won't be joining in the search?"

"Shut yer blasted mouth, Fletch! Of course I'd no' go desertin' the lass. The fact that I chose not ta wed her does not mean I'm no longer responsible fer her care. Ta answer yer nasty question, I will take the team ta my house and unhitch them. Then Horace and I will ride them ta join ya. I'm imaginin' the man will want ta participate in findin' his former mistress. Three of us against that kidnappin' Wallace gang will be able ta put up a fair ta middlin' fight. Get up, Timber! Lift yer great hooves, Best!"

Fletcher jolted back on the seat as Culloden urged the horses into a gallop.

****

"Bollocks!" Fletcher uttered a curse that should not pass a gentleman's lips as he stared at the place where three horses had entered the stream. He'd managed to track what he believed had been Isabella and her abductors a quarter mile through the woods from the place where hooves had churned up the trail. Now he stared stymied at the clutter of prints leading into the shallow, fast-running stream.

With a faint hope of finding some visible signs that would enable him to follow the trio further, he dismounted and waded into the water. Behind him, Galahad lowered his head to drink. Finally, abandoning his search, Fletcher remounted and rode slowly up the brook, watching left and right for any sign that the group he pursued had left the water.

Upstream, the terrain became rocky, small stony plateaus on either side of the stream. With a sinking feeling in his gut, Fletcher realized that three horses could have left the water at any point in the area, with only the slightest trace to be found. By now, any wetness they might have shed would have dried up.

Nothing to do but turn back, meet up with Cully and Horace, and continue the search farther up the brook and along any woods roads bordering it. The forest was dense in the area, and horses would need cleared spaces in which to travel.

****

"I know it's that bastard Brodie MacMillan who's taken the lass!" Culloden slammed a fist down on the table where he sat with Fletcher and Horace in his manor, sharing whisky with them. "And, by God, he and his bunch of Highland rogues will pay. That includes the Reverend Edward Morgan."

It was nearing midnight. The three men had reluctantly abandoned the search as darkness and cloudy night made further hunting impossible.

"The minister?" Fletcher stared at the big buckskin-clad man.

"Aye. Remember, he, Harry Wallace, Brodie MacMillan, and even the reverend's wife were a band of outlaws in the Old Country. Riverhaven has become a place of refuge for all kinds of riffraff to call home. Even our magistrate and his deputy were privateers during the war."

"Privateers who served in this country's defense when it had no official navy and the British were too occupied in quarrels about the world to send help." Fletcher, weary of Culloden's blame-placing, could no longer listen to it.

"Aye, aye, go defendin' them, why don't ya. Ya who was once a gentleman, ya who strained his family's honor ta the point yer own family forced ya out of the country in disgrace."

Fletcher's hands around his tankard tightened until the knuckles turned white. Silenced, he stared down at them.

"Hold now, sir." Horace spoke up for the first time. The big man faced Culloden squarely. "I understand you're right upset about Miss Isabella's disappearance, but I see no call for making such nasty remarks about your friend. We've all had things in our past we'd rather leave buried—perhaps yourself, as well. Dragging such incidents out at the moment can have no good effect. What we have to do now is try to come up with some way of finding Miss Isabella."

"Right ya are, my good man." Calmed by the groom's words of common sense, Culloden drew a deep breath and stood. "We'll get ourselves a bit of rest and start out fresh in the mornin'."

Culloden and Horace made for their pallets that Lucy had allowed to remain against the kitchen wall, but Fletcher stayed seated, staring into his drink.

Isabella, where in God's name are you? If anything has happened to you...

"Fletch, go ta bed." The words were a grunt as Culloden settled himself in his bed. "We start out at first light. Ya need ta be rested."

"I'm going." He drained his tankard and stood. He'd do as Culloden had said, but he doubted sleep would come easily...not with visions of Isabella and her possible fate at the hands of her abductors flashing through his mind.

****

Pistol stuck in his belt, dressed for a day of hard riding and searching, Culloden MacPherson pulled open his kitchen door and froze. A piece of paper, a knife holding it to the panel, greeted him.

"Bloody hell, what...!" As he yanked it free, Fletcher came to join him.

"What is it?"

"A message of some sort. Here, read it to me." He thrust the dirty missive into his friend's hands.

"MacMillan holds woman." Fletcher read the three words, astonishment causing his forehead to furrow.

"Aha! It's as I first thought and knew all along! Come along, men." Culloden swung on Fletcher and on

Horace standing behind him. "We're ridin' ta the bastard's homestead."

"No!" Fletcher caught the mill owner's arm as he made to head for the stable.

"Whit? Man, have ye lost yer senses? Someone has kindly told me of Miss Isabella Marston's whereabouts." He shrugged free to glower at his friend.

"I think not." Fletcher looked down at the dirty paper. "I think this is another attempt to start a war between the Wallace-Fowler enterprises and us. I know Brodie MacMillan well enough to be convinced abducting women isn't anything he'd ever consider doing. This fight, in his mind, is between men and will remain that way. At any rate, he'd never take a captive to his homestead where women and children might become involved in a battle."

"Blast ye, lad! I'm right sick of ya defendin' that bit of Highland trash. I'm headin' out there now." Culloden made another attempt to make for the stable.

"Cully, for God's sake, if you ride out there, you'll start an all-out war!" Fletcher stepped in front of him. "And you could be wrong."

"Air ye sayin' ye'll not stand beside me in a fight against those kidnappin' buggers?"

"No, no, not at all. If we fail to recover Miss Marston, I'll ride by your side into hell, if you wish."

A static hiatus followed. Fletcher fancied the air between him and his friend crackled with emotion.

"Verrae well. But only until midday. Then we ride after that MacMillan and his bunch of bastards."

Fletcher nodded and strode off toward the stable with the other two men.

****

As the three men rode into the village, Lucy Welsh ran into the road, waving her arms.

"Do you know where to find her?" she cried. "Has there been any news of her fate?"

"Not as yet, lass, but we'll find her, never fear." Culloden halted his horse and, to Fletcher's chagrin when time was of the essence, dismounted. His annoyance melted into absolute astonishment when Culloden pulled Lucy into his arms and kissed her.

"I'll be givin' ya something ta think about while we're searchin'," he said when he finally released the astonished young woman who stared up at him. "I want ya ta marry me, Miss Lucy Welsh, and I won't be easy takin' 'no' as your answer." He kissed her again, this time hastily, before remounting. With a brisk salute to the young woman who stood looking dazed, he swung Timber away and headed off at a gallop.

"Miss Lucy." Fletcher touched his hat brim before following Culloden. Horace urged Best into a canter behind him.

When Culloden finally slowed Timber to a trot, Fletcher rode up beside him and gave him a sly look.

"Well, whit is it?" Culloden snapped. "Don't go givin' me that crafty glance. Spit it out. Whit air ya thinkin'?"

"I'm thinking you've made an excellent decision, asking Miss Lucy to marry you."

"Oh, ya do, do ya?"

"I do. Now let's go. We've a lady to locate."

They followed the road to where the churned hoofprints had indicated Isabella may have been intercepted, then rode into the trees following the weak trail that led to the stream. For hours the trio rode up and down its length but failed to spot any place where three horses might have exited the water.

"That shower in the night has taken the trail." Culloden stopped Timber to pull the back of his hand across his sweating forehead. "We'd best go back and set up a wider search with the men from my mill."

Reluctantly Fletcher followed the man and Horace back to the road to the village. As they rode into Riverhaven, the idea hit him.

"You go gather a search party," he called out to his companions. "I'm stopping in the village."

"Don't go near the tavern, laddie." Culloden rode close beside him and spoke softly. "I know yer right flummoxed with Miss Isabella missin', but gettin' drunk or mixed up in more gamblin' won't help. And for damned sure, stay away from that whore Molly."

"Jesus, Cully, as if…"

"I'm just givin' a warnin', laddie."

****

"Mrs. O'Malley, will you put a collar on Percy? If you have a bit of cord, I might attach to it, I'd be obliged." Fletcher stood in the kitchen of Mrs. O'Malley's cabin and made the request. He was about to try a last resort. "I'll also be requiring a small, strong sack."

"What are you planning to do?" Lucy, her face paler than Fletcher had ever seen it, asked. Her former mistress's disappearance was taking a harsh toll on the formerly brash young woman.

"I'm going to take Percy out to the last place I've been able to trace Miss Marston." Fletcher faced the two women. "Our searches so far have led to nothing. I'm hoping Percy can find her scent and lead me to wherever she is."

"He's hardly a hound, Mr. Atkin," Mrs. O'Malley, already engaged in fastening the collar about the little dog's neck, commented. "And we did have that shower in the night." Her task completed, she picked up the Pug and handed him to Fletcher. "I'll fetch a bit of cord to tie to his collar, and a sack. I'm assuming you plan to place him in it to travel with you on your horse? The wee lad can hardly be expected to keep pace with that animal's great long legs."

She hurried into a small pantry. Lucy came forward and kissed the dog's snout as he snuggled in Fletcher's arms.

"Please, please, Percy, find Isabella," she whispered as Fletcher saw a glitter of tears in her eyes.

"Miss Welsh...Lucy," Fletcher spoke softly while Mrs. O'Malley rummaged noisily, searching for a bit of cord. "Have you given any thought to Cully—Mr. MacPherson's proposal?"

"My mind's been more than occupied with fears for Isabella," she replied. "But I don't need to contemplate my decision. I'd already made up my mind to marry the great oaf even after he treated my friend so badly. I knew Isabella didn't sincerely want him and that if she married him it would be only out of a sense of obligation. I believe I'm just the woman to drill manners and the rules of polite society into Culloden MacPherson. No disrespect to Isabella, but she isn't the one to do it."

"Very good, very good." In spite of the present situation with the woman he loved, Fletcher experienced a lightening of spirit. Isabella could now truly feel free to do as she pleased...and marry who she chose.

"Now it's all up to you, Percy," he said when Mrs. O'Malley returned with a length of cord and began to tie it to the Pug's collar. "Find Isabella alive and well, and I'll personally knight you Sir Perceval."

"Mr. Atkin, you must find her." Mrs. O'Malley caught at his arm. "Word is fast spreading that Brodie MacMillan has challenged Mr. MacPherson to meet him and his men in the meadow at the edge of the village. It's war he's proposing to prove his honor, and if you don't find Isabella, a war it will be."

****

As Fletcher rode away from Mrs. O'Malley's house, the Pug's head sticking out of the sack tied in front of him, he realized what a faint hope he was following. Percy was no bloodhound nor any kind of hunting dog. His chances of catching his mistress's scent in the damp woods and following it to the desired conclusion were probably dim to none. Still, Fletcher felt he had to try—and try soon, before Cully started a war.

He slowed Galahad to a walk as they reached the location where the tracks of their quarry entered the stream. The Pug grunted as the horse lurched down into the water.

"Sorry, Percy." He didn't want to jounce the little fellow into illness. The Pug was still recovering from his encounter with a bear, after all.

When he reached the place where the rock face leaned down to provide what he saw as the best exit from the stream, he urged the gelding onto dry ground and dismounted.

"Now, Percy, do your best." He freed the Pug from

the sack and placed him on his paws on the smooth rock surface. "Lives may be riding on what you can find."

The little dog looked up at him before lowering his head, his sides heaving. A moment later he vomited.

"Ah, poor boy." Fletcher, in spite of the severity of the situation, felt compassion for the Pug. He recalled someone, Isabella or maybe Lucy, telling him how seasick the dog had been on the voyage. Apparently the jolting he'd received in the sack had revived his inclination to motion sickness.

With a final cough, Percy finished purging and began to sniff the air. He wandered a few steps in one direction, then in another, and finally, nose to the ground, he headed under the limbs of trees that stretched to the ground.

"Wait!" Fletcher barely had time to catch up the cord Mrs. O'Malley had supplied to his collar before Percy was off, tugging the man along behind him, over stony ground that allowed for no hoof prints.

"Galahad!" Afraid to deflect the Pug's attention to return for his mount, Fletcher called out to the animal. To his relief, the gelding responded, and he was able to gather his reins in one hand while holding onto the determined Pug's leash in the other.

About a quarter mile farther on, the trio, led by Percy, burst out onto an old logging road. Here, Fletcher saw the prints of horses, more than two, possibly three.

"Good boy," he praised the little dog softly. He had no idea how near or far they were from the kidnappers, if indeed the Pug was on the correct trail. He didn't want to warn them.

****

"Percy, halt!" He pulled on the cord to stop the little dog. The road had emerged into a ragged clearing with a ramshackle log cabin in its center. Tied to a tree by its side was Duchess. As Galahad made to announce his presence with a whinny, Fletcher stifled him. The gelding, not willing to be denied calling out to his stable mate, wrenched free and neighed loudly. Duchess's head went up and she replied.

So much for approaching noiselessly.

Fletcher waited. If the kidnappers were in the cabin, they'd definitely been alerted. When no signs of arousal issued from the structure, he tied Galahad to a tree. Clutching the pistol in one hand and the Pug's leash in the other, he eased forward. At the door, he paused to listen. Not a sound. Ignoring further caution, he kicked the door open.

Chapter Thirteen

It took a few seconds for his eyes to become accustomed to the gloom inside, but when they did, he saw a person bound to a chair, a black hood over her head. Riding trousers, shirt, and small stature identified her immediately to Fletcher.

"Isabella...Miss Marston." He was instantly behind her, pulling away the hood.

"Mr. Atkin." Her first words rasped over dry lips and throat. "I was...I thought..."

"Don't try to talk." He stuffed the pistol into his belt and bent to release her wrists. Then, kneeling in front of her, he untied the bonds that held her ankles, his fingers trembling. "Right now we have to get out of here quickly," he said, helping her to her feet.

She staggered and might have fallen when Percy jumped up on her if Fletcher hadn't steadied her on her feet.

"Percy." She bent to touch the Pug's head. "What are you doing here?"

"He led me to you." Fletcher held her arm to secure her. She weaved against him, making him wonder how long she'd been bound in place. Outrage coursed through him. "He'll get his hero's treatment later. Right now we have to get away from here before your kidnappers return...and before there's an all-out timber war. Do you think you can ride?"

Blinking, she nodded.

"Come on." He drew her outside and left her leaning against the cabin wall as he picked up Duchess's saddle and cloth where they'd been dropped on the ground. As he threw them onto the mare and began to fasten the girth, he asked, "Who kidnapped you? Who brought you here?"

"I don't know." Her words sounded hoarse, a croak. He realized she needed water. "They threw that hood over me when they accosted me on the trail. They hardly ever spoke in my presence, and when they did, I'm sure they disguised their voices with an awkward attempt at an Irish accent."

"Bastards!" He pulled the girth tight. "Big men? A pair of them?"

"Yes. They spoke like Mrs. O'Malley...Irish accent."

"Tom Bracken and Clem Reid, disguising both themselves and their voices, I'll wager. Out to avenge their mistress by raking up trouble in the valley." He took a canteen from his saddle, opened it, and held it out to her. "Not too much or too fast. You can make yourself ill."

She nodded before raising the flask to her mouth. When she lowered it again, he was relieved to see she was recovering, her eyes brightening.

"Let me help you aboard." He retrieved the water container and hung it on his saddle, but as he put out a hand to help her mount, his control snapped. With a passion held too long in check, he pulled her into his arms and covered her mouth with his. She uttered a soft gasp, but after a moment of stiff surprise, melted into his embrace. Returning his kiss with an inexperienced fervor that delighted him, she silently told him she welcomed his advances.

"Isabella," he breathed against her hair when he finally released her lips. "When I learned you'd been kidnapped, something in me died. I knew then that life without you would be a void, a great emptiness."

"Fletcher Atkin, are you telling me you love me?" Green eyes wide, she looked up at him.

"Yes, I believe I am." He felt his face breaking into a smile. "Yes, indeed I am, Miss Isabella Marston. I'm hoping you will some day find your heart to be harboring a similar emotion."

"I do believe I shall." She was smiling back, color that the events of the last few days had taken away now seeping back into her face.

"Good...very good." He drew her out at arm's length. "But we must wait until we've prevented a timber war before continuing our courtship. Much as I long to linger here with you, to make love to you—as a gentleman—duty calls." He released her and held out his hand to help her mount her mare.

She nodded and accepted his assistance. Once on Duchess's back, she swayed. He reached up to steady her.

"Should I ride pillion?"

"No, I can manage. Please see to Percy."

In his relief at finding Isabella and in the emotional upheaval that followed, Fletcher had almost forgotten the reason he had been able to locate her. Turning, he saw the little dog staring up at his mistress, tail wiggling, ears alert, apparently as delighted as Fletcher to have found her.

"Yes, of course. Come here, Perceval, second

knight of the Holy Grail." He picked up the Pug and headed for Galahad. "Although you're the hero of the day, you'll have to submit to another ignominious ride in that sack, but I think you should be allowed the privilege of travelling with your mistress."

He placed the Pug in the sack, then carried it to Duchess to tie it in front of Isabella. With the little dog in place, they set off. While he longed to burst into a full gallop that would take them back to the village and meadow in short order, he held Galahad to a walk, aware not only that the Pug could again become seasick but also that his companion was weak from her captivity. Riding ahead along the narrow trail, he kept glancing back to make certain she was still in the saddle, still able to manage. Once she smiled at him reassuringly. Something that previously had felt like a stone in his chest fluttered like a feather as he turned back to guide his gelding through the trees.

Shortly they were at the stream. As both horses entered the water, Fletcher stopped his mount to allow Isabella to come abreast of him.

"I have news I can't wait any longer to share with you, news that may in some way influence you to feel comfortable with our…attraction." He grinned. "Before we left to search for you, Cully proposed to Lucy. Furthermore, I have it on good authority she plans to accept."

"Lucy…marry Mr. MacPherson?" Isabella stared at him.

"Think about it. Who better to take him on? She knows how to handle him, how to train him, how…to love him."

"You're right. She is the perfect mate for him. I

237

hope they will be very happy."

An explosion rent the quiet.

Later Fletcher would deduce that it was the sound of the babbling brook that had hidden the ambushers' approach, but at the moment he was only aware of Galahad's shriek before the horse collapsed beneath him, and of Duchess's frantic thrashing and snorting beside them. Percy howled and struggled in his sack.

"Mr. Atkin...Fletcher!" Isabella screamed his name as he struggled to extricate himself from the fallen animal.

Beside him, the gelding was thrashing, hooves flaying as he tried to rise out of the water. Fletcher yanked his pistol from his belt and fired into the trees. A scrambling among the brush marked the retreat of the attackers.

"Whoa, whoa." Stuffing his weapon back in his belt, Fletcher turned his attention to his horse. He fought to keep his voice calm as he held the reins while he stood in the rushing water at the animal's head. "Easy, easy."

The animal's desperation slowed. As Galahad's head dropped, Fletcher fell to his knees to hold it above the surface of the shallow water.

He swung on Isabella, who was struggling to hold a prancing Duchess in check. "Isabella, ride! Get out of here! Before whoever fired that shot has time to reload and try again."

"No! I won't leave you!"

"Go, or there will be more than a horse that is shot! Get to the meadow at the edge of the village...now! Lives are at stake!"

"Fletcher..."

"Do you want your friends to lose husbands… fathers? Now go!"

After one last look at the man holding his horse's head, she swung Duchess about and headed off downstream at a gallop.

When horse and rider had vanished from sight, he turned his attention back to Galahad. The horse had stopped his wild thrashing. Now he lay on his side, gasping. He looked up at Fletcher, eyes wide with fear and desperation.

Fletcher pulled the pistol from his belt and began to reload. His hands shook.

****

Isabella galloped Duchess until she began to sway in the saddle. She had to complete the mission Fletcher had sent her upon. Falling from her horse wouldn't allow her to accomplish it. She slowed to a trot, brook water splashing up her mare's legs. Finally she drew rein as she saw a place along the shore where it appeared horses had left and entered the stream.

"This must be where we will have to try to find a trail," she said to the Pug in front of her. Putting her heels to her mount, she urged the mare out of the water and into the trees. For a few yards, following the hoof prints was not difficult. Then they appeared to vanish into hard, dry rocky ground.

"Which way from here?" She gazed about into the forest. She was puzzling her next move when the shot rang out.

Oh, God! Galahad!

She closed her eyes. Fletcher had made the only decision possible. Still she could imagine his agony at shooting his horse, the animal that was his most prized possession. Swallowing hard, she forced herself back to her present predicament. Which way to turn? If she could only get to the trail where she'd been abducted, she knew she could find her way to the village and then to the meadow where a battle was looming...if not already in progress.

In front of her, Percy burped and gagged.

"Poor little fellow." She dismounted to place him on the ground.

Sides heaving, the Pug expelled a mouthful of bile before looking up at Isabella with sad eyes.

"I'm sorry, Percy, but we must continue." She reached to pick him up, but he staggered ahead, nose to the ground. She watched, a sudden, probably impossible hope starting to rise.

"Percy, do you know the way to the trail?" She gathered up Duchess's reins.

The little dog glanced up at her again before starting off into the undergrowth, nose to the ground.

Deciding she had no other choice, she set off to follow him on foot, her mare in tow.

For a time they struggled through thickets and low-hanging branches. Suddenly they burst out onto a well-worn wagon road. The Pug looked up at her and wiggled his tail.

"Wonderful, Percy!" Holding Duchess's reins, she bent to pat the little dog. "Now, I fear you'll have to go back in your sack. We must get to the meadow quickly."

The squeaking, grating sounds of an approaching wagon caught her attention. She turned to see a conveyance appearing around a bend in the road and recognized the Clydesdales Brodie MacMillan had driven that day in the churchyard. Margaret Wallace held the reins. Her expression grim, she stopped the team when she saw Isabella.

"Miss Marston." She halted the horses. "You are a welcome sight. We'd heard you were missing, kidnapped perhaps."

"I was, but Mr. Fletcher found me. Mrs. Wallace, it wasn't any of your family who abducted me. Although they kept a hood over my head and I can't positively identify them, I'm certain they weren't anyone connected with your relatives."

"Of course they weren't!" Margaret Wallace's indignation flared. "Someone is trying to invoke a war between our men, some nasty bastards intent on causing all manner of evil in this valley. I'm on my way to intervene…as my husband would do if he were able."

"We must put a stop to it, Margaret. We have to get to that meadow as fast as possible. But first, a favor." She bent to pick up Percy. "My dog helped rescue me, directed me to this road. Riding in a sack attached to my saddle has been hard on him. Will you allow him to ride in your wagon?"

"Certainly. I've heard about his bravery with that bear. The poor little lad deserves a rest. Put him in the back, and we'll be off."

****

"Where is she?" Isabella heard Culloden MacPherson bellow at Brodie MacMillan as she, riding faster than Margaret Wallace could travel with the wagon, reached the meadow and drew rein on its edge. The two men headed their small armies composed of mill workers, weapons drawn. "We can stop this right now if ya'll 'fess up to the dastardly thing ya've done."

241

"*I've* done!" Brodie MacMillan, his hand on the hilt of his sword, shouted. "I'd no' harm the lass. I'm not a renegin' son of a bitch who promises marriage and then snivels away from it. I wouldn't blame her for runnin' away!"

"She's no' run away! She was taken by ya and yer bloody rogues. Now I can see ya've no plan ta give her up without a fight. Get ready, men!"

There was a rattling of swords, muskets, axes, and pikes as both sides made ready for the fight.

"Wait!" Isabella slapped her heels against Duchess's sides and galloped between the two factions.

"Glory be!" Brodie MacMillan's expression brightened. "She's come back!"

"Air ye well, lass?" Culloden lowered the musket he carried to stare at her. "Where have ya been? Were ye harmed?"

"No." She sat up straight in the saddle. "And there's no reason for this trouble. The two men who abducted me didn't belong to the Fowler-Wallace business."

"Air ya sure, lass?" Culloden frowned up at her. "Did ya recognize them?"

"I'm not sure. That little matters at the moment. Although they kept a hood over my head, I heard them discussing how they'd stirred up a war in the valley to revenge their mistress's death. That was the only time they spoke within my hearing. They thought I was asleep at the time."

"Sweet Jesus!" Culloden muttered. "Traitors—worse than traitors—in our midst.'"

"Speakin' of avengin' their mistress's death, were they?" Brodie MacMillan's handsome face went taut with anger. "I'd no' have to be a genius to figure out who they are—Tom Bracken and Clem Reid. I'd stake my life on it. They've blamed me for the death of their mistress, Cassandra Carmody, because my stallion ran her down when she was attemptin' to murder my wife. Now the bastards are out to take their revenge for her and the entire Carmody family by destroying Riverhaven and those who call this valley home."

"I've heard of what happened last year." Culloden MacPherson spoke. "The woman falsely accused ya of seduction and bastardy. Seems ya have a right talent for getting' yerself inta scrapes, laddie. Perhaps I'm owin' ya an apology, MacMillan." He stepped forward to offer his hand to Brodie.

"You think it's that easy, do you?" Brodie refused the gesture. "The fact that you find me innocent of kidnappin' the lass here in no way exonerates you for spikin' trees on our patch, for causin' an accident that all but killed my friend Harry. No, you've a ways to go yet, MacPherson, before I'll be shakin' your hand. Mark me, this squabble may be over for now, but not forever. This is a truce, not a treaty." He swung on his group. "Come on, lads. We've got two cowardly bastards to catch."

Margaret Wallace's wagon rattled into the meadow. Her big team running at a shambling gallop, she drove her conveyance between the lines of troops and reined them to a halt, her strength surprising Isabella.

"Brodie MacMillan, you'll shake the man's hand and put an end to this feuding!" she cried, standing to face the man. "Don't you see? All this trouble was caused by Tom Bracken and Clem Reid as revenge for

243

what they saw as your causing Cassandra Carmody's death. It would have been that precious pair that spiked the trees and fed tea to Mr. MacPherson's horses. Think, man, think!"

"Mrs. Wallace is right." Striding across the meadow toward them, Magistrate Captain Caleb Cameron, followed by Duncan MacDougal, spoke. "From now on, you'll leave justice to the law, Brodie MacMillan...and you as well, Culloden MacPherson."

"Now don't go holdin' us up, Captain." Brodie faced him as the man stopped in front of him. "Every minute we stand here talkin', that pair are gettin' farther away."

"No need to go getting your tail in a knot, Brodie." Duncan MacDougal spoke. "We've been told they disappeared from the village sometime in the night. We're thinking they made for Upper Canada or the American border. In either case, chasing after them would be pointless. We'll have to be content that Miss Marston has returned to us and that those two cowards won't risk coming back to Riverhaven, where they'd be strung up from the highest tree the moment they entered the valley."

"Argh!" Brodie's expression reflected his frustration.

"Furthermore, you might be interested to learn that before they left, they were overheard confessing to spiking trees and feeding tea to horses," Captain Cameron informed him. "Bragging, drunk in their cups at the tavern yesterday, boasting how they'd caused the war between you two with a few spikes in choice pine."

"It seems now *you're* owin' *me* an apology, MacMillan." Culloden MacPherson drew himself up to his impressive height and stuck his thumbs in his belt.

Brodie hesitated, then stuck out his hand. "Aye, aye, MacPherson. Right you are."

"Now enough!" Isabella could contain her concern for Fletcher no longer. "We were ambushed on the way here. I think those two men made a last-ditch effort to do damage before they left. Mr. Atkin's horse was shot from beneath him in a stream back in the bush. Please, someone, ride with me to help him."

"Aye, ride with the lass to lend a hand." All turned as a group at the sound of another's voice.

Isabella saw a tall, dark-haired man walking his horse into the meadow between the two factions. His left arm was in a sling, his face gaunt, but he was one of the most commanding, handsome figures she'd ever seen. He was mounted on the outstanding horse Brodie MacMillan had ridden on their first meeting on the day of her arrival. This had to be Harry Wallace, the suspected legendary Highland Harry.

"Harry, what are you doing here?" Margaret stood in the front of the wagon, her expression bellicose. "I cannot believe Louisa allowed…"

A second rider burst into the meadow. Louisa MacMillan, riding her ivory-colored horse, galloped up and reined to an abrupt halt.

"Just going to the privy, were you, my good man?" She glared at Harry. Turning to Margaret, she continued, "I in no way sanctioned this ride. It appears Highland Harry has lost none of his powers to inveigle his way out of situations, although how he knew about this…" She waved her arm to indicate the assemblage.

"I overheard my boys talking outside the bedroom window." He shifted the reins in his free hand with a slight grimace. "I had to stop them. Margaret, climb down from that wagon. Brodie, take the reins. We'll be riding to fetch Fletcher Atkin and his horse. We'll be needing a conveyance to bring the beast back…either way."

"Harry Wallace, I'll have you know I can handle this team and wagon as well as any man." Margaret Wallace reseated herself and adjusted the reins through her fingers. "Brodie may ride with me if he chooses. But first, I have a question for you, dear husband." The last sentence reeked of sarcasm.

"Oh, aye?"

"Just how did you manage to saddle that mare and mount in your condition?"

"Our two eldest daughters are fine, strong young lasses." He avoided her piercing gaze. "They weren't about to let their brothers be maimed or killed in a senseless battle." Turning with a grimace, he glared at the four young men in the forefront of Brodie's ragtag troops. "And you'll not be behaving in this way ever again, do you hear?"

"Yes, sir." Their response was a mumble.

"That is, without my consent." Isabella caught the roguish gleam in Harry Wallace's eyes as his wife scoffed in exasperation.

"Good God, Harry, you're approving everything our children have done in this instance. You've even drawn our daughters into your conspiracy."

"The lasses believed I could prevent bloodshed. After they got Scotia saddled, Bella and Lizzie hoisted me aboard. Now enough blathering. Brodie, join my darling wife. I'm sure she'll concede she's not quite up to lifting a"—he glanced at Isabella—"an injured horse aboard, and your muscles will come in handy."

Isabella flinched at Harry Wallace's slight hesitation. He'd been about to say "dead."

Please, God, let his spoken words be correct.

"We'll be needing a strong canvas to hoist the beast into the wagon." Duncan MacDougal was galloping toward the village as he yelled back the information. "I'll fetch a sail. Follow me with the wagon, Mrs. Wallace."

"Hie, there." As Duncan dashed off, followed by the conveyance, two more riders galloped into the meadow. Isabella was astonished to recognize the pair on the big horses as Reverend Edward Morgan and his wife, mounted in saddles on Percherons. "There will be no battles today!" The clergyman rode between the two groups, holding up a hand.

"Yer a tad late with yer peacemakin', Reverend." Culloden MacPherson squinted up at the man. "We've resolved our troubles…well, at least most of them. We're about ta ride ta help Fletcher Atkin with his beast that's been injured."

"We'll help." As the minister's wife spoke, Isabella couldn't help staring. "Iona is safe with Mrs. O'Malley. We've time."

The group started, a small combined army of Brodie MacMillan's and Culloden MacPherson's people, with Isabella riding ahead to show the way. Glancing back at the mixed entourage, she drew a deep breath. This motley crowd consisted of the citizens of Riverhaven, the people with whom she'd decided to spend the rest of her life.

But how would she, Isabella Marston of Hollybranch Hall, manage to fit in among these

Riverhaven rogues?

Chapter Fourteen

"How is your beast?" Culloden MacPherson entered the stable on Fletcher's homestead.

"Getting stronger with each day." Fletcher stood in the gelding's stall, his hand on the animal's arched neck. "When we loaded him into Harry Wallace's wagon that day two weeks ago, I had serious doubts he'd survive. You and the Wallaces took a great risk, driving a team and wagon along that stream bed to fetch him. Margaret Wallace is one amazing woman. It took a master teamster to handle the journey. I'm grateful for all your efforts, Cully."

"We know what the lad means ta ya." Culloden came to lean against the doorway. "My beasts mean a fair share ta me as well. All our creatures work hard for us. They deserve proper care and respect."

"I agree." As Fletcher made to return to brushing Galahad, Culloden drew a rumpled paper from inside his shirt.

"This came for ya, laddie. I was at the wharf, checkin' ta see if the ship newly docked would be lookin' for any lumber ta take south. The captain knows me, knows that ya work with me. He trusted me ta deliver it ta ya."

Fletcher hesitated, then slowly took the paper. His lips tightened as he recognized the crest pressed into the wax seal.

"Ya look as surprised as a man who's found a snake in his bed. I'm guessin' ya weren't expectin' its likes. Well, I'll leave ya ta it." He strode out of the stable.

Fletcher stood staring at the missive. Finally he stuck a thumb under the wax and opened it.

For a few moments he read, transfixed. Finally, with a moan, he sank back against the boards of Galahad's stall.

"Good God! I didn't expect this."

****

Isabella sat on the veranda of Mrs. O'Malley's small log house, basking in the sunshine, Percy stretched out beside her on the warm planks. Two weeks after the incident, she could look back on her kidnapping as a bad dream, something that was not likely ever to be repeated now that her abductors had fled. Furthermore, with both sides of the timber dispute at least temporarily at peace, their reason for taking her didn't exist.

A smile curling her lips, she threw back her head and closed her eyes, letting the sun's rays warm her face.

"Enjoying this fine morning, Miss Marston?" Her lids flew open to see Fletcher walking into the dooryard.

"Most definitely." She smiled. "Thanks to you and Percy, I've survived to do it."

"I doubt those men would have killed you. I think they meant to hold you captive until a battle broke out. But your rescue was mostly the little chap's doing." He stopped at the bottom step. "Are Mrs. O'Malley and Lucy about?" He glanced around the yard.

"Both gone to their housekeeping duties...after I assured them I was quite comfortable being alone. How is Galahad?"

"Doing well, I'm happy to report. At present, he's enjoying the sun with Duchess in the paddock at my farm. It will be a couple of weeks before I can ride him again, but the results of that shot could have been much worse."

"Yes, indeed. When I saw him go down, I was horrified. It's wonderful that he's recovering. Our attackers must not have been very good with firearms. From the noises in the bush after the shooting, I deduced they were nearby."

"I don't think it was their intent to shoot me...or you." He came up the steps and seated himself on the veranda railing in front of her. "Killing a horse carries a much lesser penalty than murder. I believe their plan was simply to delay us from getting to the meadow and preventing the outbreak of a timber war."

"But they were already guilty of kidnapping."

"Yes, but there they were careful. They made certain there was no way you could positively identify them. At any rate, Tom Bracken and Clem Reid are long gone now and not likely to ever show their ugly faces in this valley again. I'm assuming they were on their way to either Upper Canada or America when they ambushed us, both places too distant and foreign for us to lay a hand on them." He shifted on the rail. "Miss Marston...Isabella, I didn't come here to discuss those two blackhearts. After our...moment at the cabin, after Percy and I found you, after I knew Galahad would survive, and that the danger of a battle between men who should have been allies was averted, I decided I had to tell you exactly who I am and what constitutes my not so stellar past."

"Mr. Atkin, please, that's not necessary."

"Oh, but I think it is." He drew a deep breath. "I'm the second son of Lord Docane, Sir Walter Atkin, the one of his three boys of which he was least proud."

Isabella stifled a gasp.

"You're astonished? Small wonder. In my present station, I hardly appear to be of the aristocracy." A corner of his mouth quirked. "As a young man, I was sent to university, where I behaved badly. I enjoyed the company of ladies of the evening and fine wine. I also began to gamble. Finally my debts and carousing became more than my father could bear. He bought me a commission in the army, and I was shipped off to France." He paused and looked away, squinting up into the trees before returning his attention to Isabella and continuing. "The senseless killing, the young men maimed before they'd had a chance to live…I hated every minute. As soon as I could, I resigned. I wasn't greeted with open arms at the family estate. My father decided the only solution was to send me so far away he'd never have to deal with me again. Thus, within two weeks of my return from the war, I found myself, not all that reluctantly, on a ship bound for New Brunswick—Riverhaven, in fact. I wasn't sorry. I'd finally be out from under my father's control."

"And so you came here and met Mr. MacPherson, and…"

"It wasn't all that simple. On board ship, I fell into my old ways, gambling and drinking far more than was good for me. Too deep in drink to be clever, I lost heavily to sailors and fellow passengers. When I arrived at Riverhaven, wasted from weeks of drunken debauchery, I was in debt to several of the rougher passengers. Before I could leave the ship, before they continued the voyage to the Caribbean, they decided to vent their anger at my failure to pay up. They left me in a bloody heap on the wharf."

"How horrible!" Isabella put a hand over her mouth.

"It was a bitterly cold November day." He wet his lips and continued. "I might have died there if Cully hadn't been delivering a load of lumber to the wharf. He found me behind a pile of planks. He was helping me to his wagon when some of the men to whom I owed money stopped him. There were too many for even Culloden MacPherson to fight off, so he paid my debts. Then he took me back to a cabin he had near his mill, and he cared for me until I was once more back on my feet. When I was able, he set me to work with his woods crew. That first winter was nearly as hard as fighting the war in France, but at least there was no carnage."

"How long did you work there?" Isabella, enthralled by the tale, asked.

"When Cully discovered I was literate, that I had a head for words and figures, he made me his foreman, keeping track of wages, prices, and the like. I realized this was my last chance to straighten my sails and make a life for myself. I believe I have." He paused to draw a deep breath.

"You have, you most definitely have."

"Isabella, when I asked you to marry me, although I esteemed you, indeed loved you at the time although I forced myself not to believe it, I was, as you accused, offering you a solution to the untenable situation into which Cully had forced you. Now I'm in a position to offer you more…"

"Fletcher, please." She felt a hot blush creeping up her cheeks. "There's no need. Mrs. MacMillan has visited earlier today, read some of my prose, and thinks it will find favor in her publisher's eyes. Also, Captain Cameron has been to see me on another matter that will enable me to earn my keep. He's suggested I operate a school. The provincial government has allocated a sum to this district for the erection of a small building and the salary for a teacher. I've agreed to take the position. So you see, I'm no longer destitute. I'll be able to make my own way."

"I'm delighted by your good fortune, but"—he spoke carefully—"I can assure you that my proposal on this day has nothing to do with finances or your ability to support yourself. I know you came to this country expecting to marry a man of means, a man whom I, not erroneously, referred to in Cully's advertisement as a baron, albeit a lumber one. My words quite possibly deceived your family into thinking you would be marrying into a sort of aristocracy. That was very wrong of me."

"Fletcher…"

"Isabella, allow me to continue. I've told you I am the second son of Lord Docane, Sir Walter Atkin. When he died two years ago, my elder brother Arthur inherited the title. Today"—he pulled the travel-weary letter from his waistcoat pocket—"this missive has arrived from the family solicitors in London. My brother was killed in a hunting accident. Therefore…"

"Therefore, you have inherited the title." Isabella

stared at him. "Therefore you are now Sir Fletcher Atkin, Lord Docane."

"If I so choose. This inheritance, however, holds only one possibility that I cherish. Isabella Marston, will you marry me?" He dropped on one knee before her. "I can now offer you at least some of what you hoped for in coming to this country. Will you do me the honor of becoming my wife...and Lady Isabella?"

She looked down at him, his blue eyes sincere and imploring, and knew she returned his feelings, that she had for some time. She simply hadn't felt at liberty to acknowledge them.

"Fletcher...are you quite sure? Perhaps you should take time to consider. This letter arrived only today..."

"It did, but these thoughts and desires were in my heart almost from the first moment I saw you. Then I had nothing to offer...nothing but a small homestead and a murky past. Now there's a sizeable estate in Kent and a respected title awaiting you...if you'll see fit to take on this reforming rake."

Catching the twinkle tempered with hope in his gaze, Isabella had only one answer.

"Yes, Fletcher. Oh, yes."

He stood to catch her into his arms with a suddenness that took her breath away and kissed her until she was engulfed with a wave of desire such as she'd never dreamed existed.

"Oh, Fletcher," she breathed as he pressed her full length against his strong body.

"Yes," he breathed against her temple. "I understand. But"—he pulled back reluctantly—"we'll be waiting until Reverend Morgan can make us husband and wife in the eyes of God and the law."

"Of course." She stepped back, heart pounding a mad tattoo against her ribs. "Of course. Fletcher, there is one matter, however, I feel we must discuss before we proceed with further plans."

"Yes?"

"I realize you now have family obligations in England, that you..."

"Isabella, what are you saying?" His brightening expression told her he'd guessed at least some of her thoughts.

"I'd rather not go back to the Old Country. I'd rather not become Lady Isabella, hosting fetes and tea parties, being watched as the possible mother of the next Lord Docane."

"You wish to stay here?" He was grinning, chuckling.

"I do, but, Fletcher, please think. In England, you'd be lord of the manor, respected, powerful."

"And while you were hosting those fetes and tea parties, I'd be managing farms and rents and possibly being forced to consider taking my father's and brother's seat in Parliament? No, thank you. But"—he drew her gently back into his arms to speak softly into her ear—"I do reserve the right to call you 'my lady' when we're alone."

Chapter Fifteen

Later, as they walked toward his homestead with Percy prancing beside them, she drew a deep breath of the fresh summer's morning air and smiled up at her companion.

"So Lucy didn't immediately accept Mr. MacPherson's proposal?"

"I think she was holding back a reply to taunt to him, to make him doubly glad when she accepted." Fletcher chuckled. "For the last two weeks he's been going about like a bear with a thorn in its paw. Then last evening, as Lucy was about to leave off her housekeeping duties at the manor and head back to Mrs. O'Malley's for the night, he came downstairs and into the kitchen where Horace and I were lingering over what Cully calls 'a wee dram' before bedding down. He was dressed in the outfit he wore for that ill-fated dinner party with Sir Henry. His expression was about as friendly as an annoyed bull, and he ordered Horace and me out of the house. A half hour later he bellowed from the door that we were to return. Inside, we found a very different man, one smiling from ear to ear, as the saying goes, and Miss Lucy looking smug as a cat in cream."

"So she finally said yes?"

"Yes, and not a moment too soon. I don't know how much longer Horace and I could have abided his bellicose attitude. They're to be married next week."

"Next week? Isn't that sudden? What about posting the bans?"

"Reverend Edward Morgan is, as you may have noticed, not a conventional clergyman. He says there are ways around such formalities."

"I see."

"And what of us, Miss Isabella? Shall I visit the minister and see if he can manage a similar situation for us?"

"Fletcher, so soon? I don't know…"

"This is the New World, my lady. There's no necessity for long engagements, the purchasing of wedding clothes, and the like. Actually, I think you look very fetching in that outfit you wear to tend the garden…curls peeping out from beneath a venerable sunbonnet, feet bare."

"Now you're teasing." She chuckled. "Poking fun at my unladylike behavior."

"No." He sobered. "I'm rejoicing in the amazing woman you've become…and the wonderful wife you will be." He took her into his arms and into a long kiss.

"We'd best be getting on," he said, finally releasing her. "Even a week seems a desperately long wait, but I will be patient. The prize is well worth seven days' frustration."

"I believe I must write Mama." An imp of mischief rose in her as they continued on. "I believe I'll first tell her I'm marrying Sir Fletcher Atkin, Lord Docane. Then, after a couple of paragraphs describing your charms, I'll tell her you're renouncing the title and we'll be remaining here on your homestead." She chuckled. "I wonder that I won't hear her screams right across the Atlantic. Poor Papa! What he will have to endure in consequence. Do you think we could invite him to visit next year? He could leave the estate in the hands of his steward for a few months. He'll surely need a reprieve from Mama's constantly declaring me a fool and a total loss."

"I'm sure I'll like your father." He paused to kiss her cheek. "After all, he's made it possible for me to find the love of my life. And my younger brother will be only too happy to become Lord Ducane."

A
Trollop's Treasure

by

Gail MacMillan

Riverhaven Rogues, Book 6

Chapter One

Head bent against the wind, rain and sleet, he led the stumbling horse through the night. Hunger and exhaustion raked every fiber of his body as he fought to control the cough that would send pain raging in his chest.

"Come on, Gallant," he urged the old gelding. "Not much farther, that's a good lad."

The animal blew and struggled ahead.

Midnight. It had to be nearing midnight. Darkness had fallen what seemed like hours ago. By his calculation, this journey from hell had to end soon. Narrowing his eyes against the storm, he squinted back at the young man slumped astride the horse.

"Not much farther now, laddie." He tried to reassure him. "You're almost home."

"Home." Clinging to the horse's scraggly mane, the rider breathed the word with the same intonation he'd heard others use when they spoke of heaven. He couldn't blame the lad. All three of them had been through hell.

A fit of coughing he couldn't suppress overtook him, and he had to pause until it receded. *Bloody hell!* He spit mucus and wiped his mouth with the back of his hand.

"Come along, Gallant." With a gentle tug on the animal's reins, he started forward again. "Chust a wee bit farther."

"Lex?" His companion weaved in the saddle.

"Aye?"

"It would be wise"—he fought to speak—"to disguise your Highland brogue. My...father has no love of Scots."

"If that's your wisdom, then I shall, niver fear, laddie."

He refrained from asking the reason for the parent's aversion to his people. It had taken a supreme effort for Captain Archibald Spencer to get out that warning. The young lad was in no condition to offer further explanations.

Lights. Ahead he saw the twinkle of lights. Relieved, he paused to get his bearings. The horse rested its head against his shoulder. Lex felt its breath exhaling in long, warm puffs against his wet shirt.

"Almost there," he muttered.

****

"He says he's brought Master Archie home, sir." The footman stood aside to allow his lordship access to the kitchen doorway.

"Who are you?" Sir Maxwell Spencer peered out into the storm. "And what do you want?"

"I have your son, your lordship." Remembering his companion's warning, Lex spoke with the English accent he'd cultivated for use on such occasions. "He was wounded in France."

"The devil, you say!" In drenching rain, Lord Dunstan stepped out of the shelter of the doorway and around the horse's head to peer up at the young man on its back. "It can't be! They told us he was dead."

"Papa." The young man's word reeked of relief.

"I've come home."

He toppled from the horse, only his father's arms preventing him falling into the mud of the dooryard.

****

"Hie there, who are you...and what do you think you're doing?" A young lad, holding a cudgel, confronted Lex as he led the horse into the stable. "We allow no tramps shelter here."

"I'm not seeking shelter for myself, sir." Lex spoke respectfully. He didn't want any rudeness on his part to cause the starving, exhausted animal to be turned away. "Just for this gallant beast. He's been walking injured for days with barely enough food to keep him on his feet."

"And why should I be taking in this ragged scrub?" The lad circled the pair, club at the ready, but Lex could see compassion easing into his expression as he perused the old gelding. *A boy with a kind heart.* He pressed home his suit.

"This brave soul has carried the young master of the house, wounded, across the battlefields of France and to the very door of his home. I'm sure Sir Maxwell will sanction the best of care being giving to such a beast."

"Master Archie is home?" The boy's eyes widened. "Saints be praised! We thought him dead. His lordship was fair beside himself with grief." He took the horse's reins from Lex. "This old lad carried him home, you say? Let me see to him." He led the animal into a box stall.

Guid, verrae guid. Lex allowed his natural brogue to speak in his thoughts. He hated hiding his heritage beneath a veneer of smooth English intonation, but

3

Archie's warning echoed in his mind.

He should be on his way before anyone discovered his true identity. Still, the relative warmth of the stable and the shelter it provided from the miserable night held him in its thrall. *Just a few more minutes, just a few more...to see how the old Gallant fares.*

He knew the last wasn't entirely true. Already he could hear the stable lad talking softly to the horse, telling him he could not have too much hay, else he'd make himself sick, and how he'd have him rubbed dry in no time.

Not overfeeding the beast, and saving the poor bugger from a chill. The old lad is in good hands. I can leave.

Another bout of coughing overcame him. Doubling over, he surrendered to the ragged pain racking through his chest. *Sweet Jesus!* When the spasm ended with a gagging retch, he fell back against the stable wall, drenched with cold sweat.

"Are you all right, sir?" Frowning, the stable lad peered out at him.

"Just a bit of a cough," Lex muttered the reply.

The door of the stable opened, letting in two figures in black cloaks. Their size suggested women, but he wasn't sure until they threw back their hoods to reveal an elderly one with an age-wrinkled face and another, little more than a girl, behind her. The woman carried a covered basket, the lass a sack.

"You are the gentleman who brought Mr. Archie home?" The woman spoke with a French accent.

"Yes." He stifled his natural response of "aye."

"We are most grateful." She held out the basket. "Here is a small recompense, a bit of food and drink to warm you after your journey. Violet has a dry shirt and bedding. You must stay the night. I'm sure his lordship will wish to speak to you in the morning…once he's overcome the joyful shock of having his beloved son at home once more."

"Thank you, mistress." Gratitude for the Frenchwoman's kindness welled inside him. Although he'd been prepared to head out once more into the night, food, dry clothes, and a bit of rest before he resumed his journey appeared a boon from heaven. He put the back of his hand over his mouth in an effort to stifle another outburst of coughing. The result was a muffled grunt.

"Are you unwell, young man?" Giving him a shrewd look, the woman caught his gesture.

"Thank you, mistress, just a bit of a cough," he said, repeating his earlier explanation, but her expression told him he hadn't deceived her.

"Show him into a comfortable place, Bobbie," she called out to the boy involved in caring for the horse. "I take responsibility."

"Yes, ma'am." The boy Bobbie came out of the stall. "There's a clean stall with a gate at the end of the stable…if that would suit you, sir."

"That will be excellent." He took the Frenchwoman's wrinkled hand and bowed over it. "Your grateful servant, Madame…?"

"*Mademoiselle* Marie Roi," she replied. "And you would be?"

He hesitated. "Lex, Mademoiselle, just Lex." When it had become necessary to hide his true identity, he'd chosen a moniker he believed would be difficult to trace, unlike the name he'd received at the christening fount as a babe in the Highlands.

"Ah, a man of mystery as well as charm." Her dark eyes sparkled out at him. "If I were many years younger, you would prove a danger to a woman such as myself."

With a mischievous glance, she turned and headed out of the stable. "Come along, Violet. We must be getting back to the house."

Violet looked at Bobbie, blushed, then lowered her head shyly, and hastened to follow the older woman.

When Lex looked at the young stable hand, he saw him staring after the girl, a slight smile curling his lips.

"Your...friend?" He gave special meaning to the last word.

"Oh, no, sir." Bobbie shook his head ruefully. "A stable lad such as myself can entertain no such hopes." The defeat in his tone touched Lex's heart. "Let me show you where you may sleep."

Lex picked up the basket and sack and followed him down the corridor to a box stall at the end, bedded with clean straw.

"You can stay here," Bobbie said, shoving open the gate. "But have a care. Lay low tonight. Mr. Brant, the head groom, is due back from the village. He'll be in a right state, what with the rain and..."

"And drink?" Lex made a knowledgeable guess. Forays into the vicinity of taverns often proved fraught with overwhelming temptations.

"We don't say such things." The young lad turned away and hastened back to his work.

Once alone, Lex closed the stall door and sank down in a corner of the enclosure bedded with clean straw. He leaned his head back against the board wall and closed his eyes. It was good to be out of the wind and rain, even if only for a night. Maybe it would be enough to cure whatever malady was haunting his chest.

Tempting smells issuing from the basket the Frenchwoman had furnished brought him back to the moment. He opened his eyes and withdrew the cloth that covered it. Inside he found a bowl of steaming broth thick with meat and vegetables, a few slices of bread, a square of cheese, and a flask.

Could it be? God in heaven, let it be.

He grasped the latter, pulled the cork free, and raised it to his nose. It was.

He swilled the brandy until it made him choke as it hit his throat, soothing the soreness from coughing. Then he let his shoulders sag as he relaxed and allowed the drink to ease its restorative power through his body. Slowly, warmth entered his belly and moved out through his being.

He turned his attention to the food. Bloody hell but he was hungry. He grasped the bowl in both hands and slurped down its contents. Then he turned his attention to the bread and cheese. When he'd finished all he could manage, he remembered the bag the girl had carried.

He opened it to find a shirt, a quilt, and a blanket. All dry, all clean! It had been so long since he'd been dry or clean. He stood and staggered. *Weariness and too much brandy too fast.* He paused to get his bearings.

The moment he was sufficiently steady on his feet, he stripped naked, tossed his ragged, wet clothing aside, and donned the fresh shirt that hung to below his thighs. He took another long drink of brandy before kneeling to spread the blanket over the straw.

Moments later he lay curled up on it, the quilt tucked about him, lost in sleep.

Chapter Two

"Stop her! Catch the bitch!"

His shout followed her as she bolted for the brothel door. Clutching her torn bodice, she reached the entrance and had her hand on the latch when she was seized about the waist and yanked back into the hot, smoky room.

"Let me go!" She fought at the brawny arm holding her and lifting her feet off the floor as its owner dragged her back to face the man who had issued the order to detain her. Bent over, clutching his lower regions, the man glared her, his face distorted with pain and outrage.

"Lock the whore somewhere she cannot escape!" he muttered. "In the morning, she'll face a magistrate's court. We'll then see how fine and arrogant you are!" He focused on her, his small, bear-like eyes narrowing. "I doubt you'll enjoy time spent in one of our elegant prisons, you bloody little wench." He swung on the establishment's owner as he sank into a nearby chair. "Take the damned trollop out of my sight!"

"I have a number of other young ladies who will be only too happy to see to your lordship." The owner of the house rushed to put a solicitous arm about the man's fat shoulders. "I really do not know how this one"—she glared at the young woman still writhing against her constraints—"got in here. She's definitely not one of

9

mine. Take her away, John," she ordered the guard. "Lock her in the garret room."

Thrown into the small cell of a room at the top of the house, its only furnishings a small stool, the door barred behind her, the accused girl paced like a restless lioness. Treat her like a common trollop, would they? Just wait until they experienced the kerfuffle that would occur when she identified herself to the magistrates. A smirk twisting her lips, she paused to reflect on the scenario. On further consideration, her jubilation faded as other thoughts crowded into her mind. What would her father do if he got wind of the incident? Marry her off in a whipstitch to that simpering Duke of Cumberly, or if His Grace wouldn't have her, maybe ship her off to any convent willing to have such as her...for a price?

Bloody hell, this adventure had turned into more of a fiasco than she'd anticipated. She had to find some means of escape. Taking a look about the room, she saw a small window a few feet away. Her red satin skirts swept the dusty floor as she moved to examine it. A rub removed enough of the grime for her to see what lay outside. Indeed, she was high above the rear of the house, and the window was exceedingly narrow, but several feet below was the roof of a porch. If she could somehow manage to get through the small opening and, clinging to its sill until she hung by arm's length downward, she might be able to drop to freedom.

In a moment, she was struggling out of her gown. There was no way its generous skirts would fit through the narrow opening. Then, dressed only in her barest of undergarments, she grasped the stool by its legs and lunged to smash the glass from the window. When its shards had ceased to tinkle to the floor, she paused to listen—no sounds of anyone approaching, only the continuing cacophony from below. No doubt all were too caught up in their pleasures to give a second thought to the prisoner above.

With her hand and forearm wrapped in her gown, she set about freeing the sides of the window from shards of glass. Although it slowed her escape, she knew it had to be done, that it would be foolish to find freedom only to bleed to death from a cut. The frame seemingly cleared, she stuffed the garment outside and watched as it fell through the rain to land on the roof below. Good. She'd need it when she made good her escape. She couldn't go running along London streets in only her undergarments on her way back to Lady Balfour's house.

****

"Hold there!" Drenched and trembling from cold, she raised a hand and limped into the darkened street to stop the lone cab travelling along it. "Hold, I say!"

The driver drew rein. Even through the night and bucketing rain, she could see skepticism colored with annoyance in the man's expression. Certainly a woman dressed as a lady of the evening, clutching the torn bodice of her soaked gown to her bosom, didn't represent a profitable fare.

"Take me to Lady Balfour's residence." She pulled open the door and stumbled inside before he had time to whip his horse away. "You'll be well compensated."

"Argh!" The man shook his head and spit into the gutter before shaking the reins over the horse's back to set it into motion. "We've nothing better to do, now, have we, Butter?" she heard him mutter to the animal.

The moment the cab drew up in front of Lady

Balfour's elegant residence, she jumped out, grimacing and all but collapsing as her injured ankle shot pain up her leg.

"Wait here." She hobbled up the steps and raised the ornate door knocker.

Shortly, Gravesfield the butler was peering out into the inhospitable night. "Good evening, Lady Anna."

"Gravesfield, please see to the cabbie." She pushed past the man and into the foyer.

"Yes, my lady." Without comment or question, he pulled a cloak from a rack and headed out to do as he'd been bidden.

He returned in a few minutes, shaking water from his cloak and replacing it on its peg.

"A most inhospitable night, my lady," he said.

"Most inhospitable indeed, Gravesfield." In spite of her physical discomfort, she couldn't help marveling at the man's composure and lack of question or comment in view of her condition. Years of service to her mother's friend and her present hostess, the unconventional twice-widowed Lady Balfour, had schooled him in the art of discretion. "I assume my maid is in my rooms?" She hobbled toward the wide, curving staircase.

"I don't believe so, my lady." Gravesfield was standing straight and still as a pillar in the foyer when she turned back to ask the question. "I believe…er…she went out."

"Went out? Went out?" Her annoyance boiled over. "Who gave her permission? Certainly not I. Where did she go?" She paused, then continued, suspicion tainting her tone, "And with whom?"

"I cannot say for certain, my lady, but Mitchell,

one of the footmen, has had the evening free."

"Bloody hell!" She turned back to continue upstairs. She was wet and cold, her ankle ached like the worst toothache she'd ever had, and the long scratch on her arm needed washing and bandaging.

That girl has been nothing but trouble, hardly worth my efforts to train her.

"Shall I send Lady Balfour's maid along to you, my lady? Her ladyship is out for the evening and won't be requiring Cecile's services for some hours."

"Yes, please do, Gravesfield. I admit tonight's…activities…have left me feeling a bit spent."

Once in her room, she didn't wait for Cecile but stripped off her sodden clothing and pulled on a silk robe that had been thrown across the end of the luxurious bed. Sitting down at the dressing table, she surveyed her wet, tangled hair and the darkening bruise on her left cheek where she'd struck something on her descent from her prison. Shoving up the sleeve of the robe, she examined a long, bloody scratch.

Hell and damnation! I can't go home until I mend. My appearance will raise too many questions. And I certainly can't attend any of Lady Balfour's social functions. I could encounter someone who might recognize me from the brothel. Lord knows, at least half of London's elite gentlemen frequent the place. So I'm housebound here…a prisoner for a week or so.

"Good evening, my lady." Cecile, Lady Balfour's lady's maid, slipped quietly into the room. "How may I be of service?"

Another perfect servant, not questioning her appearance. She very much doubted she'd ever be able to train Rose to such excellence.

Damn it, where is that girl! Hopefully not getting herself into trouble with a footman named Mitchell.

Frustrated, she began to pull pins from her hair as she directed Cecile's ministrations. That disgusting, pot-bellied man had called her a trollop. Now where had she heard that word used before?

Aha! The tale of a trollop's treasure. She remembered. Marie, her lady's maid at home, had told her the story. Was it simply an old folk tale, or was there perhaps some truth in it…and maybe the source of another adventure? She'd investigate when she returned home.

A word about the author...

Gail is the award-winning author of almost forty traditionally published books. She is delighted to be an author with The Wild Rose Press, "where writers are encouraged, tutored and mentored in the best of ways."

Contact her at:

macgail@nbnet.nb.ca

Twitter: tollerbeagle44

Facebook: Gail MacMillan

Thank you for purchasing
this publication of The Wild Rose Press, Inc.

If you enjoyed the story, we would appreciate your
letting others know by leaving a review.

For other wonderful stories,
please visit our on-line bookstore at
www.thewildrosepress.com.

For questions or more information
contact us at
info@thewildrosepress.com.

The Wild Rose Press, Inc.
www.thewildrosepress.com

Stay current with The Wild Rose Press, Inc.

Like us on Facebook

https://www.facebook.com/TheWildRosePress

And Follow us on Twitter
https://twitter.com/WildRosePress